MW01505551

BEFORE AND AFTER

LANGSTON HOTELS
BOOK TWO

ANNA HACKETT

Before and After

Published by Anna Hackett

Copyright 2025 by Anna Hackett

Cover by Hang Le Designs

Cover image by Ren Saliba

Edits by Tanya Saari

ISBN (ebook): 978-1-923134-74-4

ISBN (paperback): 978-1-923134-75-1

ISBN (special edition paperback): 978-1-923134-76-8

This book is a work of fiction. All names, characters, places and incidents are either the product of the author's imagination or are used fictitiously. Any resemblance to actual persons, events or places is coincidental. No part of this book may be reproduced, scanned, or distributed in any printed or electronic form.

WHAT READERS ARE SAYING ABOUT ANNA'S ACTION ROMANCE

The Powerbroker - Romantic Book of the Year (Ruby) winner 2022

Heart of Eon - Romantic Book of the Year (Ruby) winner 2020

Cyborg - PRISM Award Winner 2019

Unfathomed and Unmapped - Romantic Book of the Year (Ruby) finalists 2018

Unexplored – Romantic Book of the Year (Ruby) Novella Winner 2017

Return to Dark Earth – One of Library Journal's Best E-Original Books for 2015 and two-time SFR Galaxy Awards winner

At Star's End – One of Library Journal's Best E-Original Romances for 2014

The Phoenix Adventures – SFR Galaxy Award Winner for Most Fun New Series and "Why Isn't This a Movie?" Series

Beneath a Trojan Moon – SFR Galaxy Award Winner and RWAus Ella Award Winner

Hell Squad – SFR Galaxy Award for best Post-Apocalypse for Readers who don't like Post-Apocalypse

"Like Indiana Jones meets Star Wars. A treasure hunt with a steamy romance." – SFF Dragon, review of *Among Galactic Ruins*

"Action, danger, aliens, romance – yup, it's another great book from Anna Hackett!" – Book Gannet Reviews, review of *Hell Squad: Marcus*

Sign up for my VIP mailing list and get your *free box set* containing three action-packed romances.

Visit here to get started: www.annahackett.com

CHAPTER 1
ALLIE

With a bone-cracking yawn, I pulled my favorite cardigan on over my pajama shorts and tank top, then stumbled out of my bedroom.

I'd kill for another hour of sleep, but alas, that wasn't happening anytime soon.

I flicked on the light switch in the living room, narrowly avoiding stepping on a toy car, but managed to put my right foot on a tiny piece of plastic torture also known as a LEGO brick.

"*Ow*." Hopping on one foot, I raised my voice. "Ollie, are you up and dressed? I'm making breakfast."

The pain subsided. Quickly, I rushed through the tiny living room, collecting toys and books, and shoving them in the huge basket in the corner. Wandering into the kitchen, I yawned again, then put the coffee machine on. I'd stayed up too late. I'd realized I was behind on laundry and had done two loads after Ollie had gone to bed. I'd also needed to stitch a button back on a pair of

1

his jeans. A seamstress, I was not. It had taken me way longer than it should have, because the button had fallen off twice after I'd finished stitching it.

There were never enough hours in the day lately. I pulled out some plates and glasses. Next, I put some Pop Tarts in the toaster. I winced. My brother would kill me, knowing I was feeding his kid Pop Tarts.

"Sorry, bro. I'm running short on time today." I poured a glass of orange juice, just as my nephew came in.

He did it quietly. Ollie had never been the loudest kid in the room, but he'd become even quieter and more withdrawn since his parents had been killed.

Who could blame him? My heart squeezed. Fuck, I missed Sean. My brother had been the person I was closest to in the entire world.

Our parents had divorced when we were in our teens. Dad had remarried and moved to Denver. Mom had focused on mom, getting into yoga, the spa, and cruising. She lived in Arizona now and had a wealthy boyfriend. Sean and I had thankfully had each other. He'd understood me. He hadn't judged. He'd supported me, no matter what.

I pressed a palm to my chest, letting the grief sit there.

Now, it was just me and Ollie.

As the five-year-old climbed onto a stool at the small kitchen island, my heart squeezed even harder. He was so quiet. Too quiet. And he looked like a mini-Sean, with his dark hair and gray eyes. It also meant he looked like me, too. People always assumed that he was mine.

"Morning, kiddo."

"Morning, Allie."

I circled the island and pressed a quick kiss to the top of his head. "It's a Pop Tart morning." That got me a flicker of a smile. We both shared an unhealthy love of Pop Tarts. I pushed the glass of juice across the island in front of him. "Drink that, so I can pretend that you're getting some vitamins."

I served up the breakfast of champions, then gratefully drank my coffee. As I gulped it down, I could feel the caffeine hitting my veins, my brain cells soaking it up.

"Right. I have work. You have school." I paused. "Who are you going to play with today?"

He toyed with his glass. "I don't know."

My heart squeezed, yet again. I'd gotten a lot of 'I don't knows' since he'd started kindergarten the month before. I knew he was having trouble making friends, but the teacher kept telling me to have patience.

Sean, I hope to hell I'm not screwing up your kid.

The last thing I'd expected was to become a single mom at age twenty-nine. After ten months of it, it had me questioning everything I thought I'd known. I honestly didn't know how parents did it.

But I had a grieving five-year-old to care for, so there was no time to worry or wish like hell that my brother and sister-in-law hadn't been carjacked by a maniac.

"Okay, go brush your teeth, my man, and grab your backpack."

Once he'd disappeared down the hall to his room, I sprang into action. I grabbed a discarded hoodie off the floor, some socks, and a scarf. I dashed to the laundry room and dumped them in the hamper. The condo wasn't tiny, but it wasn't huge, either. I'd had to sell the four-bedroom house my brother and sister-in-law had owned. There was no way I could afford to pay the mortgage. My nose wrinkled. I still felt bad. So much had changed in Ollie's life, and maybe it would have been better for him if he could've stayed in his own home. Or maybe it would have been worse, filled as it would have been, with all the memories of his parents. I had no idea.

Shaking my head, I raced into my bedroom. I quickly dressed in my uniform.

Before everything in my life had changed, I'd worn sleek suits, and lived and worked in New York City.

I tried not to think about Before too much. Now, it was all about After. In my life now, I was a housekeeping supervisor at the Langston Windward—the best resort in the small mountain town I'd grown up in. Sean and I had attended the same school that Ollie went to. All through my childhood, I'd dreamed of escaping Windward to a glamorous life in the city, with a fast-paced career, great shoes, an exciting nightlife.

After I fastened my brown pants, I tugged the tunic-style top into place. Now, I was back in Windward. Back walking the same streets I had as a kid, back shopping in the same grocery store, back smiling and waving to the same people I'd known all my life. Pretending not to see their sympathy and pity was new, but I was mastering that well.

I brushed my short, black hair with my fingers, then swiped on some minimal makeup.

Now, I had a kid to worry about. Nothing else

mattered. Not that I'd given up my New York dream, not that I had no time to sleep or exercise, or that I worried constantly I'd make a mistake with Ollie. I looked at my reflection in the mirror. Yikes, it was impossible to miss the dark circles under my eyes. I sighed.

Suck it up, Ford.

I strode out. "Okay, Ol-ster, let's roll."

He was already waiting for me at the door, with his backpack on and his face solemn. He nodded at me.

We headed out of the condo and I locked the door behind us. Our place was at the end of the second floor on the corner. The bonus was that we had extra windows —with views of the thick trees outside that I loved—and our door was tucked around a corner, so it was private. I'd put a cute little planter beside the door with a plant I desperately tried to keep alive. There was also a tiny fairy statue stuck in the soil. She peeked out through the leaves with a mischievous look on her face. Ollie called her Sparkle since she was dusted with gold.

That was my little secret—I collected fairy statues. Sean had bought me one when I was ten, and I'd loved collecting them ever since. My dresser in my room was covered in them.

We headed down the hall and passed our neighbor's door. Mrs. Jenkins was a lifesaver. She often babysat Ollie, if I had an out-of-school-hours shift, or had a chance to go to cocktail night with my girlfriends. She baked, and he liked her and her cookies.

Outside, a brisk wind whipped down the sidewalk. The condo building didn't have a garage, just assigned parking places in the tree-lined lot in front of the building. It was great in summer, but I wasn't looking forward to the winter and digging the car out when it snowed.

We headed toward my beat-up Toyota RAV4. I hadn't owned a car in New York, but when I came back to Windward, I'd needed one. I hadn't saved much money since living in the Big Apple was expensive, and I'd made the most of living in one of the most exciting cities on Earth. Sean had talked about looking into life insurance, but he hadn't gotten around to it. He and Sylvie had been young, fit, and healthy.

No one could have predicted they'd be violently murdered by a criminal out on parole.

My stomach did a sickening turn. Swallowing, I unlocked the car. "In we go, kiddo."

Sean and Sylvie hadn't owned their house for very long, so they hadn't built up much equity in it. I'd used what little I gained from the sale of the house to buy the small, second-hand SUV—and the rest I'd socked away for Ollie.

Once Ollie was buckled into his booster seat, I drove to school. It killed me that Sean and Sylvie had missed seeing their little man start school. I managed to find a parking spot in the drop-off chaos outside the main school building. I cursed, as a woman in a Mercedes SUV cut me off and stole it. But I did it under my breath so little ears wouldn't hear. After snagging another spot, I walked Ollie to the gate.

"You make sure you eat all your lunch."

"Okay."

"And remember, it's not just about learning to read, it's making friends, having fun."

His nose wrinkled. "I know."

"All right, you have a great day." I crouched down in front of him so that we were eye level. God, I never knew how much you could love someone until you stared at a kid you were responsible for, and they looked back at you with pure trust.

Ollie nodded.

"We're going to go and see Miss Catherine this afternoon, okay?"

He looked at his feet.

Catherine was his therapist. She assured me that he was doing well, and just needed time to deal with his grief.

"Ollie?"

He looked up. "I like Miss Catherine. It's just... When I talk about mommy and daddy, I feel sad."

"Oh, kiddo, that's normal." I hugged him. "I feel sad sometimes, too. I miss them so much."

He looked at me with those solemn, gray eyes. "I do, too."

I ruffled his hair. "Want me to walk you in?" I didn't have the time. I'd be late to work, but I didn't care.

He nodded.

We walked side by side, his arm brushing mine. He hadn't let me, or anyone else, hold his hand since his parents had died. My heart hurt. *It'll be all right, Allie.* I walked him to his classroom, and smiled at his teacher. When a little blond boy motored over, talking a hundred miles a minute to Ollie, I felt relieved.

Ollie gave me a small wave as I left. Back in the car, I

headed to the hotel. Glancing at the dash, I accelerated. I *might* still make it in time.

Windward attracted a lot of visitors. It was especially busy in the winter, and as soon as we got snow, the skiers and snowboarders would descend like an avalanche. The central part of the town was quite glitzy, with lots of high-end shops and restaurants that catered to the tourists. The eastern part of town was where the locals lived.

Then, the Langston Windward came into view.

It was a solid, sprawling building with a gabled roof, constructed of natural stone, dark wood, and glass. Until recently, the historic hotel had been owned by a Windward local, but after he'd sold it, it had been purchased by the Langston Hotels Group. I drove around the back and parked in the staff parking lot, then hustled to the staff entrance. I fumbled and pulled my ID card out. I was only five minutes late, so that wasn't too bad.

The lock beeped and I shouldered through the door, my brain turning to everything I needed to get done. I'd start with checking in with my team, who'd be in charge of cleaning the guest rooms this morning.

I'd barely taken a step inside, when I slammed into a brick wall.

A brick wall that shouldn't be in the middle of the hallway.

I almost fell backward, but the wall had hands and grabbed my waist. I looked up into brown eyes that were so dark they looked black.

Oh, hell.

"You're late, Ms. Ford."

Of all the people to catch me running behind. "Five minutes, Broody."

His dark gaze narrowed at the nickname. Broody was actually Caden Castro, head of security for Langston Hotels. After the sale, more than just the hotel logo had changed. We now had the Langston Hotels executives underfoot, as they renovated and updated the hotel. Broody had been skulking around every corner of the hotel for two months. I was pretty sure that *paranoid* was his middle name. Or maybe *distrusting*. Maybe both.

"Late is late," he said.

I rolled my eyes. "So sue me. You're making me even later."

And sending my stupid body haywire.

That was my huge secret—bigger than collecting fairy statues—and I hadn't told anybody. For some insane reason, Caden Castro flipped every switch I had. Anytime the man was near me, my pulse took off, my stomach felt fluttery, and I got tingles. *Tingles.*

I wasn't a woman who got tingles.

And I didn't have time for tingles. I barely had time to sleep.

Any time Caden's dark gaze swung my way—assessing and intense—it reminded me that I hadn't had sex in over a year. I hadn't had an orgasm in months. I was too tired.

And don't get me started on the man's thighs. I'd never in my life ogled a man's thighs before, but any time I saw him shift in a way that had his suit pants pulling taut on those long, muscular—

Snap out of it, Allie.

Jeez. I cleared my throat and realized his big hands were still gripping my waist, digging into my skin. My traitorous heart did a weird thump.

"I can't get to work until you let me go." God, my voice was husky. Please don't let him notice.

His hands flexed, his dark eyes locking on mine. Then he released me.

I sidestepped him and took off.

"No time for dark, broody men," I muttered. "Even if they have killer thighs. And inky-black eyes, and..." I cursed and forced Caden out of my head.

After dumping my things in the locker room, my heart rate finally evened out. I met my team of housekeepers in our main area. They all wore the same brown uniform as me. Their carts were all stocked and lined up, like they were ready for battle. Sometimes cleaning the hotel actually did feel like a battle. Most days, things were normal, but every now and then, some guests sprung a disaster on us. I'd seen it all: blood, snot, vomit, semen, and some bodily fluids I couldn't identify, which was probably for the best. I clicked my radio onto my belt and snatched my tablet off its charger.

"Morning, all." I got nods and hellos. "I hope you had a good breakfast and are well-caffeinated." Now I got a few chuckles. "All right." I swiped my tablet screen. "No changes to the room allocations today, or special instructions. I have a note from the night team that someone was ill in room 407. They had to change out the sheets and towels. Amy, can you check in on them and see how they're doing today?"

The brown-haired housekeeper nodded. "Sure thing, Allie."

"If it's contagious, don't share the germs," another housekeeper called out.

There were murmurs and nods.

"Luckily, our cleaning products contain commercial-grade disinfectants." I smiled. "Let's all get to work. You know the drill. If you have any issues, radio me." I held up a hand. "And never forget that we're the backbone of this place. Because of our work, the Langston Windward is such a great hotel. Go, make it shine."

There were grins as my team headed off, carts rattling.

"Allie?" One of my younger team members, Wade, stepped in front of me. "I'm *really* sorry, but I need a few days off next week." He clasped his hands together like he was praying.

Great. Last-minute roster changes always sucked. "Why?"

"My mom is moving house. I need to help her pack and move." He shot me a pleading look. "If she didn't need the help, I wouldn't ask."

I blew out a breath. "Message me. I'll sort it out for you."

He smiled. "Thanks. You're the *best*, Allie."

I ran through the notes from the night supervisor. I shunted a few maintenance requests to Everett, our head of maintenance. He was another Windward local. We'd gone to school together. Tucking my tablet under my arm, I headed through to the staff office area, when a female voice called out my name.

"Allie, there you are." Tessa Ashford bustled toward me in her tight-fitting, navy skirt, and white shirt.

She was the hotel manager and my best friend. We'd grown up in Windward together. Unlike me, all Tessa had ever dreamed about was managing this hotel. She'd made her dream come true, and had recently also fallen in love.

"Hey," I said.

"Morning." She was sipping a coffee from Mountain Brew. It was the best coffee shop in Colorado. Yeah, I was biased.

I stared at that cup long enough that Tessa huffed out a breath and handed it to me.

"It's only half full." Her brow knitted as she scanned me. "You look like you need it."

"I stayed up late doing laundry."

"You wild thing, you."

I gulped the coffee down. *Oh.* I closed my eyes and savored the latte goodness. It was so delicious. I didn't have the money to buy expensive coffees anymore. I'd also had to give up my favorite chocolates. I'd learned quickly that kids outgrew their clothes and shoes insanely fast.

"Do you need a moment?" Tessa asked, amused.

I opened my eyes. She was glowing. I guessed that was one of the perks of being crazy in love. Tessa had fallen for the new owner of the hotel, billionaire hotelier Ambrose "Ro" Langston. She could afford good coffee, and got regular orgasms from her hot guy.

"You woke up wrapped around a billionaire, who no doubt gave you multiple orgasms before breakfast, *and* got you a Mountain Brew. I stepped on a LEGO brick, ate Pop Tarts for breakfast, and dropped my kid off at school." I held up the coffee cup. "This is as close to orgasms as I'm getting." I took another sip.

"How's Ollie?"

I noticed she didn't refute the multiple orgasms thing. I sighed. "Sad, too quiet, won't hold my hand."

She grabbed my arm. "He knows you're there for him. He just needs time. His mind is still processing everything."

I nodded. Tessa would know. She'd lost her parents at eight years old in a car accident, and had been raised by her aunt. I knew that was a big reason why she'd bent over backward to give me a job at the hotel and help me out. But I also knew she'd done it because she was a good person and a good friend.

"I'd better get to work. Broody already razzed me for being five minutes late." I rolled my eyes.

My friend's lips twitched. "Did you call him Broody to his face?"

"Yep." I held up the coffee cup. "I'm keeping this."

She waved a hand at me. "My gift to you."

I took a step away.

"And Allie?"

I glanced back over my shoulder.

"If you need help with anything, laundry, babysitting, whatever, just ask."

I stared at Tessa's earnest face. She was such a good friend and had already done so much. There was no way I'd take advantage of that friendship, not when she was busy integrating the hotel into the Langston Hotels group, and especially not when she was enjoying time with her new man.

Pasting on a smile, I winked at her. "You bet."

I moved through the door and into the lobby. Next on my To-Do list was checking on the new floor cleaner we were using. If it wasn't doing the job, we'd need to switch again.

A smile hit my lips. I loved the lobby. With its high ceiling, wooden beams, and polished wood floor, it shouted rustic mountain elegance. But the large, triangular bank of windows was the real star. Those panes of glass showcased the mountain view. Right now, the trees outside were a riot of yellow, orange, and red.

A long, stone reception desk sat on the other side of the lobby. A huge vase of fresh flowers scented the air. There were several groups checking in, but one of the receptionist's gazes snagged on me.

Oh, great. Coral. She was older than dirt and had worked at the Langston since before I was born. Her gray hair was always styled in an unforgiving bob around her wrinkled face. She gave a new meaning to the term battleaxe. Coral wasn't afraid to share her bad mood with anyone.

I picked up my pace, but a second later, the woman intercepted me.

"You look like crap."

"Thanks, Coral. My new face cream must be working, then."

She sniffed. "You should sleep more."

"It's on my To-Do list." Along with five hundred other things.

The older woman paused for a second. "How's your boy?"

I softened. "He's okay."

She nodded. "By the way, the new floor cleaner is shite."

Aw, at least I could trust Coral to share nothing but the unvarnished truth. "Thanks for the feedback."

I'd already noted that the wood floor wasn't as shiny as I liked. Lifting my tablet, I made a quick note.

Loud voices, followed by deep, masculine laughter, interrupted my thoughts. I glanced over at the reception desk. A group of young, fit guys in their late twenties was checking in. They had large bags of outdoor gear. I saw one gesture toward the front doors, and I swiveled around to look through the glass. Four rugged mountain bikes were parked outside.

"Trouble." Coral sniffed and stalked back to the desk.

One of the guys was tall and cute, with ruffled, blond hair. I remembered him. This group had been here last winter, snowboarding. They were into extreme sports. They'd been spending most of their time on Windward's famous Back Runs. Wilder terrain for more experienced skiers. He'd told me they'd be back for mountain biking and paragliding in the fall.

I couldn't remember his name. Brandon? Blake? Bryce?

The blond looked up and caught my gaze. He gave me a slow smile.

He'd asked me out last winter, but I'd had to say no. I was coping with selling Sean's house, and Ollie had been sleeping in my bed every night. I'd been sorry to turn him down because the timing was bad and I'd thought he was attractive.

Funny thing, now, I didn't even feel a blip.

No, instead, I thought his hair and eyes weren't dark enough, and his body was too lean.

Dammit, Broody had broken me.

I shot Brandon/Blake/Bryce a polite smile, then kept walking.

I had work that needed to get done. And I definitely had no room for men—either young, blond ones, or darker, older, intense ones.

All I had room for was my nephew.

CHAPTER 2
CADEN

I had the security camera installation plan to check, resumes to peruse, and several emails from other Langston Hotels security heads that needed my attention.

Crossing the lobby, I headed for the concierge desk. As I walked, it was habit to check the camera locations, take note of all the people milling in the lobby and the vehicles pulling up in front of the glass doors.

Nothing tripped my internal radar. No troublemakers or possible threats.

Okay, one thing pinged on my radar.

My gaze locked on the Langston Windward's concierge. He was talking with a young couple in hiking gear, handing them a trail map. He had a wide, white smile and handsome looks that made him popular.

His name was Enzo Rossi. The background check I'd run on him was as clean as a fresh damn fall of snow, but my radar was pinging. Loudly. There was more to Rossi and I would find out who the hell he was. Eventually.

Thankfully, he appeared dedicated to the hotel and staff, so for now, he wasn't a problem.

He caught my gaze, and I stared back steadily.

He shot me an amused smile. "Castro."

"Rossi." I circled the concierge desk and strode through the security room door.

The sound of hammers and power tools assailed me. I glanced around at the construction, and nodded to myself. It was coming along nicely.

The old security room had been tiny, but now the walls had been blown out to four times the size. Once everything was finished and the new technology installed, it would be state-of-the-art.

The previous head of security for the Langston Windward had happily retired. Deem hadn't been bad, just the kind of guy who put in the bare minimum and thought that was enough. It was never enough. I knew it paid to stay on top of things before trouble brewed.

The new security room would help us do that. For now, the security guards were monitoring the hotel's CCTV feeds in the conference room. It wasn't ideal, but we'd manage until the space was finished.

I stalked out. I'd oversee the installation of the new cameras and sensors myself. The current system was woefully outdated, and had more holes than a slice of Swiss cheese. I'd already done up a detailed plan, but it still needed some tweaking. I'd also hired some good locals to add to the security team. They all had military experience and were great additions. However, I still needed to find the right person to lead the team once the renovations were completed and I left.

I liked my job. Traveling around the world to different Langston hotels and upgrading the security was interesting and kept me busy. I never imagined I'd be running security for a hotel empire.

All I'd wanted growing up was to be a soldier. Like my grandfather. I'd been good at it.

Too good. Eventually, I'd gone into special forces. A muscle ticked in my jaw. I had no regrets. I'd done a hard job. I'd protected. I'd fought.

But I'd also seen things no man should see. Done things...

My steps slowed and I closed my eyes. For a second, I felt the humidity of the jungle, heard mud squelch underfoot, felt the trickle of sweat down the back of my neck. And I heard my friends screaming, moaning in pain...

Choking that thought off, I opened my eyes and continued across the lobby. My right hand clenched. It had been a different man who'd giddily signed up for the Army. A man following in his grandfather's footsteps, with dreams of making a difference.

The man who'd come home...

I didn't believe in dreams anymore. I didn't believe in anything.

Lifting my ID card to the reader on the staff door, I waited for the lock to beep, then I entered the staff office area.

Ahead, I spotted a tall, lean brunette and stopped. She was talking with one of her housekeeping staff. I kept my face blank.

I was known as cold and hard to read, mostly

because it was second nature for me to keep what I was feeling off my face. But what was usually very easy for me seemed to be hard around her.

I had no idea what it was about Allie Ford, but whenever she was near, I wanted to get closer, I wanted to look, I wanted to touch.

My fingers curled into my palm. She turned her head and looked my way. Gray eyes—almost silver, and always churning like a storm—locked on me. I knew she worked hard, was a loyal friend, and was also a single mother to her orphaned nephew.

I'd thumbed through her background report so many times the pages were smudged. Previously, she'd lived in New York, and had a fancy job and a nice apartment.

Until she'd left it all behind to come home to Windward and take care of her nephew.

She held my gaze and her chin lifted. Like she was challenging me. Or telling me to fuck off.

My fingers curled some more.

I couldn't get Allie Ford out of my damn head.

She turned away and I released a breath.

She had attitude, that was for sure. She wasn't the kind of woman to keep her thoughts to herself. Case in point, the fact that she called me by that ridiculous nickname.

And those legs...

Allie was slim and tall, and while her legs were currently covered by her sensible work pants, I'd seen her a couple of times in tiny jean shorts. My gut clenched. I bet Allie wouldn't want to know how many times I'd taken my hand to my cock in the shower, thinking of her long, smooth legs.

One of the security team stepped out of the conference room and spotted me. "Caden, there you are. We're ready."

Shoving thoughts of Allie away hastily, I managed to give Paul a brief nod. *Get your mind on your work, Castro.*

Paul was a new hire. He was ex-Army and working out well. Clean-cut, and married with two kids, he'd been working construction and barely making ends meet. He'd jumped at the chance to take the job I offered him.

Following him, I strode into the conference room, but as I passed through the doorway, I shot one more glance down the hall over my shoulder. Allie was watching me, but quickly looked away.

Yes, I was attracted to her, but I didn't get involved with women. I had zero to offer. I was also well-aware I wouldn't be in Windward forever. She had a kid and she deserved better.

I focused on the man sitting slumped in the chair at the long shiny conference table. He was scowling at the floor. Hastily erected flatscreen monitors covering the back wall showed security feeds from around the hotel. Gretchen was leaning against the wall. Another new hire, the forty-five-year-old former Marine was straight down the line and good in a fight. She was medium height, with gray-streaked, blonde-brown hair, and all packed muscle. Just the other week, I'd seen her take down an enraged man a foot taller than her. The guy had been trying to beat his wife in their suite, and Gretchen wasn't about to let that happen.

I circled the table and let my gaze lock on Morgan Brown.

He was older than me, in his late forties, and worked in the hotel's busy Bluff Bar and did some shifts as a server in the great room and restaurant.

He also liked to help himself to guests' handbags and wallets.

I sat in the chair. "Mr. Brown, I'm Caden Castro."

The man sniffed. "I know who you are. Langston's attack dog." His voice was belligerent.

I leaned forward. "Do you know why you're here?"

"Nope."

"I have you on camera stealing from the handbags of several of our guests."

The man stiffened.

"My team is also currently conducting a search of your locker."

A muscle ticked in his jaw.

"Stealing isn't tolerated at the Langston Windward."

Brown lifted a shoulder. "Whatever."

"Your employment is terminated. Effective immediately."

The conference room door opened, and another member of my team walked in. Hugh was a tall man, with the build of a football player, and sandy-blond hair. He set some items on the table. I saw credit cards, a diamond bracelet, two watches, a wad of cash, and a pair of ruby earrings.

"These are from his locker," Hugh said.

"Never seen any of that before," Brown sneered. "It's—"

"Shut up." I lowered my tone and Brown's mouth snapped shut. "If I see you in the Langston Windward again, or any Langston hotel, there'll be consequences."

Brown stiffened, as did my security staff. I knew my tone was enough to scare most people.

But Brown rallied. "Fuck you. These people can afford it. They're off having fun vacations in fancy hotels—"

I slammed my fist down on the table and he flinched. I lowered my voice to Arctic levels. "Some can't. Some scrimp and save for a special trip. And even if the wealthiest person in the world was staying here, you have no right to violate them and take something that isn't yours." He couldn't hold my gaze and looked away. "And now, I get to make your day even worse." I waved a hand.

Gretchen opened the door, and Officer Melissa Sanchez from the Windward Police Department stepped inside. The young woman was fit and wore her dark-blue uniform well. Her glossy, black hair was in a no-nonsense braid. She nodded at me. "Good morning, Castro."

"Officer Sanchez. He's all yours."

Brown's face drained of color. "The police? *No.*"

"You thought you'd get to walk out of here?" I rose and tugged my suit jacket into place. "This is the evidence from the locker."

Sanchez nodded. "Thanks. We're also executing a search warrant at his condo."

The man made a choked noise.

"And thank you for giving us the name of his fence," she added.

I inclined my head. It hadn't taken me long to dig up dirt on Brown. "Langston Hotels appreciates your help."

I watched dispassionately as Officer Sanchez cuffed the man and led him out. Then I nodded at Hugh to escort them out of the hotel. Just in case Brown got any stupid ideas.

"Thanks, Paul, Gretchen."

"Sure thing, boss," Gretchen said. "I'm off to do a walk around."

"I've got the monitors," Paul added.

I headed into the corridor and strode toward the owner's office at the end of the hall. The door was open. As I entered, I saw my boss sitting behind his desk and one of the executive team perched on the corner of it.

"He graces us with his presence," Piper said.

Piper Ellis was a workaholic blonde who liked high heels and things running smoothly. She was the COO for Langston Hotels.

I nodded at her, then at my friend and boss, Ambrose "Ro" Langston. He had his hands steepled under his chin. He had thick, dark hair, brown eyes, and bronze skin. The Greek heritage he'd inherited from his socialite mother was evident. Photos of him were always plastered all over the pages of glossy magazines.

"I was busy firing a thief." I sat in a chair in front of the desk.

"Busy morning," Piper noted.

"Any other security concerns?" Ro asked.

"Nothing to report yet. I'm collating and checking

out any suspicious behavior and activities around the hotel." I shrugged. "Most of those turn out to be nothing."

"God, you're paranoid." Piper crossed her legs.

"It pays to catch problems early."

"You're good at that," Ro said. "How are the security office renovations coming?"

"On schedule. It's going to be fit for purpose. I've made several new hires for the team. I'm still searching for a new head of security for the Langston Windward. I have a few feelers out."

Ro nodded. "Piper?"

"The renovations to the guest rooms are on schedule. We're doing as many as we can before the winter season. The rest will be after. The new paint and minor updates are going well."

Ro rested his hands on the desk and smiled. "Great work."

"Oh, and I'm working with Tessa on the final details for the Halloween Spooktacular next week." Piper arched a brow at our boss. "I hear that this was your idea."

Ro's smile widened. "I thought a second event, in addition to the Mountain Masquerade, to raise money for the Windward Valley Children's Charity was an excellent idea."

I grunted. "Send me the details so I can work up the security plan."

Piper smiled. "Oh, I will. You'll love to hear that it's going to be outside."

Dammit. Outside events were always harder to secure. "Fine."

Glee entered Piper's face, which should have given me a warning.

"And Tessa is making it mandatory that everyone wears costumes. Including hotel staff."

A muscle ticked in my jaw. "I'm not wearing a fucking costume."

"It's mandatory," Ro said. The asshole wasn't even trying to hide his grin.

I crossed my arms and scowled.

"I'm busy recruiting a new chef." Ro's brows drew together. "If I can lure him away from the restaurant in London."

"Who?" Piper asked.

"Jasper Harvey."

"Oh." Piper pressed a hand to her chest. "I had a meal at his restaurant, Noir, once. *Divine.* His desserts are some of the best things I've ever tasted." Then she frowned. "I hear that he's a bear to work with."

"Yes. He says less than Caden does and roars when he's unhappy. He can be... temperamental, and grumpy as hell. Luckily, his food is beyond good." Ro rose from his chair. "We'll have to leave it there. I have a call scheduled with Kavner Fury and Tristan shortly."

"How are the plans for the Langston New Orleans going?" Piper asked.

"Coming along, but slowly. We've hit a few snags, but just the usual things. Tristan is working his magic."

Tristan Banks was CFO for Langston. The man loved numbers almost as much as he loved his closet of expensive suits.

Ro smiled. "Oh, and I need you both back here this afternoon at 2:30."

"Why?" I asked warily. If there were costumes involved, I wasn't interested.

"Tessa has samples for the planned great room and restaurant renovation to show. Paint colors, fabrics, furniture. She wants everyone's opinions."

"Not my area." I didn't care what color the restaurant was.

Ro raised a brow. "You don't show, she'll track you down."

I frowned. This was true. Tessa was all smiles and professionalism, but it covered a determined and surprisingly stubborn personality.

"She's roped Jazz, Sierra, and Allie into it as well."

Allie would be there. I kept my face blank. Jazz was Tessa's assistant, and Sierra was a bubbly blonde in charge of outdoor activities. Allie being there meant I shouldn't attend.

My mouth moved of its own accord. "Fine. I'll be there."

"Good." Ro slipped into his jacket. "Now, I might check on my hotel manager before my call."

Piper rolled her eyes.

My lips quirked. Ro was cross-eyed in love with Tessa. Watching the two of them together made me...

I mentally shook my head. I was happy for them. Despite being a billionaire, things hadn't always been easy for Ro. He deserved a good woman like Tessa.

"I hope 'check on' isn't an euphemism for something." Piper rose. "Don't cause an HR issue."

Ro's grin widened. "I'll do my best."

Shaking my head, I strode out. I had resumes to go over and I had no doubt my emails were piling up by now. I had more than enough work to keep me busy. Like I'd said to Piper and Ro, being focused on stopping trouble before it started was what made me good at my job.

I needed to focus on work, not on distractions that weren't for me.

And definitely not storm-gray eyes and legs that went on forever.

CHAPTER 3
ALLIE

*T*ime to clock off.

Standing in the locker room, I stripped off my uniform and hit the showers. My shift had run smoothly. It was always a good day when there was no disaster to clean up. I let the hot water run over my head, releasing a sigh.

I wished I could stay in here longer, but Tessa had texted strict instructions for me to meet her in Ro's office.

Shutting off the water, I grabbed a towel and dried off. Then I pulled on my clean clothes. She wanted me to look at paint samples or something. A decorator, I was not. My plan was just to hum and nod at any questions I was asked. To be fair, she'd sweetened the deal by bribing me with afternoon snacks from the local bakery. As kids, we'd been in there every week to buy honey cakes.

Pulling on some leggings, I snatched up my favorite slouchy sweater in a silvery-blue and yanked it over my head. It instantly slid off one shoulder since I'd managed to stretch it in the last wash. I ran a hand through my hair.

There. Ready. It was so easy having short hair. I wrinkled my nose. The downside was that it needed to be cut regularly to stay in style. With my tight budget these days, I knew I might need to think about growing it longer.

I grabbed my bag and checked my watch. I had thirty minutes until I needed to pick up Ollie from school. Perusing paint colors better not take too long.

I headed up to the offices. I knew Sierra would be there, along with Jazz and Piper. Striding down the hallway, I caught a hint of scent in the air and my steps slowed.

Caden. I knew his cologne anywhere. It was dark and spicy, and made me think of dark nights and dirty fantasies.

I drew in a lungful. He must've recently passed this way.

Then I stiffened. *God, I was pathetic.* Sniffing a man's cologne like a junkie. Seriously, I had no idea why the man got to me, apart from his magnificent thighs, and the confident way he carried himself, and his black eyes.

Shaking my head, I continued down the hallway. I liked conversation and cuddles and having fun when I was with a guy. I was pretty sure Caden didn't believe in any of those things. If he did, he'd probably self-destruct.

Voices came from Ro's office and I set my shoulders back.

I had snacks to eat and fabric swatches to pretend I liked. I was putting Caden Castro out of my mind.

As I entered, I heard Tessa's laugh, but my gaze went straight to Ro. The hotelier was wearing a navy-blue suit, no doubt tailored for his broad shoulders and lean hips. He looked like he should be on the cover of GQ. His dark hair had a touch of a curl and he had a handsome face many women drooled over.

He was smiling as he looked at Tessa like she was the rising sun.

Ugh, they were so in love.

"I was promised food."

"Allie." Tessa bustled over and grabbed my arm. "Just in time."

"I can't stay long, I need to get Ollie from school soon."

"Of course. Come and see the samples. We have some great options." She pulled a face. "If only we could use all of them somewhere. Piper did help me narrow down the selection."

Ro's desk was filled with paint chips, fabrics, tile samples, and pictures of lighting and furniture.

Tessa waved a hand at the selection. "Every opinion you give, I'll feed you a snack."

I snorted. "Like I'm a dog doing tricks."

She ruffled my damp hair. "There's a good Allie."

With a laugh, I knocked her arm away.

"I knew that without a bribe, you'd just eat and nod, and agree with everything I say."

Crap, sometimes it sucked when your friend knew you so well.

31

At the other end of the desk, Sierra laughed. The blonde was standing there drinking tea with Jazz. Sierra was the Outdoors Events Coordinator. She'd moved here a few years back from California. I'd liked her as soon as we'd met—despite her fondness for early morning exercise. She was tiny, barely five feet, and her blonde hair was in a perky ponytail. Jazz was Tessa's right-hand woman. She was a curvy Afro-Latina, with gorgeous curls I envied, and was happily married to her hubby Hector.

"Well, I at least need a coffee first," I said.

Soon, I was sipping a cappuccino and trying not to let my eyes glaze over. I loved my best friend, but this is *not* my area of expertise.

Sierra, Piper, and Jazz were all oohing and ahhing over everything. Ro was on his cellphone taking a call. Smart man.

"Allie, what do you think of these colors for in the restaurant?" Tessa held up two squares of blue.

Crap. I tapped a finger against my lips. "Well, the one on the right is blue. And the one on the left is...blue."

Tessa rolled her eyes. "They're Cerulean Sky and Windy Morning."

Was naming paint colors ridiculous names an actual job? "I like the one on the left."

"Me too." My friend shoved a pastry at me.

I happily took a bite. Sugary goodness hit my taste buds. Okay, so I was sleep deprived, sex deprived, and needed to collect Ollie shortly, and maybe buy some vegetables, then attempt to make a healthy dinner for the two of us, but right now, while eating this pastry, life was glorious. I took another bite.

"Tessa, these chairs will be *perfect*." Sierra tapped a finger at a photo on the desk. Jazz leaned over and nodded.

"I really like them too," Piper said.

I craned my neck. They looked like comfy chairs. "They get my vote. They'll—" Movement in the doorway caught my attention. My belly tightened.

I'd recognize that silhouette anywhere.

Caden, in his usual, dark suit along with his usual scowl stood there, scanning the room.

My stupid pulse picked up, and when his dark eyes flicked my way, it did a crazy jump.

Stop it, stupid pulse.

"Caden." Ro had finished his call and was sliding his phone away. "Come and look at paint samples."

I saw a muscle tick beside Caden's eye, and a laugh escaped me.

Those ink-black eyes focused on me.

"If Ro had asked you to come and look at some grenades, I think you'd look happier."

He walked toward me, and I smelled his spicy cologne. My inner hussy released a whimper.

Jeez. I ignored her.

"This...isn't my area of expertise," Caden said.

"Mine either, Broody." I held up a pastry. "But there's food. So for a few minutes, pretend you're human and decide which shade of blue you like best."

CHAPTER 4
CADEN

Drinking my black coffee, I pretended to give a shit about decorating. The women were all talking, with Ro interjecting with the odd comment or opinion.

"You're pretending to care about this even less than I am," Allie murmured so only I could hear.

"I don't care what color the wall is."

"No, you just care where you can stick your cameras."

I sipped again. "Yes."

"So why come?"

"My boss told me I had to." *And I knew you'd be here.* I cleared my throat. "Plus, I don't want to get on Tessa's bad side." I eyed her. "Why did you come?"

"My best friend told me I had to." Allie grinned. "And she bribed me with food." Allie reached past me and nabbed another pastry with a ridiculous amount of frosting on top.

Her scent hit my senses. She'd showered and she smelled like something fruity. Mango, maybe.

I knew I should leave. I'd been telling myself over and over to avoid distractions. To avoid her.

I'd made an appearance, so I could get out of there. I should not be standing next to Allie Ford. Smelling her, talking to her, watching her lips as she ate. She threatened my control.

My gaze drifted down her body. Her leggings showcased those damn long legs of hers.

I wondered how they'd feel wrapped around my hips.

Pressing my lips together, I fought back my irritation. *Find some damn control, Castro.* "I hope you won't be late for work tomorrow."

She cocked a brow. "Ah, there's the Broody we know and love."

Hearing the word love on her lips made me stiffen.

"I was late today because my kid needed me to walk him to his classroom. If he needs it again tomorrow, I'll be five minutes late again." She turned to face me, a fierce look in her eyes. "You going to give me a detention slip, Mr. Castro? Send me to the principal's office?"

"I was just—"

"Being an uptight, rule-following asshole." She poked my chest. "I do my job and I do it well. No one can accuse me of slacking."

"I never said you weren't doing your job. You're excellent at it." And way overqualified to work in housekeeping.

"*Oh.*" Faint color appeared in her cheeks.

"Your team members love you. You get excellent comments in the staff surveys."

She tucked a strand of hair behind her ear. "I'm glad to hear that."

"And I know you're giving everything to your nephew. You should be proud of the job you're doing."

She blinked at me and tilted her head. "Who are you, and what have you done with our head of security?"

She made me want to smile. I realized I like seeing her pleased and happy. How would it feel to make her happy all the time? She had shadows under her eyes and I knew she wasn't getting enough sleep. I knew she didn't have much free time. What if someone helped share that load?

Not your job, Castro.

"Okay, you two." Tessa appeared. "This one or this one?" She held up two small squares of fabric.

Shit. They were both shades of brown with some sort of stripe in them.

"That one." Allie pointed to the one on the right.

"I agree," I added quickly.

Tessa beamed. "That was my choice as well. I think the shades go really well with our luxury mountain lodge theme." Then she pulled something out of her pocket.

It was a bar of chocolate. It was wrapped in patterned white and gold paper.

"Your reward." She handed the bar to Allie.

Allie's eyes widened. "Dandelion!" Her lips curled into a smile. "You're a goddess, Tessa." She clutched the bar to her chest like it was made of gold.

I frowned. "Dandelion?"

Allie spun, pure joy on her face. "The *best* chocolate in the world. It's small batch chocolate made in San Francisco. They make single-origin dark chocolate using just two ingredients: cocoa beans and organic cane sugar. That's it. And it tastes like heaven."

She looked like she'd been given an all-expenses paid vacation.

"The only place they sell it in the entire state of Colorado is in The Nook here in Windward. Tessa's aunt owns the store." She ripped open the package, broke off a bit of dark chocolate and took a bite. "*Mmm.* I'm going to savor this. Thanks, Tessa."

I watched Allie eat another piece of chocolate. I tried not to look at her lips.

She broke off another piece and held it out. "Try it."

"I don't really eat chocolate."

She smiled. "Of course you don't, but try this."

I took the square and popped it in my mouth. The rich, nutty flavor hit me and my eyebrows rose.

"Told you," she said smugly.

She was right. The dark chocolate was good.

Then she carefully folded the wrapper over the chocolate and slipped it into her pocket.

"You're going to hoard it?"

"It's a treat and I need to make it last. I can't afford fancy expensive chocolate anymore." She shook her head. "It's all Reese's peanut butter cups these days. They're Ollie's favorite."

My chest tightened. She couldn't afford her favorite chocolate? I hated that.

The ring of a cellphone interrupted, and Allie fished around in her bag. "Crap, that's mine."

She pulled her phone out and an unreadable look

crossed her face. My best guess, it was part annoyance and part resignation.

She held up the phone in front of her and pasted a fake smile on. I'd never seen Allie fake anything before.

"Hi, Mom."

"Allie, sweetie." There was a pause. "Those bags under your eyes need attention, Allison. Really. You need a better concealer."

I moved enough to catch a glimpse of the older blonde woman on the screen. She looked nothing like Allie. She had artfully styled hair and a lot of makeup.

"Sure thing, Mom. I'll get right on that."

"I hope I didn't catch you at a bad time?"

"I've just finished work, but I need to leave shortly to pick up Ollie from school."

"Oh, of course. My sweet grandbaby."

Allie's mouth tightened. "How are you?"

"Wonderful, sweetie. After my yoga session today, I had a long lunch with friends, then headed to the shops. Fendi is having a sale. You need a good handbag, Allie. You should check it out."

"No, I don't need an expensive handbag, I have a kid to feed and nowhere to wear an expensive handbag."

"A good-quality piece in your wardrobe never goes to waste. I've told you that you need to put some effort into your appearance. It shows your commitment, makes a good first impression. If you look like a tomboy, no one will ever take you seriously."

"How's Harold?"

I listened to the less-than-stealthy change of subject.

"My darling is great. He's at golf right now. He's booked us a cruise around the Caribbean next month."

"That's great. Ollie's doing well at school."

"Excellent. Give him a hug from his Coco."

Allie blew out a breath. "Sure. You could call on the weekend and talk with him."

"This weekend? Oh, sweetie, Harold and I are *so* busy. I have a meditation retreat on Saturday, then we're out with friends on Sunday."

"Another time then." Allie's tone was flat.

"Yes. Okay, Allie, I have to run. And why don't you grow out your hair. You know how much I hate it that short."

"Bye, Mom." Allie stabbed at the phone.

My gaze on her face. Everything in my file said that Allie had an idyllic childhood here in Windward, except for when her parents divorced when she was in her teens.

I was thinking maybe I didn't have all the facts.

"Coco?" I asked.

"Oh, Mom had no desire to be called grandma, granny, or nana. She said it made her feel old. She picked Coco instead." Allie was tense, her voice tight. "I need to go."

"You aren't close with your mom?"

She met my gaze. "I really need to get Ollie. I always make sure I'm never late to pick him up."

"Does your mom help out with Ollie?"

Because it sounded like she was too busy buying fancy bags and going on vacations while her daughter worked her ass off to care for her orphaned nephew.

"She sends him birthday and Christmas gifts." She slung her bag over her shoulder.

I didn't want her to leave. I didn't want to see the tension on her face. "Allie—"

"This is starting to feel like an interrogation. No more answers until you answer my questions. Are you close with your mother?"

Discomfort came hard and fast. My mouth flattened. "I used to be."

Her gaze traced my face and her stiff shoulders relaxed. "Sorry, I didn't mean to pry somewhere I shouldn't."

Which was exactly what I'd been doing. "After I left the military..." Jesus, this was hard to talk about. "I wasn't the same. I was closed off and it was difficult for my mom and sisters having me around. I call them occasionally. They live in Texas."

"I really didn't mean to pry," she murmured.

"Looks like I'm missing out on the party," a deep voice said.

Everett Murray, the head of hotel maintenance, stood in the doorway, wearing a brown flannel shirt and worn jeans.

"Oh, hi, Ev," Tessa said with a smile. "Come in."

"The snacks look good." He shot the room a lazy smile. "And I can't wait to offer my opinions on the renovations."

By Ro's desk, Piper stiffened like she'd been electrocuted. "I really don't think that's necessary."

"As head of maintenance, I'll be maintaining things. I think I have a lot to offer."

Piper snorted. "You wouldn't know style if it conked you on your hard head." She shot a glare at his flannel shirt.

"And that's my cue to leave," Allie said. "Before blood starts flying. Bye, everyone." She glanced at me. "Bye, Broody. Have some of those pretty pastries."

I eyed the fancy pastries. "Hell, no."

She laughed, and I greedily absorbed the sound.

"You never lie or pretend, do you?" Her eyes twinkled. "I like that." Then she turned and headed out.

I watched her go.

I couldn't let her like me. I couldn't let her get too close.

Because then she'd realize there was nothing to like.

"I need to go too," I announced.

Ro raised a hand and Tessa and Jazz called out goodbyes. Piper was too busy telling Everett off about something to notice my departure.

I shoved my hands in my pockets and stalked out of the office. I needed to find some work to do.

CHAPTER 5
ALLIE

Another shift almost done.

Today had gone fast. Lots of guests had checked out and there had been plenty of rooms to clean and restock.

I pressed my hands to my lower back and the dull ache there. I still hadn't gotten used to being on my feet for most of the day. At least I didn't need to go to the gym or run anymore.

Last night, I'd had a quiet night in with Ollie. We'd even managed to eat some vegetables with the spaghetti I'd made.

Right, now I needed to finish up, then collect Ollie from school, and go and get some groceries. We didn't have much left in the refrigerator.

Then, I had the weekend off. Yay.

I spotted Marcy, one of my best housekeepers. There was a frown on her face as she parked her cart.

"Marcy? All good?"

The older woman nodded. "I still need to finish vacuuming on level three in the east wing." Her frown deepened.

"What's wrong? Are any guests causing any trouble?"

She blew out a breath. "No. It's nothing. Some new guests who arrived yesterday are on level three. They're loud. One day here and they already have visitors. Mostly female visitors." The woman sniffed.

"The extreme-sports guys? They're here to mountain bike."

She lifted her chin. "That's them. They give me a bad vibe."

"Did they do or say anything to bother you?" I touched her arm. "Tell me and I'll take care of it."

The woman's face softened. She patted my hand. "You're a good girl, Allie. A good boss, too."

My chest tightened. "Thanks."

"And it's no thanks to those parents of yours."

I bit my lip. "Mom and Dad are...Mom and Dad."

"They should be here helping you with their grandson." She shook her head. "It's so unfair you lost your brother. Anyway, those boys...men on level three haven't done one thing to bother me. The blond one, thinks he's all that—" she rolled her eyes "—and is heavy on the charm."

"I noticed that."

"I have no proof that they're up to no good, but I raised three sons. Those men are up to something."

"Maybe they're just a little wild?" A part of me envied them. They traveled around, doing what they loved, with no responsibilities. "I don't want you to worry. I'll keep an eye on them, starting with finishing the vacuuming on level three. You clock off and get home to that gorgeous husband of yours."

Marcy smiled. "Such a good girl."

"I'm not. I can be mean and ornery."

"Pfft. I'll tell my Darren you think he's gorgeous."

"Do that, but be careful, I might steal him away from you, Marcy."

With a laugh, the older woman hurried off.

I grabbed the vacuum cleaner and headed to level three. When I stepped off the elevator, everything was quiet. I eyed the doors to the guys' rooms. No sign of wild orgies or criminal activity. I flicked on the vacuum cleaner and felt it vibrate up my arm. I worked my way down the hall.

I was almost finished when the elevator dinged. I heard loud voices and glanced up.

It was the extreme-sports guys. Four of them. The blond one—Brandon/Blake/Bryce—was clearly the leader. There were two dark-haired guys—one tall and lean, the other shorter, but muscular. The fourth had long, dirty-blond hair with a medium build. He looked like he should be out surfing.

There were also three women and another man with them. They were all laughing and joking. Nothing tripped my radar.

They opened the doors to their rooms, and the blond guy had an arm around a cute little brunette. Then he glanced my way and his lips quirked. He shot me a wink.

The doors closed behind them. I vacuumed closer,

then switched off the machine. There was no loud music, no screams. Nothing.

Shaking my head, I headed for the elevator, dragging the vacuum cleaner with me. I needed to go, or I'd be late to pick up Ollie.

This was my new norm. Forever running five minutes late for everything.

The elevator dinged, and I turned to look back down the hall, but nobody had stepped out of the rooms. I backed into the elevator, towing the vacuum cleaner. And that's when I smacked into something. Something hard.

Firm hands gripped my hips, steadying me.

With a gasp, I whipped my head around. And stared up into Caden's rugged face.

"Um, sorry." My silly heart was trying to leap into my throat. I hadn't seen him at all today.

"It's all right."

His deep voice shivered through me. The elevator doors closed.

"Where are you going?" I asked.

He hadn't let go of me, and I could feel his fingers burning through the cotton of my uniform.

"I'm conducting an elevator test. We've been having problems with this one tripping out. Everett's team is working on it."

"God, it's not breaking down again, is it?" It had happened. Quite a few times in the past.

"Luckily, we'll be getting new ones after the winter, but we need to keep it functioning until then."

"Right." The elevator went up.

Caden's hands loosened on me. God, I wanted him to touch me. *So stupid.* I barely knew the guy. I wasn't entirely sure I liked him, and I wasn't entirely sure he liked me. Or anyone.

We reached the top floor, then after a beat, we started to descend. Good. I couldn't be late for Ollie.

"I never thanked you," I blurted out.

He cocked one dark brow. "For what?"

"For saving Tessa."

A disturbed man had targeted Ro after he'd bought the Langston Windward. I'd thought Rupert was a nice, quiet IT guy, not a deranged stalker. Instead, he'd believed he should be the owner of the Windward, and had a massive crush on Tessa. An icky, obsessive one.

He'd targeted Ro, but had almost killed Tessa in the process, then kidnapped her.

In the hospital after she'd been poisoned, I'd lost it, but Caden had talked me down. He'd promised to catch the man and he had.

A muscle ticked in his hard jaw. "It took me too long to find the guy. I should've caught him sooner."

"Broody—" I grabbed his arm. "Tessa and Ro are all right. It all worked out. I know how hard you searched for him. None of us suspected it was Rupert. I'd known him for years and I didn't know he was capable of kidnap and attempted murder. Tessa told me you broke into the cabin to rescue her with Ro, guns blazing."

"I only had one gun."

My lips twitched. Maybe that was a joke. I couldn't tell. "Fine, *gun* blazing. I'm grateful. So, thank you."

"Allie—"

Suddenly, the elevator lurched to a hard stop. The lights went out and we pitched forward. Strong arms caught me and yanked me against a hard chest.

That's when I smelled him. That dark, spicy cologne wrapped around me and made my belly flutter. I dragged in a deep breath.

"You okay?" His lips brushed my ear.

"Yes." I pulled in a few more breaths. God, I wanted to keep sniffing him. Dim emergency lighting flicked on and that's when I realized our situation. "Oh God, are we trapped?"

"Looks that way."

"*No*." My voice was sharp. "I can't be trapped. I'm off shift. I need to go." Panic coursed through me. I needed to pick up Ollie and I couldn't be late. I couldn't let him feel forgotten, abandoned. My breaths were coming too fast.

Caden spun me. "Allie—" He frowned, studying my face intently.

I held up a hand and backed up until I hit the wall. "*God*. I need to get *out*."

His hands grabbed mine and I startled.

"Talk to me," he ordered. His voice was strong, sure. "Breathe."

I dragged in a breath.

"Again."

"I'm okay."

"Are you claustrophobic?"

"No, but I have to pick up my kid. Oliver. Ollie. I have

to pick him up from school in twenty minutes. I can't leave him there, alone. He'll think I abandoned or forgot him." I sucked in a ragged breath. "Or that something happened to me."

Something moved across Caden's face.

I gripped his arm. "I *can't* have him thinking something's happened and that he's all alone."

Caden gave a brisk nod. "Okay." He pulled out his cellphone and texted a message.

"Anything? Are they working to get us out?"

"The technician is on the way, but it's gonna be an hour."

I made an agonized sound.

"Allie."

I met his gaze.

"I'll get you out." He shoved his phone away.

"Really?" Hope bloomed. I was so used to dealing with everything on my own, but I couldn't fix this problem.

"I promise."

Then he reached up to the ceiling of the elevator car and I frowned.

A second later, he pried open a panel. It dropped down, a black hole looming above us.

"Step back."

I shuffled backward. Then he jumped up and grabbed the edge of the hole with one hand, and, with a move of pure athleticism and grace, pulled himself up, curled his legs upward, and disappeared onto the top of the elevator car.

Lots of feelings rushed through me and I blinked.

That move was hot. That easy flex of muscle. He was fit and strong, and looked like a spy. *Hello, Ethan Hunt. Or James Bond.*

I licked my lips. Crap, I was damp between my thighs.

"Allie?" He leaned down through the hole, holding out a hand. "Come on."

Reaching up, I took his hand. Strong fingers wrapped around mine.

Then he hauled me up.

I let out a startled yelp and grabbed the edge of the hole. I couldn't believe he could lift me like that. I was tall. Sure, I was slim and lean, and my curves would never be described as generous, even though I'd desperately wished for boobs and hips when I was growing up, but I wasn't light.

Then I was on top of the elevator car beside him in the darkened elevator shaft.

My heart beat like crazy.

"What are you doing?" I asked breathlessly.

"Getting you out so you can get your kid." His face was in shadow, but I knew he was looking at me. "You with me?"

"I'm with you," I whispered.

When was the last time anyone had gone so far out of their way to help me?

I had good friends, and they helped when they could, but I tried not to lean too hard on them. Tried not to take advantage of them. They had their own lives.

Apart from my brother, no one had ever been there

for me. No one had ever been my shelter in the storm. Been my rock when I needed one.

Caden rose fluidly. My gaze drifted down his body, then snagged on his thighs. The guy filled out a suit so well.

Then he reached up and I saw the closed doors that led onto one of the floors. I watched as he gripped them and strained, pushing them apart slowly.

Oh God, mini orgasm.

"Let's move." He gripped my waist, and again like I weighed nothing, lifted me out.

My heart gave a flutter as I crawled out of the elevator shaft. My heart never fluttered. I wasn't the flutter kind of girl.

He leaped out behind me.

"Go. I already texted Enzo, and one of his guys is bringing your car around to the front."

That shook me out of my stupor, and I looked at my watch. "I can still make it." I spun and took two steps toward the stairs.

Then I turned back and saw Caden watching me with those black-ice eyes.

"Thanks, Broody. I owe you."

Then I raced off, heading for the stairs.

I needed to get to my kid. I definitely didn't need to be fangirling over Caden Castro and his James Bond maneuvers.

"So did you have a good day?" I unlocked the front door of the condo and followed Ollie inside.

I'd made it to school to pick him up in time...just. He hadn't been the last kid there, so I was counting that as a win.

"Yeah." He paused, swinging his backpack off his shoulders. "I played with Austin."

"He's a friend?"

Ollie shrugged, then gave a tiny nod.

Yes. A friend. This was good. I felt a giddy sense of relief way out of proportion to this news, but I was going to ride it.

"All right. You go and play while I'm cooking dinner."

He eyed me skeptically. "Tacos?"

"No."

"Hot dogs?"

"No." Those were my go-to meals, but I figured we both needed more greens. "A chicken stir fry."

He was quiet for a beat. "Okay."

I watched him head to the toy basket, my heart squeezing. God, I loved him. I wanted him to be happy.

I knew we would be. Eventually.

But I knew life could knock you in the teeth when you least expected it. It wasn't always smooth sailing and roses.

Hell, it was rarely that. It was divorces, disappointments, and losing the ones who meant the most to you.

I pulled up the recipe on my phone and got chopping. I was good at chopping, thankfully. I felt a permanent groove forming between my brows as I started putting everything together. I turned on the stove. Soon I had things boiling and sizzling. As I stood by the frypan, my brain turned to Caden.

It was way too easy to picture him pulling himself up through the ceiling in the elevator. A little shudder ran through me. He'd gotten me out.

He'd gone above and beyond to get me out so I could get to Ollie on time.

And he'd captured Tessa's stalker/abductor/would-be killer. Just as he'd promised.

Caden Castro might be a rare unicorn. A man who kept his promises. A man you could depend on.

A man who wasn't close to his family since he'd left the military. I was itching to know what the story was there.

"Allie?"

I looked over at Ollie who was sitting on the rug. "Yeah, buddy?"

"What's that burning smell?"

Oh, shit. I kept the cursing mental, something I'd had to learn when Ollie and I moved in together. I quickly pulled the smoking frypan off the stove. Everything inside it was burned to a crisp.

"Damn. It said medium heat for five minutes. That wasn't even three."

Ollie wandered over and glanced at the recipe. "Did you stir it?"

Right. Instead of stirring, I'd been daydreaming about a man I wasn't even sure liked me.

Sighing, I scraped the ruins of dinner into the trash, then set the frypan in the sink. "Looks like we're having pizza, Ol-ster."

He smiled. "Yeah."

Yeah, my little man loved pizza. "We're getting a supreme." At least it had some vegetables on there. That counted, right?

Rubbing a hand over my face, I fought back the tiredness and the pinch of failure. I couldn't even manage to cook a healthy meal.

I couldn't afford any self-pity. I had to feed my kid.

CHAPTER 6
CADEN

I sat in the dark.

My suite at the Windward was nice. A generous size, and done in classy creams and browns, with touches of wood and stone. It suited the mountain location. The best thing was the view out the windows. The mountain was breathtaking, and I'd watched the green leaves give way to the vibrant fall colors.

But right now, all I saw was darkness.

It matched how I felt inside. A muscle in my jaw flexed. I just kept staring at nothing. I didn't get nightmares. Instead, I just didn't sleep.

I didn't bother going to bed and staring at the ceiling. I didn't need much sleep, anyway.

Staring at the darkness usually dredged up old memories, old failures. I heard my mother's sobbing and saw my sisters staring at me like I was a stranger. The memories nipped away at the edges of my consciousness, like predators trying to find a way in.

But not tonight.

Tonight, like many nights since I'd come to Windward, my head was filled with Allie Ford.

My fingers curled. I could picture her long legs, her lean, intriguing body. Her eye roll. Her smile.

Her panic when she thought she'd be late to get her nephew.

I cursed. I wasn't going there.

Jerking to my feet, I snatched up my key card and phone off the side table and headed for the door.

It was midnight and the corridor was empty. Piper was in the suite next door to mine. She'd be sleeping. She always said she needed a solid seven hours.

Ignoring the elevator, I took the stairs. I did wonder if Allie got to Ollie in time after I'd gotten her out of the elevator. My footsteps were silent as I headed down the stairs.

Pushing through the door at the bottom, I found the lobby empty and quiet. I loved hotels in the dead of night. All hushed and in go-slow mode. There was no one at reception, but I knew someone would be around to deal with any late-night check-ins or emergencies.

Not all hotels were this quiet at nighttime. Some in the big cities never quite turned off.

Crossing the lobby, I absorbed the different vibe the place had when it was empty.

"You're up and about late."

I lifted my head. Enzo stood nearby, leaning against the concierge desk. I hadn't heard or sensed the man, and that disquieted me.

It was clear the guy had training. But I'd been special forces, and no one fucking snuck up on me. Except Enzo.

"I couldn't sleep. Figured I'd do a walk around."

Enzo lifted his chin. "It's a quiet night. That's the way I like it."

I cocked my head. "You worked in Las Vegas before here."

"Yes. It's never quiet there."

Our gazes met. I saw the demons in his. It took one to know one.

"Any problems, let me know," I said.

He gave me a nod. "It was good of you to help Allie out of the elevator earlier."

I stilled.

"She's all about that boy. She's been through enough, then losing her brother. Now, she's juggling so many balls. I don't know how she does it."

I turned. "What's she been through?" I'd read her background report and nothing had popped.

Enzo shrugged. "Not my story to tell. Her parents... They're not terrible, but they weren't great either."

I frowned. "I heard her talking with her mother on the phone."

Enzo made a sound. "From the two times she's visited, Clarice Ford doesn't seem like good mother material, or grandmother material. Allie's brother was her real family."

And she'd lost him.

For a second, I thought of my mother and sisters, but I locked that down really quickly. "I'll always help out staff members when they need it. That includes you, Rossi."

"I don't need help."

I didn't reply to that, and continued on into the staff offices. In the conference room, one of the new guards, Paul, nodded from his seat in front of the screens.

"All quiet, boss."

"Good."

I snatched up a stack of files off the conference table. I'd spend some time reviewing the resumes for the head of security. So far, no one was what I was looking for.

I headed into an empty office and clicked on the lamp. Settling into the chair, I set the folders down, then started flicking through.

Several hours ticked by and finally, tiredness tugged at me. I closed the files and turned off the lamp. I'd try to snatch a few hours sleep now, then get up early for a workout in the hotel gym.

Rising, I headed back into the corridor, but I paused, turning to look back at the door leading to the staff locker room. I pivoted and changed directions.

In the locker room, I punched in the code on my locker. It contained my gym gear but on the top shelf was the small parcel I'd purchased in town today. I opened it, hesitated, then pulled out one bar of chocolate wrapped in white and gold paper.

It only took me twenty seconds to find Allie's locker and pick the lock. I placed the chocolate bar inside, then relocked it.

I didn't let myself think too much about why I'd visited Tessa's aunt's store and bought the chocolate.

Back in the lobby, I was nearing the elevators when I heard loud voices, followed by raucous laughter that echoed across the lobby.

I swiveled.

A group had just entered through the front doors. They'd clearly been in town, drinking somewhere. There were four guys and three ladies. Three very young ladies. Two were clinging to guys, and the other was holding hands with one.

"Let's continue this party upstairs." One dark-haired guy threw his hands in the air. "*Yeah.*"

I assessed the girls. The best I could tell, while they were young, they all appeared to be adults.

The guys looked like frat bros out for good time, ignoring all responsibilities. They clearly lived a privileged life, and hadn't suffered responsibility slapping them in the face.

We had plenty of groups like these ones that came to Windward and other Langston resorts for a good time, but something about these guys set off my radar. I crossed my arms, watching them wait for the elevator.

"It's late," I said. "It'd be good if you to keep the noise level down."

The group jolted and the laughter dwindled.

"Dude, where did you come from?" one guy said.

Another of the guys got a belligerent look on his face, while the girls looked wide-eyed and worried.

"Man, we're just having a good time," one man who looked like an unkempt surfer said.

"It's three o'clock in the morning. The hotel guests

are sleeping. You can still have a good time, just do it quietly."

One of the guys—tall, fit, and blond—caught my gaze. We shared a look, and he nodded. He wasn't as drunk as the others. He had a little redhead tucked under his arm.

"We'll keep it down, sir."

A moment later, the group disappeared into the elevator. They resumed talking loudly, but were quieter than before. The doors closed and the noise faded.

My gaze narrowed. I'd add them to my list of things to keep an eye on.

CHAPTER 7
ALLIE

Ollie looked cute as hell in his woolen hat and jacket. I grinned at him. Thank God it was Saturday and my day off.

The sun was shining, but the air was cold. I stared up at the bright-blue sky. We'd get our first snow soon. One thing I loved about Windward was its four distinct seasons. When I got sick of the hot weather, winter rolled in. And when I'd had enough of snow, the trees turned green, and summer would appear.

But right now, I was enjoying the fall. Halloween was coming up and I wanted to make it fun for Ollie.

He and I walked down the main part of the town. The main streets were pedestrian only, and lined with stores selling art, clothes, souvenirs. On the weekends, the stores were busy. Day trippers from Denver filled the shops and bustling cafés.

"Have you decided on a costume for the Halloween Spooktacular next week?"

His nose wrinkled. "Not yet."

"A superhero, something spooky, a Jedi?" I'd been peppering him with options for weeks.

He made a non-committal noise.

Okay, I'd have another run at that later. "You want to go and play in the playground?"

Ollie glanced over at the colorful playground equipment that was crawling with kids. "No, thanks."

I kept my face even. "All right, well, we can get a coffee at Mountain Brew."

He rolled his eyes. "Allie, I'm too young for coffee."

"You are? Hmm. Well, what else can we do?"

"Get ice cream."

Now I rolled my eyes. The kid had a one-track mind when it came to ice cream. Summer or winter, hot or cold, he wanted ice cream.

I felt that familiar prickle of guilt. I should be feeding him less sugar. "I don't know, Ol-ster." That's when I noticed he was glancing at some older kids throwing a baseball. "Are you keen to play baseball?"

He looked away. "No."

God, parenting should come with a manual. *How to Read Kids 101*. Along with *How Not to Screw Kids Up 102*.

We wandered a bit more, moving close to the trail that ran along the bottom of the mountain and along a pretty, burbling creek. My gaze snagged on a man running along the trail, and I forgot all about my urgent need for coffee. I forgot about Ollie and eating too much sugar. Hell, I forgot my name.

He wore black running shorts and no shirt, although I could see it was tucked into his back pocket. He had powerful legs and abs, and so many sweat-slicked muscles I didn't know where to look first. He moved with athletic grace and ease, obviously knowing the limits of his body. Something told me that he could run all day, if he needed to. My gaze drifted higher, and I noted he had ear buds in his ear, and that's all I got before I noted dark eyes that were locked on me.

Caden.

Oh, God.

My lovely appreciation of his hot, muscled body turned to pure lust. It arrowed through my belly and between my legs.

Now, I was imagining that powerful body moving on mine, inside mine, my hands digging into hard muscle. I watched as he ran toward me.

"Allie?"

Ollie's voice jolted me out of... Whatever the hell my hormone-saturated brain was doing. "Yeah?" My voice was one level above a squeak.

"Are you okay?"

"Yep. Yes. I'm fine. Really fine."

Caden stopped in front of us, giving me an up-close view of his slick chest. I almost whimpered. I'd guessed he was fit, but had no idea he was hiding all of this under his suits.

He took the earbuds out. "Hey, Allie."

"Hi, Broody."

His lips quirked. "I have a real name."

"But Broody suits you better. You run?"

"Yes."

My gaze started to drift lower before I jerked it back up. "A lot."

"Yes." His gaze dropped to Ollie.

Get your brain cells functioning, Allie. "Um, Caden, this is my nephew, Oliver, Ollie, the Ol-ster."

"Al-*lie*," Ollie complained.

"He usually just goes by Ollie. Ollie, this is Caden. He works at the Langston Windward."

Caden crouched and held out a hand. "Nice to meet you."

Ollie gingerly took his hand and shook. "You work with Aunt Allie?"

"I do."

My nephew cocked his head. "In housekeeping?"

Caden rose, a tiny smile on his rugged face. "No, in security."

Ollie's eyes went wide. "Security. Cool. So you stop bad guys in the hotel?"

"Sometimes. My job is to keep everyone safe. The guests—" his gaze hit mine "—and the staff. Your aunt."

Those words shouldn't give me tingles.

"What are you two doing today?" Caden asked.

"We're going to get ice cream. Wanna come?" Ollie looked up at Caden with hope in his gray eyes.

Hell, I knew he missed his dad. Here was a prime male specimen with a cool job. I was pretty sure that body didn't consume much ice cream. I tried to imagine Caden holding an ice cream cone... Nope.

"Caden's probably busy, Ollie, I—"

"Ice cream sounds great. My treat."

I blinked at him. *What the hell?*

Ollie beamed.

I blinked again, my heart squeezing. I hadn't seen him smile like that in a long time.

Then he did a little skip in the direction of the ice cream shop and motioned for Caden to follow. Caden froze for a second, then he fell into step with Ollie.

The pair walked ahead of me and for some reason, seeing him walking with my nephew was just as hot as seeing his bare chest and abs.

Jeez, Allie, get a grip.

We reached the ice cream shop—Sunday Sundae—and Caden took a second to pull his T-shirt on. It was a crying shame. There was seating inside and outside, and it was busy, even with the cooler weather. We joined the line inside.

"What's your flavor, Ollie?" Caden asked.

"Chocolate."

"Good choice. I like chocolate, too."

"You do?"

"Yep." He glanced at me. "Allie?"

"Hazelnut."

He nodded and ordered. Soon, I was doing something I'd never imagined when I'd first met Caden Castro —sitting in the sunshine, eating ice cream with him.

"You have the day off?" I asked.

He gave me a clipped nod. "I'll do a few hours of work this afternoon."

"It must be hard to switch off when you live at your workplace."

"I like it. It suits me."

"You live in a hotel?" Ollie asked.

"I do, bud."

"That's cool." Ollie gave his ice cream a giant lick. He had chocolate all around his mouth. "So you live in Windward?"

"For now. My job takes me to hotels all over the world."

"Oh." Ollie stilled. "So you'll leave?"

"Eventually."

I gave my ice cream cone a long lick. When I glanced up, Caden's gaze was locked on me.

Those damn tingles hit again. Then I did something I shouldn't have. I gave my ice cream another long, delicate lick.

Heat flared in Caden's eyes.

Oh God. My belly clenched.

"Have you always worked in hotels?"

Ollie's voice cut through the tension.

Caden cleared his throat and looked at my nephew. "No, before I worked at Langston, I was in the Army."

Ollie's eyes went round. "Really?"

Caden gave him a faint smile before he took a bite of his ice cream. "Really."

"Did you shoot people?"

I noticed a faint stiffening of Caden's shoulders. "Ollie, you don't ask things like that."

My nephew screwed up his face. "But he was a soldier."

"I was," Caden said quietly. "I fought for my country and to help others. It's not always easy. And I can tell you something, bud. Shooting someone is the hardest thing a person ever has to do." There was something in his voice. A touch of darkness. His gaze met mine for a long beat, then he focused back on Ollie. "It's a hard job, but an important one. Now, I'm lucky because my job at Langston Hotels isn't so dangerous. I can still help people and keep them safe."

Ollie nodded.

I felt...something. Not sympathy, exactly. A man like Caden didn't need or want that, but something.

"It's important to keep people safe," Ollie said. "Someone shot my mommy and daddy."

My throat closed. *God.*

Caden stilled. "I'm sorry, buddy, that's tough."

Ollie nodded. "I miss them."

I cleared my throat. "Lick that ice cream, little man. It's going to melt."

Soon, our ice creams were all finished.

"We'd better go." I wiped my sticky fingers on my napkin, then wiped Ollie's mouth. "We need to head to the grocery store."

Caden rose with a nod. "I need to get back."

"Thanks for the ice cream, Mr. Caden."

"You're welcome, Ollie."

Then my nephew looked up at me. "Can I go to the playground?"

"Go." I watched him dart away. He seemed lighter than he'd been in ages.

"He's a good kid," Caden said.

"He is. Sometimes, I think he's teaching me more than I'm teaching him."

Suddenly, Caden reached out. He touched the corner of my mouth, and I sucked in a breath. A tingling sensation spread over my cheek.

"You had a bit of ice cream there." His voice sounded deeper, grittier.

"Oh."

Then I watched him stick his thumb in his mouth and suck it clean.

My womb spasmed. I couldn't breathe. I felt the urgent and desperate need to jump him.

I swallowed.

Caden gave me a long look, then nodded. "I'll see you at work."

He turned and moved into a powerful jog, and I watched him move away. Okay, I watched his ass. It was a damn fine one.

I pressed a palm to my chest. Oh, this was bad.

I was in lust with Caden "Broody" Castro.

Crap. I shook my head. I needed a cold shower— which I sure as hell wouldn't do because I liked my showers scalding hot. But I did need to get a grip on this madness.

From the playground, Ollie waved. I needed to focus on Ollie and not the dark, muscled man that was getting under my skin.

WHY WERE Mondays at the hotel always crazy?

I hustled down the corridor, carrying a stack of muddy towels. My quiet weekend with Ollie seemed like a distant memory. I'd spent most of Sunday cleaning the condo and doing laundry. How one small five year old got so many clothes dirty was still a mystery I hadn't solved.

I'd had no time to think about sharing ice cream with Caden. Okay, that was a lie. I'd thought about it. A lot. I'd especially thought about him swiping ice cream off the side of my mouth and licking his own ice cream. Caden licking had given me lots and lots of ideas. Of him licking me in lots of places.

I spotted Wade, pushing his cart, and jolted myself out of my Caden spiral.

The young man gave a groan. "Why are Mondays always so crazy?"

"I don't have an answer for you, my friend." I held the towels up higher.

"Dump them in here." He grimaced. "What happened?"

"Don't ask." Gratefully, I dropped them into his cart.

"You working the later shift today?" he asked.

I nodded. I tried to stick to school hours, but it didn't always work out. Mrs. Jenkins was collecting Ollie from school. She'd hang with him and make him dinner.

"I need to wash my hands. Catch you later."

"Bye, Allie."

In the locker room, I washed my hands. My stomach growled, reminding me that I'd worked through lunch. I thought I might have a packet of pretzels stashed in my locker.

This morning, I'd been in a rush and shoved my gear in without thinking. I opened the locker and waded around my bag and jacket.

My hands closed on glossy paper. I pulled out the Dandelion chocolate bar and gasped.

I would have definitely remembered leaving that in here.

Had Tessa left it for me? I stroked a finger over the gold foil wrapping. But how would she have accessed my locker?

The only other person I'd recently confessed my Dandelion obsession to was...

No way. There was no way Caden Castro had left me chocolate.

I broke off two squares and stuffed them in my mouth. Biting back a moan, I enjoyed the rush of chocolately goodness.

Was Caden hiding a thoughtful, kind guy under the scowly exterior? And what exactly did this mean?

My radio crackled. "Allie, are you there?"

It was Karen, who I knew was working up on level four. My chocolate mystery would have to wait. I plucked the radio off my belt. "I'm here. Go ahead."

"We have a locked safe in a room. The guest checked out a couple of hours ago."

I sighed. "On my way." I glanced at Wade. "See you later."

Ignoring the elevator, I took the stairs. The incident the other day had left me wary. I couldn't wait for the renovations and upgrades to be completed. On level four, I motored down the hallway to the open guest room with the housekeeping cart out the front.

"Karen?"

"Here." She waved from where she was making the bed, then pointed to the safe in the closet.

I pulled my keys off my belt. I had a master key for all the room safes. If someone had left valuables, I'd need to document them and call security. My heart gave a little wiggle. Maybe Caden would come up to deal with it.

Shaking my head, I unlocked the safe. Karen pressed in behind me, looking over my shoulder.

I frowned. "What the hell?"

Karen let out laugh. "Seriously? I mean, I've seen some weird stuff working here, but this is new."

I reached in and pulled out...a burrito. It was still wrapped and uneaten.

"That's from the Wandering Burrito food truck in town," Karen said. "They have *great* food."

Shaking my head, I closed the safe. "I assume our guest imbibed a little too much, bought a burrito, and mistook the safe for a microwave."

Karen burst out laughing. I couldn't help but smile.

My radio crackled to life again. "Allie, this is Marcy. I have a woman on level two who's accidentally dropped her wedding ring down the sink. Room 214."

I closed my eyes.

"Please hurry," Marcy added. "She's really losing it."

"Bye, Karen," I murmured.

"Thanks, Allie. Good luck with the ring."

"Oh, I'm calling Everett to deal with that one." I headed out of the room and dumped the burrito in the trash bag on Karen's cart.

Long after I'd calmed down a hysterical Mrs. Coggin and helped Everett retrieve the woman's four-carat diamond ring, I finished up my reports and managed to do a few employee evaluations that were overdue. I blew a strand of hair out of my face. God, my feet were aching. I dreamed of soaking them and getting a foot massage.

A girl could dream.

I turned a corner and almost mowed down Sierra.

"Hey."

My friend had a scowl on her face. Unusual for the perkiest person I knew.

Then I noted the mud splattered all over her white polo shirt.

"Did you start a mud-wrestling activity that I didn't know about?"

"Ha ha," she replied, plucking at her shirt. "There's an idiot group of guys here mountain biking. One surfer guy's been asking me out several times a day and isn't taking a hint. When I say hint, I mean several blatant, firm 'nos.' Today, the asshole 'accidentally' sprayed me with mud when he braked." Her eyes narrowed. "Accident, my ass."

"I've seen the guys. They were here last winter. They're into extreme sports."

"Yes, they asked me to organize some paragliding for them. And they wanted to know all the hardest biking trails. It's a shame they're assholes, a couple of them are easy on the eyes."

"The tall blond asked me out last winter."

"Oh." Sierra perked up. "He seems like the best of the bunch."

"Yes, well, I need a guy like I need a hole in the head."

"And an extreme-sports bro is probably more trouble

than he's worth." My friend cocked her head. "And something tells me you prefer dark-hair, muscles, and moodiness."

I blinked. "I have no idea what you're talking about."

She shot me a smug smile. "Oh, so you and a certain grumpy head of security weren't getting ice cream together with your nephew on the weekend?"

Damn the small-town gossip grapevine. "We just ran into each other. That's it."

Sierra stared at me a beat. "I'm not buying it."

"Broody is..." I cleared my throat. "Like I said, I don't need a guy and I'm not looking for one."

"They do come in handy for orgasms, cuddling, and killing spiders."

"Can you picture Caden Castro cuddling?"

"Hmm, not really. But two out of three aren't bad." She plucked at her muddy shirt again. "I need to change. I'll catch you later."

Lifting my tablet, I checked over the items still on my To Do list. I pushed through the door into the lobby and did a quick scan.

No way that I was admitting I was hoping to catch a quick glimpse of a certain dark-haired head of security.

I saw Coral and quickly detoured away from the reception desk.

"Hi, there."

The low, male voice was right behind me. I spun and looked up.

Oh. Speak of the devil. Just the wrong devil. It was Brandon/Blake/Bryce.

He was wearing jeans, and a nice, button-down shirt

that was tight enough to showcase his lean chest. He smelled good, too. It appeared he'd just showered and changed.

I waited for a blip.

Nope. Nothing.

"Hi. You were here last winter."

He smiled. And it was a good one. "You remembered. I'm Blake. And your name is...?"

"Allie. Are you enjoying your trip?" I glanced over at his friends. They were huddled nearby talking with a trio of young guests in hiking gear.

"Yeah. We're getting some good biking in. We love the trails here." He shifted closer, his arm brushing mine.

He was smooth. He made it seem accidental.

"We're going to have a drink in the bar." The wattage of his smile increased a notch. "Would you like to join us?"

"Oh, thanks, but I can't. I'm still on shift and after, I need to get home to my kid."

"Kid?" His eyebrows winged up.

"Yes. I'm raising my nephew. He's five."

"Cool. I don't know anything about kids."

"I didn't either. But I'm a fast learner."

Then suddenly he reached out and touched my hair. I made myself stay still.

"You look tired, Allie. If you want to go out, just the two of us, the offer from last winter still stands."

"Oh, um, thanks." Still no blip but it was nice to be asked. Then I sensed something. Felt someone staring a hole between my shoulder blades.

I turned my head and saw Caden on the other side of the lobby. He was scowling at me.

Correction, he was scowling at Blake.

"Look, if you change your mind. We'll be at the bar. Come have one drink." He gave me a chin lift and rejoined his friends.

I watched them another beat, and that's when I saw the guys passing something between each other. I frowned. What was that? They were being pretty furtive about it. I narrowed my gaze but whatever it was it was too small. I couldn't quite make out what. A cold shiver ran down my spine.

What were they up to?

Then the group all disappeared into the Bluff Bar.

I totally felt Marcy's vibe now. She'd warned me she thought they were trouble.

Hmm, maybe I needed to keep a closer eye on these guys.

Glancing back across the lobby, I noted that Caden was gone. I blew out a breath. I could share with him that I suspected these guys were bad news.

But Caden struck me as the evidence kind of guy. All the evidence I had was a vibe.

Well, maybe after my shift, I would go and have that drink. And see if I could find out what Blake and his friends were up to at the Windward.

CHAPTER 8

CADEN

I tightened the remaining screw and stepped down off the ladder. The new camera was installed. The scent of fresh paint tickled my nostrils. This area of the Langston Windward was newly renovated and now completely finished. I'd started installing the new security system here. The entire project would be done in phases.

Setting the screwdriver back in my small toolkit, I checked my watch. Early evening. The day had passed by fast. Grabbing the toolkit, I took the stairs.

From my calculations, Allie would be finishing her later shift. Not that I'd memorized her schedule or anything.

A muscle ticked in my jaw. I'd only seen her once today. Flirting with that young asshole in the lobby.

My hand tightened on the toolkit, the plastic digging into my palm. Did she like him? Was that the sort of guy she liked? Young, easy-going.

Jealousy hit my gut like a spiked bomb.

I blew out a breath. I had no right to be jealous. She wasn't mine.

I turned into the staff area, stopping in my tracks.

Ro had Tessa pinned to the wall. He was kissing his woman, hard. They were lost in their own world, neither of them aware of anything around them.

I shook my head. I never turned off. I was always aware of my surroundings, no matter what. When I'd first come home after leaving the military, it had been far worse. I'd been jumpy as hell, and always on edge, always ready to fight.

It had terrified my mother. My sisters had stared at me like I was a stranger.

My grip on the toolkit tightened, but then I forced my fingers to relax.

These days, I managed some sort of normalcy.

Except you don't sleep.

Ignoring the voice in my head, I cleared my throat.

Tessa jerked away. She had fair skin, and her blush of embarrassment was obvious. "Oh, Caden... Hi."

Ro just turned, grinning smugly.

"Don't you have a private penthouse? And an office?" I said. "And Tessa's house?"

She smoothed a hand down her skirt. "We have a little more work to do. Ro has a call." She rolled her eyes. "He always has a call."

He ran a hand down her braid. "I have a call with Tristan. He's got some spreadsheet I have to look at. Tessa is keeping me company."

"Is that what you're calling it?"

Ro just smiled. "Allie calls you Broody. Suits you. See

you later." He took Tessa's hand and dragged her into his office.

Despite how it may have appeared, I was happy for my friend. Ro was a workaholic, driven, and pushed by his own family demons. He seemed far happier and calmer now that Tessa was in his life.

Movement caught my attention, and Allie rounded the corner. My mind went blank.

She'd changed out of her uniform, and fuck me, she was wearing a tiny skirt and a long-sleeved, cream top that looked soft and silky.

Those legs. They were even longer than I realized. I couldn't drag my gaze off them. They were toned and smooth.

On Saturday, she'd been wearing leggings that had hugged her legs and ass. She might be slim, but she still had an ass. After ice cream, I'd come back to my suite. I hadn't been able to get my mind off those legs. Or imagining them wrapped around my hips.

I wondered what she'd think, knowing I'd taken my cock in hand and stroked it, thinking of her damn legs until I'd come.

She looked up and shot me a small smile. "Hey, Broody."

"Allie." I cocked my head. "Got a date?" The thought felt like knives to my gut.

"What?" Her brows drew together. "No, why?"

"You're in a skirt."

"Oh." She tugged on it. "Ollie's with my neighbor and my shift is done, so I decided to treat myself to a drink in the Bluff Bar."

The knives in my gut whirled. "Alone?"

She fidgeted. "Not exactly. I know some guests are having a few drinks. They said to stop by."

"So a date."

She huffed. "It's *not* a date. It's a drink. It's me pretending for an hour that my life didn't blow up, and I didn't lose my brother, or leave behind the life I'd made for myself—" She clamped her mouth shut. "It's a drink."

With the blond guy. "I saw you flirting with that guy in the lobby." My words were a growl.

Her mouth dropped open. "I was not flirting."

I crossed my arms over my chest.

"Broody, that was a conversation, *not* flirting."

"He wants more than conversation." I paused. "Are you into that guy?"

"Blake? No."

Of course his fucking name was Blake. "The flirting made me think otherwise."

Her eyes flashed. "It wasn't flirting."

I could feel my damn control slipping through my fingers like water. "Fine." My voice sounded like gravel. "Don't let me keep you."

She stared at me for a beat, then she shouldered past me. She was muttering under her breath, and I suspected calling me a few names.

I probably deserved them. My hands flexed, then I whirled and stalked toward the conference room.

I wasn't going to think about her with that guy, laughing, having a good time.

My cellphone rang and I snatched it out of my pocket. "Castro."

"Sounds like you're having a bad day, my friend."

Instantly, I recognized the voice. "Gunnar. It's been too damn long."

I'd served with Gunnar O'Neill in special forces. He was several years older than me and a hell of a soldier. He'd been a mentor to me when I'd first joined the team. Gunnar was solid as a rock, the man you could always count on.

"Good to hear your voice, Caden. How's the hotel life treating you?"

"It has its days."

Gunnar laughed. "I bet you have everyone quaking in their boots and following your orders."

I thought of Allie. "Not everyone."

"Well, I was calling to tell you that I'm out."

"Out? You left the Army?" My eyebrows winged up. I thought Gunnar would be a lifer. He had no family and the Army had been his home.

A sigh echoed down the line. "It was time."

I understood that better than anyone. "What are your plans?"

"Don't have any. I haven't got a home base or anyone waiting for me, so I'm a free agent. Thought I might come and visit you."

"I'd like that." Then a thought coalesced in my head. "You like Colorado?"

"Love the mountains. That where you are?"

"Yes, for now. Small mountain town called Windward. Just so happens I'm looking for someone to run security for the new mountain resort the company purchased."

"Really?" Gunnar was quiet. "Never thought of working in a hotel."

"Come take a look." Gunnar might just be the answer to my hiring problem. "And I'll throw in a bottle of that Barrel Craft Spirits bourbon you love so much."

"The Gray Label."

I snorted. I knew the Gray Label was way more expensive. "Sure."

"Right. Well, I'll see you in a few days."

Sliding the phone back in my pocket, I stared ahead. If Gunnar liked Windward and was keen to take on the job, I could get out of here sooner rather than later.

It should make me happy, but for some reason, the idea felt like a rock in my gut.

No, dammit. That was my plan. Getting out of Windward was what I needed.

I straightened and headed toward the security room.

I had to find something to do. Something to keep my mind off the fact that Allie was having a drink with another man in the bar. Acid welled in my throat and I viciously ignored it.

CHAPTER 9
ALLIE

The Bluff Bar had a classy, Art Deco vibe. The walls were a dark blue-gray, and trendy, gold lighting ran along the ceiling. Elegant leather armchairs and stools dotted the space, and the long, gleaming bar was backlit with shelves of top-shelf liquor.

I hadn't been here—for anything other than to clean it—for ages.

The only thing on my mind right now was punching Caden Castro in the mouth. I stomped toward the bar. All that intense grumpiness was more than I could handle. He'd been acting like a growly bear—

I jerked to a stop. Had he been jealous?

The thought tingled through me.

A loud burst of laughter rang through the room.

They were here.

The extreme-sports guys.

I glanced out of the corner of my eye, and saw they had some women, and a couple of guys, with them.

They'd pushed some tables together by the windows. There were lots of empty glasses and bottles littering the surface, so they'd clearly been at it since I saw them last time. As I watched, a stocky, dark-haired guy stood, chugging back a drink while the others cheered him on. Glancing away, I headed for the bar.

"Hey, Allie," the bartender said.

"Hi, Ross. It's been a *long* day and I have aching feet, I need a drink."

"I hear you, sister. What can I get you?"

"Some sort of gin cocktail, please. Surprise me."

He tapped a finger on the bar. "On it."

Right, I was going to have a drink, see if I could dig up anything on Blake and his friends, then head home.

I slowly glanced around the bar, pretending to look at everything, but really focusing on the sports guys.

There was definitely something off about them. I wasn't sure what I hoped to find out, but my gut kept telling me that I needed to pay close attention.

"Here you go." Ross set my drink down.

I smiled. "Thanks." I sipped, and surreptitiously watched the group.

Blake was telling some story, and all his friends were laughing. He was definitely charming. I could clearly see what had appealed to me last winter.

Now, he held zero appeal.

Yeah, well, you know why. Lifting my glass, I sipped again. *God.* I was overdue for cocktail night with Sierra, Tessa, Jazz, and Piper. Piper was a new addition to the gang. I hadn't thought I'd like the workaholic city girl.

Maybe because Piper lived the life I'd once wanted with every breath I'd taken.

One that had crumbled away in an instant.

I sipped again, taking a larger mouthful this time. Life liked to throw curveballs. It was how you dealt with them that dictated your happiness. Not some shiny, perfect dreams.

Turned out, shiny, perfect dreams didn't always live up to expectation, anyway.

It was a realization that I'd come to once I'd started work at the hotel. I liked my job here, and honestly, I'd hated my job in New York. I'd worked long hours, the work itself had often been a grind, and I hadn't found it fulfilling.

A wave of tiredness hit me and I beat it back.

Ross came past again.

"Hey, Ross, what you know about the guys sitting over by the windows?"

He followed my gaze to the raucous group, then he rolled his eyes. "Well, they're not impressed with a gay guy serving their drinks. Like they might catch the urge to want dick, or something."

I wrinkled my nose. I had no time for anyone like that. "Sorry. That's shitty."

He shrugged. "Not your fault, gorgeous. I've dealt with worse." He leaned on the bar. "They have lots of company. A new crowd every night, and they all like to party. And they *especially* like the ladies." He frowned. "Girl, you're not interested, are you? You could do so much better."

"No, I'm not interested. One of them did ask me out, but—" I shrugged. "I have my hands full."

"Pretty Allie, your hands are never too full that you can't fit in a nice, sizable—"

"Ross," I said, with a grin.

He grinned back. "Guy. I was going to say fit a nice guy into your life."

"No, you weren't."

"Which one asked you out?"

"The blond."

"Best of the bunch. Easy on the eyes, and polite. Too polite."

"Too polite?"

Ross nodded. "Can't get over the sense that it's for show. That he likes being in control of the situation."

Hmm. "Anything else seem off?"

"Just that they make lots of friends really quickly. Who has time for that?"

"Not me. I have good friends but just a few of them. I couldn't cope with more."

"But you don't have a dick in your life."

I pointed a finger at him. "See, I knew that was what you were going to say. I can manage just fine without a man. Besides, this is Windward. It's slim pickings. I went to school with most of the eligible males, and they are not for me."

"How about I make you another cocktail?"

"Why not?" I could walk home, or get an Uber, if I needed to.

Ross bought me a new cocktail, and after a few more sips, I had a pleasant buzz. Two was definitely my limit.

Mrs. Jenkins would put Ollie to bed, but I still needed to get home to him.

Swiveling on my stool, I took another sip and that's when I caught Blake's gaze across the bar.

He smiled and lifted a hand.

I smiled back and gave him a small wave. This could be my chance to find out more about him and his friends.

"Allie."

Caden's deep voice made me jolt.

He stood nearby, watching me, his eyes looking darker than they ever had.

My heart galloped into overdrive. "Caden, what are you—?"

"Don't have a drink with him."

I licked my lips and set my drink down. "I told you, it's not like that."

That all-too-familiar muscle ticked in his jaw. "I don't care. I don't want you near him, or anyone else."

I sucked in a breath. "You don't get to come in here and boss me around, Broody."

He stepped closer, his big body crowding mine, and I felt the heat of him. I also smelled him. That scent that haunted my dreams.

Now, I felt a blip. A big one.

"Don't have a drink with him." His tone was unyielding.

"Let me explain—"

"No." His hand curled around my arm. "Ross, keep an eye on Allie's drink."

The bartender nodded, his wide gaze ping ponging between the two of us.

Caden dragged me off the stool and pulled me toward the area that led to the restrooms. "What are you doing?"

"I think you need a little convincing."

Heat flickered through my lower belly, goose bumps breaking out on my bare skin. This was all very un-Caden-like. "How are you going to do that?"

He towed me past the restrooms and into a small alcove used for storage. There were a few spare stools and a step ladder tucked in there.

He pressed me back against the wall and I felt like my heart lodged in my throat.

"You want me to show you?" His hand curled around the base of my neck, his thumb rubbing over my racing pulse. "You want me to show you how I'd convince you?"

His voice was like a deep, dark caress. My chest hitched. God, he was so big, and hard, and intense. I should tell him no and get the hell out of there.

I didn't. "Yes."

He leaned in, and our chests pressed together. Air puffed out of my lips and I bit back a moan. He ran his nose down the side of mine, his breath warm on my cheek.

"Do you know how much you drive me crazy? How much you push me until my control is gone?"

God. My nipples beaded into hard points and I pressed my thighs together. I liked it. No, I loved knowing I pushed this heavily controlled man past his limit. "How much?"

His hands clamped on my waist and one big hand

slid up, then cupped my breast. This time, I couldn't stop my low moan.

His thumb flicked over my nipple. "Maybe as much as much as you want me."

I pushed into him. I felt like all the brakes were gone. There was only the two of us. "You left the chocolate in my locker."

He stared down at me. "It's your favorite."

My lower belly clenched. "Why shouldn't I go back out there and have a drink, Caden?"

His fingers tightened. Then they slowly traveled down, tugging on the waistband of my skirt, brushing the skin of my belly. "I don't want you with him. With anyone."

A terrifying tangle of emotions stormed through me. The biggest one was hot desire throbbing between my legs. Desire for this cool, intimidating man, who was the opposite of cool right now.

"Who should I be with?" I whispered.

A look crossed his face, his lips hovering over mine. His hand moved again, this time tracing over the hem of my short skirt, rubbing the sensitive skin of my thigh. I felt the hunger in him, barely contained. "I can't say me, even if I want to. I've got nothing to offer you. I've got nothing to offer anyone."

My chest hitched. He couldn't really believe that.

"I'm a selfish asshole because I don't want you with anyone else." His fingers skimmed up my thigh. "*Allie.*"

There was so much need and possession packed into that one word.

His lips touched mine, his hand travelling up to my inner thigh. And the desire in me broke loose.

Everything about him overwhelmed. A needy sob escaped my lips, then I pressed my mouth to his.

In an instant, he kissed me. A powerful, urgent kiss. His tongue slid into my mouth, firm and demanding. The desire inside me roared like a fire. I threw my arms around his neck, grinding my body against his.

"God, your mouth." He bit my lip, then kissed me again.

That hand slid higher and he stroked between my thighs. I gasped. When he realized I wasn't wearing any panties, his body jerked against me.

"You came here to meet that fucking punk without panties on?" His tone was sharper than a blade.

"No." I cupped his stubbled cheeks, locking my gaze with his. "Not for anyone. I...um...never usually wear underwear."

The flash in his eyes almost scorched me.

"All this time you've been walking around with no panties on?"

I nodded.

"*Fuck*." Then he stroked me again.

Gasping, I trembled against him. He stroked my folds, then his thumb pressed on my clit.

I cried out, pressing my face to his neck. "Please, don't stop."

"This is mine." He pushed a finger inside me. He pumped it twice, then slid a second one inside. The stretch made me bite my lip. "It's been mine for weeks now, hasn't it?"

I couldn't speak, all I could do was feel. I thrust against his hand, riding it, feeling the sharp edge of an orgasm growing inside me. "*Caden.*"

"Love hearing you say my name, baby."

My hips moved faster and I clung to him. He worked the swollen nub of my clit ruthlessly.

"*Caden.*" I was going to come. It had been so long since I'd had an orgasm that I hadn't given myself. And this one felt big.

"I want to feel it, Allie."

I exploded. Coming hard, I sank my teeth into his neck. I heard his low groan, his fingers inside me, and his other hand clenching on my ass. Rocking against him, I rode through the pleasure of the best orgasm I could remember in a long time. Or ever.

Then, it was just the two of us standing there, both of us panting. His fingers were still inside me and I felt his rock-hard cock pressed against my belly.

Swallowing, I gripped his arms to keep myself upright. My legs felt like cooked spaghetti. "Caden—"

Abruptly, he pulled back. At the loss of him, I almost pitched forward. He grabbed my elbow to steady me, but only for a second, before he took another step backward.

He stared at me, his face completely unreadable. Like he was carved from stone. "That shouldn't have happened."

His sharp tone made me flinch.

"Caden—"

"I lost control." His face twisted, then smoothed out again. "I don't have an excuse. Did I hurt you?"

"No, you didn't hurt me." But I got the feeling he was going to. Not physically, but in a far worse way. "Look—"

"I'm sorry. This was a big mistake."

A mistake. My stomach curled up into a tiny ball. I'd lost count of how many times my mother had called me a mistake. *Be more ladylike, Allison. Do better, Allison. You're such an embarrassment, Allison.*

"Allie—"

"Don't," I whispered. "Don't say anything else." I jerked my skirt back into place and pushed past him. Blindly, I found the door to the ladies' room.

Inside was just as classy as the rest of the bar, but I didn't give it any attention. I splashed some water on my face. In the gilt-framed mirror, I stared at my reflection.

Shit, I looked like a woman who'd just come and enjoyed it. My cheeks were pink, my lipstick was smeared.

And I was sticky between my thighs.

I took a few minutes to clean up, and I ruthlessly ignored everything that had just happened.

Maybe I could live like this forever. In total denial that Caden Castro had just fingered me to a magnificent orgasm in the hotel bar.

"Get a hold of yourself, Allie." I dried my hands. I was going to finish my drink, see if I could salvage anything from my botched surveillance of the extreme-sports guys, then go home.

When I headed back out into the Bluff Bar, I was shocked to find Caden leaning against the bar, talking with Ross.

What the hell was he still doing here?

I wanted to turn and hide, but instead, I lifted my chin and marched forward. Ignoring him, I sat on my stool and picked up my drink. I took a hefty sip. It didn't manage to wash away the memory of that hot, sexy moment.

He leaned in. "Why are you here?"

"Don't you have somewhere else to be?"

"I want an answer."

I huffed out a breath. "I told you, to have a drink."

"I thought you were going to meet up with him. But that's not it, is it?"

I studiously kept my gaze on the shelves of bottles behind the bar.

Caden's voice lowered. "You're watching him, and asking questions about him and his friends."

I gaped at him. "How do you know I was asking questions?"

He crossed his arms over his chest. "I know everything."

"You do not." Ross was a tattletale who'd just gotten interrogated.

"In this hotel, I do. Talk."

"I don't want to talk to you."

His mouth flattened. Then he pulled out a stool and moved it close to mine and sat. Suddenly, I found myself inches from him. He was all strength and watchfulness and ruggedness. I tried not to quiver, or stare at the way his muscular thighs pressed against his suit pants.

He thinks touching you was a mistake, remember?

"Allie?"

I blinked and shook off my Caden daze. "Something

is off about those guys." I kept my voice to a low murmur.

He eyed me.

"I don't have any proof. You seem like a proof guy, so that's why I didn't come to you. I wanted to see if I could get something more concrete. They always have people around, and I don't know why, but they bug my house-keepers too. No one likes them."

"They cross any lines with the staff? Mouth off? Touch anyone?" His tone was dark.

"No." I liked that he went instantly into protective mode for the hotel staff. "Something is just...off."

He was quiet for a beat, and I expected him to tell me to go home.

"I agree."

I blinked. "You do?"

He nodded. "I've been keeping an eye on them. Like you, I have no proof, but Allie, I trust gut-feels a hell of a lot. There've been times when they're the only thing that's kept me alive."

My heart bumped against my ribs. I wanted to know what he meant. How many times had he been in a situation where his life was in danger? I wanted him to trust me enough to share those stories.

Stop it, Allie. The man just apologized for kissing you senseless.

"My gut says they could be dangerous," he added. "Stay away from them."

Instantly, I felt a sear of annoyance. "You're not the boss of me."

He arched a brow.

"I could help. No one pays attention to the house-keeping staff. I could—"

"No." This time, his voice was clipped and filled with bossiness.

I looked away.

He touched my arm, and I felt a sizzle of sensation.

He must have too because he quickly dropped his hand. "I'm trying to keep you safe."

Oh. No one but my brother had ever done that. I looked into Caden's dark eyes. So inky black.

I'm sorry. This was a big mistake.

I stiffened. He was just doing his job. "I won't do anything crazy, but I will keep my eyes peeled."

He sighed. "Fine."

I hopped off my stool. The two drinks had caught up with me. "I need to visit the ladies' room again. Keep an eye on my drink."

I didn't walk too close to Blake and his group of extreme-sports guys. The ESG. I was going to call them that for short. Less of a mouthful to say or think. I did glance over, and saw Blake looking at me.

With a nod, I hurried to the ladies' room. I did my business, and was washing my hands, when the door opened. A woman in her mid-twenties with big, blonde curls and a tiny, blue dress with long sleeves walked in. She was weaving unsteadily.

She shot me a wobbly smile and disappeared into one of the stalls.

I looked in the mirror. *Go back and say good night to Caden, then get home to Ollie.* That's what I needed to do.

The toilet flushed, and the woman staggered to the sink. "I *love* a good party." Her voice was slurred.

I frowned, but nodded.

I headed for the door and had just pushed it open when the woman followed me out, then she gasped.

Spinning, I had no warning before she staggered into me.

"Are you okay?" I asked, grabbing her arms.

"No. I don't feel so good." Her face drained of color. "I'm so dizzy."

"Too many cocktails?"

"I've only had one." She gripped my arm, her nails digging in. "I was chatting with a cute guy. I hoped he'd ask me out." She staggered. "I feel... Sick..."

She leaned most of her weight against me and I barely kept us both upright. I found myself with an armful of barely conscious blonde.

"Help me," she whispered. "Something's wrong."

"Hang on. I've got you." I managed to move us a few steps into the bar. The ESG were gone, but Caden was still there. "Caden, help!"

When he spotted us, he launched off his stool and strode toward us.

"It's going to be okay," I whispered. "We'll help you."

CHAPTER 10
CADEN

S *hit.*

I lunged forward and took some of the young woman's weight before she dragged Allie over.

"Caden, she's dizzy, slurring her words. She said she only had one drink."

The blonde's head lolled to the side. I slid an arm around her, while Allie did the same on the woman's other side.

"We'd better get her to the hospital."

Allie's brow creased. "You think it's drugs?"

"It could be."

Together, we hobbled into the hotel lobby. The woman mumbled, barely conscious.

"Caden, she was with the extreme-sports guys. The ESG."

My jaw hardened. Then I spotted one of my security team frowning as he walked our way.

"I saw on the camera," Hugh said. "Gretchen is bringing an SUV around."

"Scan the security footage from the bar," I ordered. "See what she was drinking, and if anyone tampered with her drink."

Hugh nodded. "I'm on it. I'll call ahead to the hospital and tell them that you're on the way."

Allie and I got the woman outside just as the SUV pulled up. Allie opened the back door, and I helped the woman into the back seat. Then Allie slid in with her.

"I've got her." Allie's voice was calm, focused.

I was pretty sure that nothing shook Allie Ford.

I circled the vehicle. Gretchen handed me the keys and I got in the driver's seat.

"Keep us updated, boss," Gretchen said. "Tell us how she is."

It was a short drive to the local hospital and my hands clenched on the wheel. In the backseat, I heard Allie murmuring soothing words to the mostly unconscious woman.

I'd done the same drive, not so long ago. With Ro holding a sick Tessa in the backseat. I hoped to hell we had a good outcome again.

I pulled up at the emergency entrance. A moment later, the doors to the hospital opened, and a team raced out with a gurney.

Pushing open the door, I slid out of the SUV. "A woman in her mid-twenties. She's dizzy, slurred speech, barely conscious." I opened the back door. "She said she only had one drink."

A woman in a blue scrubs nodded. "We've got it from here."

In seconds, they transferred the woman to the gurney and were whisking her inside. Allie stood beside the vehicle looking lost, staring into the hospital.

"She'll be okay," I said.

Allie nodded.

"I'll park the SUV. You want to wait?"

She nodded again.

"Wait inside, Allie. It's too cold out here." Especially with her legs bared by that damn skirt.

After I'd parked the SUV, I found Allie inside, in a small waiting room with uncomfortable chairs. She was pacing, with a phone pressed to her ear.

"I'm sorry for such short notice, Mrs. Jenkins. I appreciate you watching him and putting him to bed." She paused. "Tell him someone at work got sick and I've taken her to the doctor. I will. Thanks."

She turned. She looked tired and worried.

"This is déjà vu. I feel like I'm back at that night Tessa got poisoned." Allie shook her head. "God, I was so scared and worried that night."

And here she was, worried about a woman she didn't even know.

"Until you promised to find who'd done it." She shot me a wry smile. "You calmed me down."

"You were ready to go off half-cocked and maybe murder someone."

"True. And you caught Rupert, thank God."

My gut tightened. "Eventually. He almost hurt Tessa again."

"You saved her. And it all worked out. Believe me, I

don't give Rupert a single thought these days." She smiled. "Nor does Tessa."

I bet Ro still had a few violent thoughts about the guy. I sat down on one of the chairs and Allie sat beside me.

She fidgeted, the chair creaking. "I really hope this woman is okay."

"Me too."

Silence fell. She shifted, crossing her long legs. Which served as a reminder that she wasn't wearing anything under that short skirt.

And that I'd touched her.

My cock—still half hard—twitched in my pants. My fingers curled into my palm. Fingers that had been inside her, pleasured her.

Then I'd hurt her.

I'd seen it in her eyes.

A part of me wanted to pull her onto my lap. I wanted to hold her, comfort her.

Fuck. It wasn't that simple. It was best for her that I kept my hands to myself.

If I'd still been the man I'd been before the military... But I wasn't. Allie deserved more than the broken shell I had to offer.

"They did this, Caden." Anger vibrated in her voice. "One of ESG drugged her."

I took her hand. *So much for not touching.* She stilled, then relaxed. Her fingers curled around mine.

Hell. I hadn't held hands with a woman for years. My fingers were covered with lots of old scars. Hers were far softer and more elegant than mine.

"The doctors will test to see if she was drugged?" Allie asked.

I nodded. "Is Ollie okay?"

"Yes, my neighbor's with him." Allie rubbed a hand over her face.

"You should go home. Get some sleep."

"There's *no way* I'll sleep. I need to know that she's okay."

The minutes ticked by, and I couldn't make myself let go of her hand.

Finally, one of the doctors pushed through the doors.

Allie shot to her feet, and I rose.

"The young lady is going to be fine. She's asleep now." The man's face turned serious. "She has GHB in her system."

I cursed.

"That's a date-rape drug, right? God." Allie ran a hand through her hair.

"I've reported the incident to the local police," the doctor added, his gaze swinging my way. "You're in charge of security at the Windward?"

"Yes. I'll follow up with the police. I won't let things like this happen at the Langston Windward."

"Good."

I glanced at Allie. "I need to make a call."

"Okay." She looked back at the doctor. "Can I visit with her? I don't even know her name, but I want her to know she's not alone."

"Yes, but keep it brief," the doctor said. "We found a wallet in her bag. Her name is Mellody Evans."

"Thanks." Allie shot me a look, then followed the doctor.

Meanwhile, I pulled out my cellphone. I texted Hugh and got confirmation that Mellody Evans was twenty-four years old and a guest at the hotel. Then I called the local police. I wasn't surprised when, fifteen minutes later, Officer Sanchez walked in.

"Late night," the woman said.

"Yeah. Not how I'd hoped it would go."

She pulled out a notepad. "Tell me what happened."

"The young woman, Mellody Evans, is a guest at the hotel. She was in the bar and said she'd only had one drink. She stumbled into Allie Ford, one of our housekeeping supervisors. She was clearly under the influence of something." I calmly told her the rest of the story.

"She was lucky it was Ms. Ford who found her."

"*Dammit*." My mouth flattened. "I hate knowing there are men who do this sort of thing."

"I'll bet, and you aren't alone." Sanchez slid the notepad away. "You said Ms. Evans was partying with a group of guests?"

"Four guys. They're here mountain biking. They're into extreme sports." My jaw hardened.

Sanchez reached out and touched my forearm. "Now, Castro, no playing judge, jury, and executioner. I'll investigate." There was a warning look in her eyes.

The door opened and Allie stepped in. She saw us and jerked to a halt. "Um, sorry. Should I come back?"

I waved her forward. "Allie, this is Officer Sanchez. Allie is the housekeeping supervisor I mentioned."

Sanchez dropped her hand, all business again. "Can I get your statement, Ms. Ford?"

"Sure."

I stood with my hands in my pockets as they talked, and Allie answered all of the officer's questions.

"I'd better get Allie home," I said.

"I can try and get an Uber."

"No." I nodded at Sanchez. "Thanks again."

"Any time, Castro." The officer smiled. "I'll keep you posted." She walked out.

"Are you...dating her?"

I frowned at Allie. "What?"

"Officer Sanchez."

"No." Did she really think I'd kiss her, touch her, if I was dating someone else?

"She wants to jump your bones."

I ushered Allie out of the waiting room and made a scoffing sound.

"God, you are dense," she muttered

"I have no personal interest in Officer Sanchez."

"Sure. A sexy young officer with big doe eyes." She fluttered her eyelashes.

I whirled and grabbed her. "I think you're the dense one."

She blinked, her gaze on mine. "What?"

Even with my brain screaming at me to step back and let her go, I backed her toward the wall. "There's only one woman who is under my skin, like a damn itch."

Allie sucked in a breath. Her back hit the wall. "Oh, I'm an itch, am I? Like a bad rash."

"I wouldn't be touching you, kissing you, or making

you come on my fingers if I was interested in another woman."

Her chest hitched, then her gaze dropped to my mouth.

I leaned forward, my lips hovering over hers.

Back off, Castro.

I closed my mouth over hers.

My blood running hot, I claimed her mouth. I teased her with my tongue, and she made a low, needy sound before parting her lips for me.

Tunneling my fingers into her hair, I held her so I could kiss her deep and hard. I kept kissing, like it was the only thing I needed.

We broke apart for a second, both of us breathing hard. Then we both went at each other again. Her arms wrapped around my neck and she pressed against me. With a low groan, I pinned her to the wall. She rubbed against me with wild abandon, and I knew she'd feel my steel-hard cock digging into her stomach.

We broke apart again and my damn mind was spinning.

No control. With her, I lost sight of everything. A damn terrorist could walk right up to me and I wouldn't know. Wouldn't care.

Shit. I stared at her, trying to drag air into my burning lungs. She was breathing heavily as well.

"Broody..."

Dammit. I shouldn't have touched her.

I'd already gone over this in my head a hundred times. She deserved far better and less complicated than me. She deserved someone who'd make her life easier, not harder.

I stepped back, and when I saw the disappointment on her face, fought from reaching for her again.

"Allie—"

"If you apologize again, I'll punch you."

I dragged in a breath and I stayed silent.

What else was there to say?

Then I gave her a tight nod. "I'll drive you home."

CHAPTER 11
ALLIE

S tepping into the hospital in the bright light of day felt different.

It was busier than it had been last night, with more people racing around, but it had the same smell of antiseptic. I turned into the corridor, carrying a bunch of flowers. I wanted to check on Mellody, and make sure she was okay.

But all I could think about was a certain dark and broody man.

One who'd kissed me like I was everything, made me come fast and hard, and then had pushed me away.

My belly tied itself into hot, little knots.

I'd never been kissed like that before. I'd never had a man touch me with such blatant possession.

Then he'd pushed me away. *Twice.*

Clearly, I was a sucker for punishment.

I lifted my chin. I didn't need Caden Castro. Hell, I had no room for kisses and orgasms that rocked my world and shook my foundation. I needed to be strong and independent. It wasn't just me I had to worry about anymore. I knew that when you leaned on someone, it hurt too much when they were yanked away. It left you stumbling and unsteady and ready to fall.

I'd barely survived losing Sean. I didn't want to do that again.

I had Ollie now, so I couldn't fall.

"Aunt Allie. You're walking too fast."

I jerked to a halt and spun. Ollie powered up beside me. It was cold today, so he was in a jacket and a different woolly hat. It was vibrant green with white dino spikes along the top and a dino face on the front. Sylvie had an entire collection of winter hats for him. A pang hit me. I wished she was here to see him.

"Sorry, buddy."

He reached out and touched my hand, then pulled back. My heart ached. I'd give anything for him to hold my hand.

"I'm sorry your friend got hurt."

He was so sweet. "Me too, Ol-ster. Let's give her the flowers, then get you to school." I handed the bouquet to him.

We'd come early before school to visit Mellody, plus I had an early shift today at the hotel. I was pretty sure the bags under my eyes had their own suitcases. I'd only had a few fitful hours. Between thoughts of Mellody and Caden, my sleep was nonexistent.

We found her room and knocked.

She was sitting up in the bed, a frown on her face. She still looked pale, her blonde hair lank and brushed back from her face, but all in all, much better.

"Hi, Mellody. My name's Allie—"

"You helped me." She swallowed. "Last night is a big haze with a lot of blank spots, but I remember you. You got me safe and got me to the hospital."

I nodded.

"Thank you," she whispered.

"These are for you." Ollie held up the bouquet of roses. "Aunt Allie let me pick. I picked yellow because she told me you got hurt and needed something to cheer you up."

"Oh, thanks." Mellody took the flowers. "These are beautiful."

"My mom liked daisies."

I pressed my hand to his shoulder. "This is my nephew, Ollie."

Mellody smiled. "It's nice to meet you, Ollie. I really appreciate the flowers."

"You already have a huge bouquet." I nodded at the beautiful flowers in a vase by her bed.

"From the hotel." She tucked some hair behind her ear. "It was really nice of them to send it."

"Are you feeling better?" I asked.

She nodded. "Much better and not groggy. My parents are flying in today."

"I'm so sorry your trip ended like this."

"It could have been a lot worse. It wasn't, thanks to you."

"Do you know who did this?"

She shook her head, her hands clenching on the white sheets. "I don't want to think it was the guys I was with. They were so nice and fun. They didn't seem like creeps." She pressed a hand to her chest. "The super intense hotel security guy was here earlier. He asked me a bunch of questions, and he promised to find who did this."

"He's a man who keeps his promises. We'll let you rest. Ollie needs to get to school."

Mellody reached out and grabbed my hand. Squeezed. "Thank you, Allie."

"You're welcome."

After I dropped Ollie at school, I headed to the Langston. I had butterflies in my stomach at the thought of seeing Caden again.

"Get a grip, Allie," I muttered under my breath. "You're an adult."

I thought of Mellody. Of what could've happened to her, if we hadn't collided in the ladies' room. My jaw tightened. It was the ESG. They were *not* good guys, and it seemed that their idea of fun included drugging young women.

Assholes.

They could target someone else. They had to be stopped.

After I'd parked my car and headed toward the staff entrance, my determination solidified. Soon, I was changed into my uniform, and went to meet with my team.

"Morning, everyone."

"Allie, is it true you saved a girl in the bar last night?" Marcy asked.

I should've known word would've gotten around. No one gossiped more than staff in a hotel.

"Yes. She's fine. I want all of you to keep an eye out for anything suspicious. Hotel security will be investigating."

"Oh, Mr. Dark and Dangerous can interrogate me *anytime*," Sarah Marie said.

There were titters and laughter from the crew.

God, they were talking about Caden. I waved my clipboard. "Okay, off to work. Go. We have rooms to clean."

Once I'd finished my paperwork, I headed into the lobby. I waved at the reception staff, who were already getting busy checking out guests. I headed toward the office area and held my ID card to the reader.

As I passed the first office, I heard Tessa's voice inside, talking with Jazz. I turned toward the conference room, which was acting as the temporary security room.

And saw Caden.

My heart gave a hard knock against my ribs and my belly clenched.

He was standing, staring at a computer monitor, and I was barely in the doorway for a second before his head whipped around.

His face was blank and composed. His eyes unreadable. Like we were strangers.

"Hi," I said.

He nodded. "Good morning."

"Any luck with the security footage from last night?"

He eyed me. "No. Whoever did it was very careful."

My nose wrinkled. "That probably means he's done it before, right?" I felt a hot lick of anger.

"I'll find him. The important thing is that Ms. Evans is all right."

"I know. I visited her before I came in."

There was a flicker in his eyes, but he was still standing there like a damn cyborg, encased in a block of ice. There was no sign of the man who'd kissed me with such scorching passion.

"I want to help."

His dark brows drew together and he cocked his head. "Help?"

"We both know who is behind this." I stepped closer. "It's one of those guys. I want to help stop them."

"No."

The word was harsh and cutting.

I straightened. "I'm *not* going to stand around while those guys hurt more women. They have date-rape drugs, Caden."

He grabbed my arm, yanked me inside the room, then slammed the door closed behind me. "You aren't going anywhere near them."

My gaze narrowed. "Haven't you learned yet that I don't follow your orders?"

"*Allie*," he growled.

I poked him in the chest. Unsurprisingly his pecs were rock hard. "I won't let another woman go through what Mellody did, or worse—"

"They're drug dealers."

I jolted. "What?"

"It's not just date-rape drugs. They're dealing out of the hotel. Cocaine, Ecstasy, Fentanyl."

I pressed a hand to my chest and tried to process. "The entire time? All the trips? They've been dealing drugs?"

"We suspect so. After what happened to Ms. Evans, I spent the night doing some digging. They haven't left much of a trail, but I found a few crumbs and connected the dots. There were no reports of date rapes previously. That seems to be new..." He paused. "Or perhaps not reported."

I felt sick.

"I'm investigating them."

I met his dark gaze. "You knew something was off about them right from the beginning."

"Stay away from them, Allie."

I couldn't make that promise. I realized he was so close. He shifted, and I pressed a hand to his chest. I felt his heartbeat.

Memories inundated me. The taste of him, his forceful kiss, the thrust of his hand between my thighs. He'd wanted me. More than anyone ever had before. And I wanted him. I wanted to see that chest bare. Touch it. Stroke it.

My gaze fell on a faint smudge on his neck. My belly tightened. It wasn't big, but I'd managed to leave a bruise on his neck when I'd bitten him.

"Caden—"

He abruptly stepped back, and my hand dropped to my side. I could practically see him shutting down.

"I don't need your help, Allie. I don't need you."

The words cut deep.

He didn't need me.

"Right," I whispered. "I think you've made that pretty clear."

Something moved across his face. "Allie—"

"No, I got it." A harsh laugh escaped me. "Loud and clear. I'll let you get back to your work."

He stared at me with that blank, emotionless face.

I gave him a stiff nod and left as fast as I could.

I LIFTED MY TABLET, tapped, and updated some stock levels. I made a note to talk to the laundry. The level of the linen sent back for re-cleaning was too high. Whatever new cleaning products they were using were not up to scratch.

Setting the tablet away, I pushed my cart out into the corridor. I'd told Marcy that I'd clean the ESG's rooms.

I wanted to have a little look around.

Caden the cyborg could go screw himself.

I don't need your help, Allie. I don't need you.

Message received. It seemed any time I was near him, the temptation was too great. I was sick of getting burned.

I needed to stay far away from Caden Castro.

Rubbing my chest, I tried to ignore the ache there. Pain hurt, but it didn't kill you.

"Hey, you."

I turned and saw Sierra waving at me. Tessa and Jazz were with her.

"Hi."

"We heard about last night." Worry was stamped all over Tessa's face. "The young woman who was drugged."

"It was horrible, but she's okay. Ollie and I took her flowers this morning."

"That's so sweet," Jazz said.

Sierra set her hands on her hips. "It's not like you to stop in at the bar."

I shrugged. "Ollie was with Mrs. Jenkins. I was thirsty."

Tessa raised a brow. "And you happened to be sharing a drink with Caden?"

Sierra and Jazz gasped.

"Really?" Jazz grinned.

"No." I shook my head rapidly. "He was just there."

"They had ice cream together on the weekend with Ollie," Sierra shared.

Tessa and Jazz both blinked.

"Caden eats ice cream?" Jazz asked in an incredulous tone.

"Nothing is going on." I slashed a hand through the air.

"Both of you took the woman to the hospital," Tessa said.

"Yes. We helped that poor girl. Her name's Mellody."

"Something happened," Sierra said. "Between you and Caden. I *knew* you liked him."

I sniffed. "Broody is bad tempered and acts like a robot. I'm steering clear."

My friends all studied me hard.

I blew out a breath. "We may have kissed." Okay, twice, and he'd made me come. I decided it was best not to share those details.

My friends' faces all lit up.

"And he left a bar of Dandelion chocolate in my locker."

"Ooh," Jazz said. "He gave you a gift. He doesn't strike me as the gift-giving type."

"It's her favorite, too," Tessa added.

I straightened. "He made it abundantly clear that kissing me was a mistake that he doesn't want to repeat."

All their faces fell.

"You kissed all that dark and dangerous? Sierra demanded. "How was it? Is he a good kisser? I just feel like with all that bottled-up intensity he would be."

I looked at the floor. "It was good. Then he apologized and backed off."

Tessa grabbed my arm. "He hurt you."

"It's fine. Really. I don't have time for a man. He did me a favor." I dredged up a smile. "Guys, seriously. I've got to go. I have rooms to clean."

Tessa grabbed my arm and squeezed. "Are you sure you're okay?"

Warmth filled me. I had good friends, and they'd all helped me through the toughest times after my brother died. "You know me. I'm good."

Tessa gave me another long look, then yanked me in for a hug. "Okay." She didn't sound convinced.

"We need to have cocktails soon," Sierra said.

"Tell me when, so I can get Mrs. Jenkins to watch Ollie." With a wave, I hurried toward the elevators. I needed to get up to the third floor. It was midmorning, and most people were out doing whatever they did when they came to Windward.

Including the ESG who would be out on the mountain by now.

Drug dealers. I still couldn't believe it. Operating right under everybody's noses.

I pushed the cart down the corridor. I stopped at the first of the ESG's two adjoining rooms and knocked. "Housekeeping."

There was no response. I knocked again, being prudent. Unfortunately, I'd walked in on plenty of stuff that I couldn't unsee. My team had some hilarious stories.

I held my card up and the lock beeped. I grabbed a stack of towels off my cart and entered the room.

It was empty. The two queen beds were rumpled and unmade. The rest of the place was a mess. There were clothes on every surface, and the carpet was littered with food wrappers and empty bottles.

My nose wrinkled. *Pigs*.

I found used towels piled on the floor in the bathroom. I set out the fresh towels, then snatched up the old ones. I looked around. Nothing looked odd or out of place, except for the mess.

After dumping the dirty towels in the cart, I remade the beds. Then I raced around, collecting trash and wiping down surfaces. As I did, I discreetly checked in the closet, the drawers, under the bed.

No sign of drugs.

Time for room number two.

The second room was only marginally tidier than the first. As I tidied the desk, I spotted some white residue on the wood, and froze.

It could just be talcum powder or sugar from some snack. My gut tightened. But I bet it wasn't.

I pulled out my phone and snapped a couple of photos. Another quick search of the room didn't yield any criminal motherload of drugs. I pulled a face. I knew it wasn't going to be that easy. These guys had gotten away with this for a long time.

I finished cleaning up as quickly as I could. I didn't want to risk running into any of the ESG. I hoped they were out biking for the rest of the day, but I disliked the idea they could also be out there, dealing drugs to people.

When I slipped into the empty hall, I released a breath.

I needed to tell Caden about the powder. That meant seeking him out and speaking to him again.

My chest tightened. Whatever. I was an adult.

I'd talk to him, calmly and rationally. There would be no touching. I'd be keeping my hands to myself.

This was more important than my hurt feelings. I headed back downstairs into the back of house, and dumped the dirty laundry, then parked the cart. I checked in with my team. We only had a few more suites that needed cleaning before the new guests would start checking in. I slid my phone into my pocket and headed for the security room.

One of the security team, Hugh, was sitting in front of the bank of monitors.

"Hey, Hugh. Is Caden around?"

"Last I knew, he was checking out the renovations in the new security room. Want me to radio him?"

"No. No, that's fine. I'll find him."

Strolling through the lobby, I noted that there were a

few late checkouts at the reception desk. Enzo was escorting some guests into their cars. I walked around the concierge desk, and into the new security room. The buzz of power saws and the bang of hammering hit me.

Wow, the place was going to be huge. I spotted a burly worker in a hard hat. "Hi. I'm looking for Caden. Mr. Castro."

The guy gave me a chin lift. "He's back there." He pointed toward some draped plastic sheets.

I pushed through the plastic. The work sounds dimmed a little, and then I spotted him with a measuring tape measuring up the wall.

I dragged in a deep breath. "Caden?"

His head jerked up. His face looked as though it was carved from stone.

I lifted my chin. "I need to talk to you."

His dark gaze narrowed. "What is it?"

Glancing around, I noted there were no workers close by. The plastic sheeting made it feel like we were all alone. I swallowed, suddenly feeling like an insect, pinned under his gaze. "I cleaned the ESG's rooms."

A dangerous look crossed his face and he tilted his head. "You went in their rooms?"

His tone made goosebumps prickle across the back of my neck. "They weren't there."

"I told you to stay away."

"News flash, I didn't listen." I put my hands on my hips. "I'm not stupid, Caden. I didn't do anything risky. Well, I did look around a little, but I didn't find any drugs."

He made a low sound.

I was done being intimidated by him. "I'm not letting my team members in there if they're dangerous."

Waves of something powerful were emanating off him.

"I saw powder on the desk." I licked my lips. "Maybe we could take a sample of it, or something." I pulled out my phone. "I took some pictures."

He moved. One second, he was standing there, the next he gripped both my arms. "You went in there."

I shoved against him. "Back off, Broody."

His face darkened and he looked intensely lethal. "I told you to stay away from them."

"I heard your order, but I had to do what I think is right. I—"

"Put yourself in danger."

My heart kicked. That was why he was pissed? "We can test this stuff and get proof."

"It would be a trace amount. It would prove recreational use, at best. They'd get off with a slap on the wrist."

I sagged. "Oh."

He leaned in, his face an inch from mine. My heart beat went into overdrive, and my hands clenched on his chest.

"If they'd caught you..." He leaned closer and pressed his face to the side of mine.

Shit, I wasn't supposed to be touching him again. It was like we were a magnet and metal. Anytime we got close, bam, we stuck together.

"They didn't catch me." I smelled dark spice. I wanted to roll around in that scent. God, I trembled, wanting to touch him. "I had a legitimate reason to be there. I'm housekeeping."

"You have no idea what they're capable of. They could hurt you." A shudder went through him.

What was going on? "Caden, I'm all right." I pressed my hand to his stubbled cheek.

Our eyes locked.

"What if they hurt you and I wasn't there to help?"

I swallowed. A part of me needed to reassure him. "I won't go there again without telling you. I want to help. Let's do it together."

His own hand came up and cupped my cheek. I pressed into his rough palm.

"Okay?" I asked.

He blew out a breath. "Okay." Then he released me and stepped back. "I'm looking into them." He paused. "If there's a way you can help... I'll let you know. *Don't* do anything risky. Promise me."

"Caden—"

"Promise me. Please."

The word was short and sharp, but I knew him well enough now to hear the seething feelings underneath it.

Besides, I knew please wasn't a word he used very often.

I nodded. "I promise."

CHAPTER 12
CADEN

"Okay, yes, send it over. Thanks." I ended the call and leaned back in my chair.

I'd made several calls this afternoon, tracking down the ESG to all the places they regularly traveled between.

ESG. *Shit.* Allie was rubbing off on me.

I scraped a hand over my jaw. There was definitely a pattern. Everywhere these guys had stayed, some guests had subsequently been busted with drugs or suffered overdoses. My hand curled into a fist, my knuckles turning white. Added to that, over the last year, several women had been drugged and raped after being in hotel bars.

There'd been no arrests or leads.

Because these assholes moved around. And they covered their tracks.

I tapped my finger on my notes. I needed evidence to take them down. Watching them wasn't giving us anything.

What I needed was to plant a bug in their rooms.

I had no reason to be in their rooms. My best option was someone with a reason who could plant it for me.

I blew out a breath. I had zero desire to put Allie at risk. I had this damn enormous need to protect her and it was getting worse with every hour. My jaw worked.

She'd do it. In a heartbeat. I knew she wanted to help.

Dammit. I closed my eyes. Remembering shouts and pained groans and blood. Remembering the men I'd failed to keep safe.

I picked up the bug sitting on the table and held it up. It was high-tech. I'd pulled some strings and got some experimental gear from an old military contact. Rising, I slipped the bug into my pocket, and strode out of the conference room.

Whatever I had to do, I'd keep Allie safe. I wouldn't fail this time.

I spotted one of the housekeeping staff carrying a stack of clean towels. "Have you seen Allie?"

The woman nodded. "She's in the locker room."

I didn't want Allie involved, but it was better to have her involved with me, than watching her trying to do things herself and getting into trouble.

I pushed into the staff locker room, and saw her sitting on one of the benches, untying the laces on her shoes. Her brown top was wet.

"What happened?"

She jolted and pressed a hand to her chest. "You scared me. You need to make more noise."

"Are you okay?"

She held up a hand. "Ease up, I'm fine. I spilled some

floor cleaner on myself." Her nose wrinkled. "I smell like a pine forest."

"There are worse things to smell like."

"Not when you smell *this* much like a pine forest. My eyes are watering." She stood and moved behind her open locker door. Then, without hesitating, she pulled her wet shirt over her head.

Fuck.

I couldn't see anything except smooth bare shoulders and her arms. Still, I turned and listened to the rustling as she got dressed. My cock was hard in my pants. My brain went where it shouldn't, wondering if she was wearing any panties today under those sensible work pants.

"Okay, I'm decent."

When I turned back, she was wearing another uniform.

"What do you need, Caden?" she asked.

You. I gritted my teeth. "I need your help."

Her eyebrows winged up and she shot me a suspicious look. "Really? After all that alpha male overprotectiveness—" she lowered her voice "—Stay away from them, Allie." She studied me. "You asking for my help was the last thing I expected."

"I said you could help me. That we'd do this together."

"I didn't think you truly meant it."

"I always mean what I say."

Her gray gaze wandered over my face. "Yes, I think you do. So, what can I help you with?"

I stepped closer. "I need you to plant a bug in their

room."

Her eyes went wide, then she clapped her hands together and grinned. "Really? My God, that is so cool."

I shook my head at her excitement.

"I'll be like James Bond." She gave a little shimmy.

Damn, I liked seeing her happy. "Allie, keep your voice down."

"Oh, right." Her gaze darted around the empty locker room.

She moved closer and I smelled traces of the pine-fresh scent of the cleaner, but it didn't fully mask the scent of pure Allie coming through.

"Isn't bugging a room illegal?" she whispered.

"Yes."

"Ooh."

"Whatever we hear wouldn't be admissible, but I'm hoping it gives us some leads. That it'll lead us to the evidence we need to stop them." Finding their stash of drugs would be best.

"Right, so what's the plan?"

I glanced around. It was just the two of us. My half-hard cock was very aware of that.

Focus on the job, Castro. I slid my hand into my pocket and pulled out the tiny listening device. "This is the bug. I need you to plant it under the desk in their room."

She took it from me, turned it over. "It's so small."

"You need to peel the cover off the bottom and stick it to a dry surface. Got it?"

"Got it."

"Go in, clean the room, plant the bug, and get out. I

checked and they're out on the mountain. They'd planned a full day of mountain biking."

She gave me a decisive nod. "No problem."

"Here." I handed over a Bluetooth earpiece. "Wear it. We'll stay connected and I'll talk you through it all."

She took the earpiece. "I can do this, Broody. For Mellody."

"I know you can." I covered her hand with mine. "But if anything worries you or goes wrong, you get out. No risks, Allie."

"I think overprotectiveness must be in your DNA."

It was. But it seemed to go into overdrive when it came to this woman.

Her finger stroked my wrist. "Don't worry. I've got this."

I sat in my office in front of the laptop. I was following the CCTV feed of Allie moving through the hotel. She was pushing a cart into the elevator. I switched to the elevator feed. She was alone, fidgeting. Probably from nerves and a little excitement.

"Relax," I murmured, my own earpiece in my ear.

On the screen, she touched her ear. "Do you even know the meaning of that word? I think you're the least relaxed person I know."

She knew me well. "Just take a deep breath."

"I can't relax. I'm on an espionage mission."

I fought back a smile. "To do that well, you need to look normal."

"Right." She straightened and her face smoothed out. She looked at the camera, then winked.

I closed my eyes and fought back laughter.

What the hell was this?

I didn't laugh. Laughter had been me before all my assignments and missions. Before long, hard days slogging through deserts or jungles, dodging gunfire. Before I'd lost people who were like brothers to me.

That me didn't exist anymore.

Except around Allie.

She wheeled her cart out of the elevator and my muscles tensed. Now she looked serious. I watched her as she headed down the hall towards the ESG's rooms.

Nerves fizzed through me. Fuck, I didn't get nervous. I'd already confirmed that the four guys were out on the mountain. I'd checked with Sierra. Our outdoor-activities coordinator didn't much like the guys, either.

"Entering target location," Allie murmured.

I couldn't hold back my chuckle this time.

On screen, Allie paused at the door. "Oh my God, you have a sexy laugh." Then she gasped. "Forget I said that." She left the cart in the hall and grabbed a stack of towels. She knocked and announced herself, then knocked again.

She headed inside. I had no visuals inside the guestrooms. I tapped my fingers on the table. I didn't like having her out of my sight.

"I'm pretending to put towels out, but I already cleaned the room earlier. Did I mention these guys are pigs?"

I imagined her moving around. A second later, I saw

her as she dumped some towels in the cart and hurried back into the room.

"Planting the bug now."

My muscles tensed. I waited in silence.

Minutes ticked by.

"Allie?"

"Dammit, it's not sticking."

"Is the back cover completely off?"

"Yes. God, trust me to get a dud bug. Hang on."

I tapped the table some more. Then I saw a text message pop up on my phone. I almost ignored it. It could wait until Allie was out of the room. But then I saw it was from Sierra.

One of the ESG took a tumble. They're heading back to the hotel.

"Fuck. Allie, abort. The guys are on their way back."

"What?" She cursed. "No, I can get this in place."

I slapped my hands on the table. "Allie!"

"I'm planting this damn thing." There was more cursing.

With a curse of my own, I grabbed a new bug off the table and sprinted out of the office. "I'm coming."

At the end of the corridor, I walked swiftly through the lobby toward the stairs. Just as I got to the stairwell, I saw the ESG enter the lobby, one of them limping. The blond asshole Blake had an arm around him, helping him.

I shouldered through the door into the stairwell. I took the stairs two at a time, moving fast. A moment later, I sprinted down the hall and used my security key card to open the empty room beside the ESG's rooms, then pushed Allie's cart inside.

When I reached the ESG's room, I touched my own earpiece. "I'm coming in, Allie."

I unlocked the door and eased it closed behind me.

She stood near the desk, holding up the bug. "It's not sticking. I thought about hiding it somewhere else."

"I've got another one." I took the base off. "We've got to be quick. I saw them in the lobby."

She paled. "Oh, God."

"Here." I handed her the bug.

She crouched and slid under the desk, then she pressed the bug to the underside of the wood.

Then she straightened. "Done."

I grabbed her arm and hurried toward the door.

Voices in the hall.

Hell. "They're coming."

Her face went even paler.

My mind went cool and focused. Just like it had on a mission. I hauled her back across the room. This room had a balcony, and I carefully pulled the curtains half closed and opened the sliding door.

"Out," I ordered.

"We can't hide on the balcony. They'll see us. And we can't jump. We're on the third floor, Broody."

"Trust me."

She stepped outside, just as I heard the front door to the room open.

Calmly, I closed the glass slider and hauled Allie back against the side wall where we were hidden by the partially closed curtains. I pressed her against the wall, shielding her with my body.

"That was a wild fucking tumble, bro," a voice said from inside.

"Yeah, my knee's throbbing like a bitch."

"Ice it, then take a bath."

"Then we'll find a pretty young thing to give you a blowjob," someone else added.

There was laughter.

Allie's expression was one of disgust.

I pressed my lips to her ear. "Stay quiet."

She nodded, her hair brushing my cheek, her small, firm breasts pressed to my chest.

"We need beers," a voice said. "I'll get them from the mini-fridge."

"Who wants to sit on the balcony?"

I tensed, and Allie gripped my shirt.

"Nah, I need to keep my leg up. The bed's comfier."

I relaxed, but only a little. At any time, one of them could step out here and see us. We needed to get off this balcony.

I edged us over to the railing and looked down. "We're going to climb over."

She shook her head. "You're joking," she whispered.

"No."

Her hands twisted in my shirt. "Caden—"

"I won't let you fall. I'd prefer not to get busted by these assholes."

She blew out a breath. "Okay. If I break my neck, I'm blaming you."

"I'll go first."

Staying out of view of the room's inhabitants, I climbed over the railing, holding it tightly and letting my body drop over and dangle. I looked down, then let go.

My feet hit the railing of the balcony below and I caught it with my hands. I steadied myself, then stood on the balcony. Thankfully, this guest room was empty.

"Okay, Allie. Climb over and dangle down."

She did. "Oh God, I'm going to die." But she eased over the railing.

Reaching up, I gripped her legs. "I've got you. Let go."

She did. The trust she had in me made my chest warm. I hauled her against me.

"One level down, one to go," I told her.

She gripped my shoulders. "Why can't we go through the room?"

"I can't open the sliding door from this side." The sliders didn't have electronic locks. I absorbed the feel of her. Her cheeks were pink, her gaze fixed on my face.

Focus, Castro.

"Okay, so there's no balcony below us."

She looked over the railing down, down at the patch of dead grass below. "I don't want to go splat. Ollie needs me."

I pressed a finger under her chin. Damn, her skin was smooth. "There will be no splat. I promise."

She pulled in a shaky breath. "Okay."

Reluctantly, I let her go and climbed over. I studied the drop below. I'd leaped from higher.

I let go.

I heard Allie gasp, but then I landed, bent my knees,

and rolled. When I rose and turned, she was staring down at me, mouth open.

"You really are like James Bond."

With a faint smile, I shook my head. "No, I'm just well-trained." I gestured. "Come on. I'll catch you."

She hesitated, then gingerly climbed over the railing. I saw her lips moving. Maybe she was praying or calling me names.

"I've got you, Allie. I promise."

She lifted her chin, then jumped.

I caught her in my arms and heard the air rush out of her.

Safe. Relief punched through me. That was all that mattered.

She gripped my shoulders. "You caught me."

"Always."

Then she wound her legs around my waist. My heart started pounding.

"Caden..." Her mouth touched mine.

With a growl, I spun and pinned her to the wall and kissed her back.

This kiss wasn't sweet or gentle. It was hot and hungry.

CHAPTER 13
ALLIE

Oh God.

I went up in flames.

The kiss was all heat and hunger, tongues stroking and hands grabbing. He kissed me like he couldn't get enough, like he had the right to do it hard and deep. Arching into him, I moaned. I bit his bottom lip, everything inside me hot and achy.

God, my pulse was throbbing between my thighs. I rubbed against him, his fingers digging into my ass.

"*Allie.*" My name on his lips sounded like a curse and a plea.

"Don't stop. *Please.*" I dragged my mouth over his hard jaw, then down his neck. When I found the mark my teeth had left, I laved it with my tongue.

He groaned. "You like knowing you left your mark on me."

"Yes."

The next kiss was even harder. He plundered my mouth. I was so close to coming.

Then I heard the sound of a throat being cleared.

Caden froze. I blinked, my nails digging into his shoulders.

I tried to get my bearings, which was damn hard when all I could feel was raging desire. Someone cleared their throat again and I glanced over his broad shoulder...

Tessa.

She was standing on the path, clipboard in hand, looking as professional as ever in her neat, fitted, navy-blue dress and jacket. Her eyes were wide and alive with curiosity.

"Um... Tessa," I croaked out.

Caden set me down. The movement rubbed me over the large bulge in his suit pants. I bit back a moan and saw a muscle in his jaw tick.

"Damn," he muttered. "Get that look off your face."

I pressed my hand to the wall. I could honestly say that this day had not gone anything like I'd imagined when I'd woken up this morning.

"Hi, Tessa." My voice was a little high-pitched. "We were just..." Hmm, I wasn't sure exactly what to say.

My friend tilted her head. "Yes, I saw exactly what you two were doing."

"I need to get back to the security office," Caden said.

My head spun. He was abandoning me? "Coward," I muttered.

He glanced at Tessa. "Yep." Then, he touched my hand. Just the briefest brush.

Abruptly, he strode away down the path, giving Tessa a clipped nod.

I pushed off the wall. "Well, I'd better get back to—"

"Oh no, you don't." She grabbed my hand and towed me down the path.

"Tessa."

She ignored me. A second later, I spotted Sierra standing outside, talking with some of her team.

Tessa nabbed Sierra with her other hand. "Come with us."

The tiny blonde shot me a startled look. I shrugged my shoulder, and we followed Tessa inside and through to her office.

Jazz looked up from her desk and her eyebrows winged up. Tessa pushed me into a chair, then closed the office door.

"Talk," she demanded.

"Well...I really have work to finish up."

She swiveled and looked at our confused friends. "I just caught her outside...with Caden."

Sierra frowned. "Okay."

"She had her legs wrapped around his waist and her tongue in his mouth. He looked about five seconds away from doing her against the wall of the hotel."

Sierra gasped, and Jazz's mouth dropped open.

"Oh, my God," Jazz breathed.

"What happened to steering clear of him?" Sierra shot me a grin. "That you didn't need a man?"

I rolled my eyes to the ceiling. "We... It's... We were doing something for work..."

"Really?" Sierra said. "Something that involves kissing his brains out?"

"No, I was helping him with a security thing. And..." I trailed off.

"You really, really like him," Tessa said.

I felt a lick of panic. I could see Tessa going into matchmaker mode. "Guys, we're all on the clock. Don't you have work to do?"

Tessa pulled a face. "You're right. Cocktails at my place. Tonight."

"I can't. Ollie and I are making burgers. And he has some sort of craft thing I need to help him with for school."

"Tomorrow." Tessa got a stubborn look on her face.

I edged toward the door. "Maybe."

"You know you aren't getting out of this, girl," Sierra said. "We all know you've had a long dry spell, and we want the details."

"We kissed, that's it."

Sierra crossed her arms. "Twice, now."

"Um..."

Tessa made a sound. "More than twice. You've been keeping secrets."

"I've got to go." I edged for the door.

"We'll get them out of you over cocktails," Sierra called out.

I escaped.

The thing was, I hadn't worked out what was going on with Caden or how I felt. I couldn't talk to my friends about it because I just didn't know what to say.

As I entered the lobby, one of the receptionists waved at me. "Oh, Allie, a kid just vomited in the restaurant."

Ah, vomit to the rescue. "I'll get someone there ASAP."

CHAPTER 14
CADEN

I sat in the conference room, monitoring the feeds, and listening to the new bug. I was trying *not* to think about Allie. Or the kiss after our risky escape.

Hell, I'd been seconds away from losing all control and fucking her—at work, outside, against a wall.

Okay, I was failing badly in keeping my hands off Allie Ford.

I blew out a breath. Grabbing my mug, I sipped my coffee. I hadn't seen her since our espionage mission, but I'd caught glimpses of her on the video feed occasionally.

So far, listening to the extreme-sports guys hadn't paid off. There was lots of talk of bikes, tires, and their friend's busted knee.

"Ah, the lone predator in its lair, monitoring prey and eschewing all contact with the rest of the species in order to hunt."

I shot Piper a look over my shoulder. She stood in the conference room doorway, Ro beside her.

Ro slipped his hands into the pockets of his suit

pants and looked at the screen. It showed room service being delivered to the ESG.

"Why are you watching these guys?" Ro asked.

"Because they're trouble. Twenty-something guys into extreme sports. As far as I can tell, they don't work, just travel around. They're here to mountain bike, and their bikes are worth thousands of dollars. They came last winter to snowboard."

"The blond one's cute, and he knows it," Piper noted.

"Blake Moreland. He's the ringleader." I leaned back in my chair. "They're also dealing drugs."

Piper stiffened. "They're the ones who drugged the woman in the bar?"

I nodded. "I suspect so."

Ro's face hardened. "Why are they still in my hotel?"

"I don't have hard proof. Right now, it's just circumstantial. I'm working on it."

Ro's gaze narrowed on the screens as the blond guy closed the door to his room. The head of Langston Hotels nodded. "Then you'll get them."

Piper's nose wrinkled. "They sound like first-class assholes."

"I'll catch them. Then we can ban them from all Langston Hotels and turn them over to the police."

"Good," Ro said.

I studied his face. "What's bothering you?"

Ro glanced at Piper. "I hate when he does that."

She shrugged. "He's trained to read nonverbal cues. He can't not do it."

Ro leaned back against the conference table. "I finally talked with Chef Harvey. The guy is gruff as hell, but despite the bluster about being too busy, I could tell he was interested. I might need to go to London to meet him in person."

"And he doesn't like being away from Tessa," Piper said.

He got a faraway look in his eyes, and the corner of his lips quirked. "I bet Tessa would like to see London."

I swiveled to look at Piper. "What's bothering you?"

She crossed her arms over her chest. "Nothing. The renovations are right on track as planned." She buffed her nails on her shirt.

"And?" I prompted. I knew the woman too well by now.

She huffed. "I hate you. Fine. I sent a bunch of uniform samples to the head of maintenance. Do you know what he did with them?"

I hid my amusement. Piper and Everett were like a cat and a dog. Piper the glossy, prissy cat who liked things her way. Everett was a laid-back, mountain man, who didn't give a fuck about uniforms.

"He used them as rags. He sent me a picture of himself wiping grease on them." Her chin lifted, her eyes on fire. "While he was wearing that old, red flannel shirt he knows I hate."

Ro was grinning.

"You're the CEO," she snapped. "You're not supposed to find this amusing."

"Uniforms are not my area, they're yours."

She tossed her head back. "I will ensure everything is up to the standards of a Langston Hotel, whatever it takes."

She looked like a woman on a mission. Everett had better watch out.

For once, I had no idea who was going to win that battle.

Ro's shrewd gaze landed back on me and I fought the urge to stiffen. "Now, time to share what's bothering you."

"Nothing."

Ro leaned against the table and crossed his ankles. "I hear you've been kissing a certain member of the house-keeping team."

Dammit. I should have known Tessa would tell him.

Piper straightened like she'd been hit with a prod. "What? Caden kissed someone?"

Ro inclined his head, clearly enjoying himself. "Allie Ford."

The COO stared at me, dumbfounded. "I've never seen you show a single glimmer of interest in any woman. Even ones who blatantly throw themselves at you."

"This topic is not up for discussion."

Piper held up a hand. "Oh no. You pry into every-thing. Turnabout is fair play, my friend."

"You've got a thing for Allie," Ro said.

"A serious thing, since I know you usually avoid rela-tionships," Piper added.

"It doesn't matter what I have. She's a single mom, she's rooted here in Windward. I'm not. And I'm...not right for her."

The pair of them just stared at me.

I looked back at the screens. "I have monitoring to do."

Ro straightened. "A good, protective man who can help her shoulder some of the responsibility weighing her down. Sounds like you're exactly what Allie needs." He glanced at his watch. "Shit, I have a call. We'll talk more about this later."

"No, we won't."

Ro shook his head, but swiveled and stalked out.

Piper eyed me. "I know talking about stuff like this isn't your thing, but Caden, whatever came before...it doesn't matter. You deserve to be happy."

With that, she strode out on her heels.

I turned the audio back on. Happy? For so long, I'd just been happy to survive. After starting at Langston, I'd found some measure of...contentment. I didn't know how to have more than that.

Another hour ticked by and nothing the ESG said proved useful.

A moment later, the conference room door opened and Allie walked in. My chest squeezed.

"Hey." She lifted a bag of microwave popcorn. "I come bearing snacks." She dropped down in the chair beside me.

"Didn't your shift just end?" I asked.

She nodded. "I have a bit of time before I need to collect Ollie." Her nose wrinkled. "Then I'm coming back for the evening shift."

"What? You're pulling a double?"

She nodded. "There's a staff member who's got sick kids. Both her kids have the flu, and she's knee-deep in

Kleenex, and stuff you put in Kleenex." She winced. "I'd prefer she keep those germs at home."

I did too.

"I figured I'd help you listen to the bug." She opened the popcorn and popped some in her mouth. She held the bag out to me.

I took a handful. "It's not very interesting so far." I turned the volume up and we could hear the guys laughing.

She sighed. "I didn't think they'd be sitting around saying, 'oh, we're asshole drug dealers.'"

My lips twitched.

She curled her legs under her. My gaze dropped to her mouth. Now that I knew how good she tasted, how those legs felt around me, I wanted more.

I looked back at the screens. *Dammit.*

Nothing about me, or my life, was compatible with hers.

She deserved better.

I cleared my throat. "They just ordered room service. The guy who crashed his bike is complaining about his knee."

They were currently talking about football.

"I assume Tessa interrogated you?" I asked.

She grimaced. "Yes. I can't believe you ran off like a coward when Tessa busted us." She playfully slapped my arm. "You left me to defend myself."

"I had faith in you."

She snorted.

"Tessa shared with Ro. He and Piper came digging."

She made a humming sound.

"Who wants to hit the bars tonight?" one guy said on the audio feed. "Mitch, can your knee handle that?"

"Yeah, if there's beer and somewhere tight to stick my cock."

Allie pulled a face.

"We already knew they were assholes," I murmured.

"I feel like you need a hot, little brunette to play nurse," someone else told Mitch. "You had a blonde last night."

More laughter.

"If you're feeling off your game, you might need a little help to persuade your chick of choice."

I leaned forward.

"Are they talking about drugs?" Allie murmured.

"Probably." But unfortunately, these guys were careful. It was why they'd gotten away with this for so long.

The minutes ticked on, and the conversation shifted to the upcoming snowboarding season.

"How's Ollie?"

She smiled. "Good. I think he's starting to settle in at school."

"He's lucky to have you."

Her smile faded. "I just wished he was lucky enough to have his mom and dad."

"Your mom doesn't help you out. What about your father?"

She pulled a face. "When mom and dad divorced, he moved to Denver. He met a woman who had two young daughters and...he replaced us. It was like he traded his old family for a new one. He got busy raising those girls, going to their games and concerts." She shrugged. "He didn't have time for us anymore. Still doesn't."

I growled.

"It's okay, Broody. I know it's better to just depend on myself. And I have good friends." She leaned back in her chair. "You said you aren't close to your family."

My muscles tensed up. "When I got out of the Army..." I paused.

"I imagine it can be a hard transition to make."

"Yeah. I...lost people. Men I fought with." I felt like my throat was wrapped in barbed wire. "I came home angry. I was hypervigilant, always assessing everyone and every situation, couldn't switch off. It scared my mom and sisters."

"I'm sorry you lost people." Her voice was low, warm. Then her brows drew together. "Your family didn't support you, help you?"

"I didn't make it easy."

"Your father?"

I shook my head. "He was a deadbeat. Ran off when my youngest sister was a baby."

"So you had no one?"

"My mom tried, but...I just wasn't the same man who left. Things worsened, then I got in a bar fight with a guy who'd put his hand up my sister's skirt. I nearly beat him to death." I still remembered Sara staring at me, horrified, like I was a monster.

Allie gasped.

"After that...I left."

"Caden." She reached out and took my hand. "You haven't been back?"

I shook my head. "I send my mom the occasional email."

Her fingers squeezed mine. "You can be pretty intense, a little paranoid, and overprotective..."

I tensed up.

"But I suspect some of that is just you. You've clearly adjusted and found a job where you can use your skills. You should call your mom, Broody. Go home for a visit."

I stared at her smaller hand entwined with mine. I couldn't go back. I didn't want to risk my mom, Sara, and Clara looking at me like I was a monster. "Maybe."

She squeezed my hand again, but didn't say anything else.

The ESG were talking about paragliding now.

"I have to go." Allie rose and set the popcorn on the desk. "You keep that. I need to go and get Ollie."

I reached out and touched her hand without thinking. "I'll see you later."

Her gaze moved over my face, a small smile on her lips. "You will, Broody."

CHAPTER 15
ALLIE

I tried to start my RAV4.

Nothing. Just a sad, teeth-rattling grind.

"Dammit." I smacked the steering wheel. I needed to get back to the hotel for my double shift.

At least I wasn't late to get Ollie. We'd made burgers for dinner, and I'd had the joy of listening to him prattle on about a new TV show he liked. I'd even gotten a few giggles. He was now bathed and in his LEGO pajamas. Mrs. Jenkins had already arrived, and I'd left the two of them reading his favorite book. I knew he'd con her into two or three more.

Crap. I was going to be late for my shift. If I ran, I could still make it. I grabbed my backpack, locked my RAV4, then set off down the sidewalk.

As a kid, I'd loved running. I'd been a member of the cross-country team in high school. I broke into a steady pace, and soon my muscles warmed up and I lengthened my stride. I had no time to run anymore, and I couldn't leave Ollie alone even if I did.

I was actually enjoying myself when I turned the corner and the Langston Windward came into view. Slowing to a walk, I took a few deep breaths and let myself into the staff entrance.

"Hi, Allie." Justin, one of the evening crew, shot me a smile. I didn't know this team as well as mine. "Haven't seen you in ages."

"Hi, Justin. I'm filling in. Jenn's kids have the flu."

I met the rest of the crew and assigned everyone their rooms for evening turn-down service. I rechecked the stock levels, then joined some of the team to clean windows in the lobby. We often saved some of the common area jobs for the night shift.

The hours moved by quickly. I wondered what the ESG were doing this evening. My nose wrinkled. Was Caden still listening to the bug?

Crossing the lobby after sweeping up the remnants of a broken vase, the back of my neck began to itch and I heard loud voices.

I swiveled. The ESG. They were loud as they entered, and they had guests with them. *Surprise, surprise.*

I leaned against my broom and watched them.

God, the girls with them looked young. I couldn't blame them for wanting to have a good time. I assessed the girls to make sure no one was under the influence. They all seemed steady.

Then I realized Blake was looking at me. I couldn't manage a smile. Not knowing what I knew now about him and his friends.

His charming smile dissolved, and there was a look

on his face that I couldn't decipher. Then he and the group disappeared into the Bluff Bar.

Shaking my head, I forced myself to get back to work.

Soon, my shift was finished. I took a quick shower in the locker room, and pulled on the long skirt, sweater, and boots I'd packed in my backpack. I pulled a face. Crap, I had no vehicle to get home, and this wasn't exactly the right outfit to jog home in. I might have to get an Uber.

Something made me detour to the conference room. Sure enough, I found Caden sitting there.

"Hey."

He looked up. "Shift okay?"

"Fine. No vomit to clean up, which is always a plus. The evening crew are all experienced. They could probably run the shift better than me."

"I doubt that."

"Nothing on the bug, I'm guessing? I just saw the ESG heading into the bar, and it looked like they'd been out."

"They went out a couple of hours ago. We'll keep monitoring. I have the bartenders watching all the drinks of any females in the bar."

"Good." I nodded. "I'd better go."

Caden rose. "I'll walk you to your car. It's dark in the staff parking area. I have new security lights ordered."

"Of course you do." I tucked my hair back behind my ear. "It's okay, I don't have my car."

He cocked his head. "Why?"

"It wouldn't start earlier. I jogged over."

His face hardened. "You getting a ride home?"

"Well, it isn't far to walk or run."

He stared at me, and I couldn't miss the unhappy vibes.

"It's fine, Broody. This is Windward. And I like running. I used to run in high school."

"You're *not* running home in the dark. It's late."

"Caden—"

"No."

I rested my hands on my hips. "It isn't far—"

He snatched up his keys and jacket. "I'll drop you home."

I sighed. "Okay."

"Let me get one of my team to monitor things in here."

Before I knew it, he was leading me outside, a hand pressed to my lower back. I felt traitorous tingles everywhere.

He led me out to a big, black SUV parked in a VIP spot out front. He bleeped the locks, then opened the passenger door for me. Before I could move, he gripped my waist and lifted me in.

Again, I felt his touch everywhere and a gasp escaped my lips. I looked up.

Our gazes meshed. He stared at me, a muscle ticking in his jaw.

Then he stepped back and closed the door.

Okay, I could handle being alone with Caden in a vehicle. In the dark.

He climbed into the driver's seat.

Then it was just the two of us. I nibbled on my lower lip. I had to get a handle on this out-of-control desire.

"So..." *Really smooth, Allie.*

He glanced my way. "Is your neighbor with Ollie tonight?"

I nodded. "He'll be fast asleep by now. That kid can sleep. A tornado wouldn't wake him. Mrs. Jenkins will be napping in front of the television. She loves spending time with him. All her grandkids are in Pennsylvania, and she doesn't see them much."

"It's good you have help."

"I'm grateful. I'm grateful he sleeps well, too. After Sean and Sylvie died—" I felt the sharp pinch of pain and breathed through it "—he slept in my bed for weeks. He had...not quite nightmares, but he'd wake up and cry out for them." I shook my head, my heart hurting.

Caden reached across and grabbed my hand. "From what I can tell, you're doing a great job with him. He has a home, love, you. Everything a kid needs."

"I feel like I get it wrong a lot. I feel like I'm not in control. I'm doing my best, but I'm worried I'll still screw him up."

"Hey, give yourself a break. Even families with two parents and tons of support make mistakes. No one's perfect, and mistakes are part of life."

I looked at his profile, his strong jaw. "Did you...have a rough childhood? With your dad gone?"

He remained quiet.

"Sorry, I shouldn't pry. Ignore—"

"I didn't. Mom's a lot like you. She worked two jobs to make a good home for us. Dad was a piece of shit. I was five when he left, and my only memories are of him getting drunk and yelling."

"You have sisters?"

He nodded, but seemed tense. "Sara and Clara." He pulled into the parking lot in front of my condo.

It appeared the conversation was over.

When he opened the door, I touched his arm. "Don't get out."

His dark gaze leveled on me. "I'm walking you to your door." His voice said he wasn't going to argue about it.

I unbuckled my seat belt. "Okay, Broody. I'll let you fight off any bad guys lurking in my condo stairwell."

He shot me a look, then grabbed my backpack.

We walked up the stairs and I unlocked the front door to the building. I saw him look around.

"It's not fancy, but it does the job. I really wish I could've kept my brother's house. But Ollie doesn't seem to mind."

"Home isn't really about the building."

"Right." We headed up the stairs and for a second, I stumbled and teetered.

He caught me, hands gripping my waist. I was pulled against a hard chest and I sucked in a breath. I glanced up and saw his face. Saw the fierce need.

"Caden."

There was a flicker in his eyes and he released me. "Walk to your door, Allie."

Suddenly I felt angry. "You're just going to ignore this?"

"I should. You should."

I set my hands on my hips. "Why?"

"Because you deserve better." He nudged me forward.

I walked toward my front door, conscious of him behind me, my mind whirling. *I deserved better? He didn't think he was good enough?*

That was crazy. He was Caden. Protective and brooding, a veteran.

What the hell had happened to him to make him believe that?

We reached my door, tucked away around the corner, and for a second, it was like it was just the two of us.

"I bet Mrs. Jenkins will have her hearing aid out. She never hears me come in." I whirled, and our gazes locked.

As we stared at each other, my heart started to pound.

"*Fuck*," he muttered, his hands clenching. "Why can't I keep my hands off you?"

"I don't want you to keep them off me."

Then he was on me. He hauled me close, his mouth closing on mine.

I detonated. I touched him everywhere, my tongue stroking his.

"You're so fucking gorgeous," he breathed.

My heart knocked in my chest. I'd always been the sporty girl, not the gorgeous one. My mom had always called me a tomboy. No curves, no style, no femininity.

He gripped my thigh and hooked it up on his hip. I moaned. Caden seemed to have a different idea.

"You drive me crazy, Broody." I slid my hands in his dark hair. "I have no control around you. I've never felt like this before."

"Same." He bit my bottom lip.

Desire shivered through me. "Before the other night, I hadn't had a non-self-induced orgasm for so long that I'd forgotten how it feels."

There was a gleam in his eye. "You liked coming for me?"

"Yes."

His mouth took mine again. Then I was pinned to my front door. His mouth travelled down my neck and I moaned, rubbing against his hard body.

His hands slid down my sides, caressing and molding.

Then he dropped to his knees.

Shock ran through me and my brain just blanked. My breasts throbbed, my nipples hard. My pulse pounded in my ears.

His hands gripped my skirt, and he pushed it up, slowly, so slowly.

My breath hitched. I looked down at the intense focus on his face. Then he pushed the skirt higher, and cool air swirled around my bare legs.

He made a low sound, then hooked my thigh over his shoulder.

Oh, God.

"Drives me crazy knowing you aren't wearing panties. I think about it all day long."

Desire exploded and my hips jerked. He made a low sound and buried his head between my thighs.

I cried out and bit my lip and then gripped his hair. I felt his warm breath on me.

He licked my throbbing pussy, pressing his tongue

deep. I bit my lip, moans ripping free of me. He worked me, lapping and sucking, and I writhed on his mouth.

Everything inside me clenched, almost painful.

"*Caden*," I breathed huskily.

When my climax hit, it was hot and wild.

I bit my lip to drown out my sobs. Pleasure washed through me in a giant wave, and I tugged on his hair, grinding against him.

When I started to come down, I was panting and my legs felt wobbly. I would've fallen, if he wasn't holding me up.

He pressed a kiss to my inner thigh. "You taste so fucking good, Allie."

I couldn't speak. All I could do was run my hands through his thick hair.

He rose, my skirt falling back into place.

Caden had just given me an out-of-the-solar-system orgasm with his mouth, against my front door.

His callused fingers ran across my jaw. "Go inside now."

I nodded, still dazed.

"Sleep well, Allie."

THE NEXT MORNING, I floated around making breakfast for Ollie, a smile on my face.

My body was relaxed and I'd slept well.

I'd had a magnificent orgasm last night. Caden had played my body like a virtuoso.

Who knew Broody would be so good with his hands and mouth?

"Ollie, breakfast is ready."

My nephew arrived and shot me a shy smile. He climbed onto a stool and pulled his bowl of cereal closer.

"How's my Ol-ster this morning?"

"Good." He shoved a massive spoonful into his mouth.

"Me too, kiddo." I lifted my piece of toast and munched.

Suddenly, I remembered my SUV wouldn't start last night. *Crap.* I'd totally forgotten. I swallowed a groan. I'd have to get an Uber or taxi and drop Ollie to school, then get to work.

Maybe the universe would be kind today and the RAV would start.

I wasn't going to hold my breath.

Once Ollie and I were ready, we headed downstairs. My gaze hit my SUV, then I paused. It was in a different parking space.

I hurried over and saw the piece of paper tucked under the windshield wiper. *What the hell?* I snatched it up.

The handwriting was a bold, dark scrawl.

It was the battery. All fixed now.

- *C*

Caden had fixed my SUV.

I felt like a balloon inflated inside my chest. He'd

dropped me home, rocked my world, then fixed my vehicle.

I looked up at the sky. How could the man think he wasn't good enough for me?

"Allie, are you okay?"

I beamed at Ollie. "I'm good. Really good. Let's get you to school.

After dropping Ollie to school on time, and giving him extra hugs at the school gate, I made it to the Windward. I called out hellos to my crew as I walked to the locker room.

I wanted to see Caden. I nibbled on my bottom lip. I was a little nervous to see him. He'd pulled back so many times and he was so hard to read, but all signs were leaning to him wanting to bang my brains out. And I really, really wanted that.

Opening my locker, my heart did a little somersault. There was another bar of Dandelion sitting inside.

He liked me.

My smile morphed into a full-on grin, and I enjoyed the pleasant shiver. Yes, I wanted to get my hands on him.

I turned, and jolted when I saw Sierra standing there, with her arms crossed, looking at me intently.

"Morning," I squeaked.

"Good morning." She stepped closer. "You look like you had sex."

"What?" I touched my hair.

She shook her head. "You don't have sex hair, it's that dreamy look you've got on your face."

Instantly I schooled my features and gave her my best frown. "I don't do dreamy."

"I know. I've never seen this look on you." She lowered her voice. "I thought you said that you and Caden only kissed."

"That's true." Technically. "Mostly."

Sierra looked like a pissed-off pixie. "A kiss doesn't make you float in here emanating sunshine."

"It does if it's done right. I promise you, we haven't slept together."

Her eyes narrowed. "So Dark and Broody hasn't stuck a body part inside you."

I squirmed. "Sierra."

"You're avoiding the question."

"Only his fingers." I felt heat in my cheeks. "And tongue."

Her eyes popped wide. "Oh my God, what happened?"

"Well, the fingers were the other night..."

Her blue eyes went wider. "In the bar?"

I nodded. "He was...not happy I was potentially meeting another guy there. Then last night, he drove me home and walked me to my front door. He's *really* talented with his tongue. And I have stubble burn...on my thighs."

Sierra squealed. "Hot. Who knew Mr. Dark and Silent had it in him?" She fanned her face. "Okay, cocktails tonight. No excuses. You're *not* getting out of it. Tessa's going to arrange for Ollie to have a sleepover at her aunt's place with the kids."

Oh, Ollie would love that. Emily had four kids. The

oldest, Josh, was in college, Leo in high school, then Caleb and Haley, whom Ollie adored, were only a few years older than him. They went to the same school. "I don't know, it is a school night."

"He's five, Allie."

"Okay, cocktails." I knew none of them would let me get out of this. "Now I need to get to work."

"Go. Lucky girl." Sierra pouted. "There have been zero glorious orgasms in my life."

I grinned at her. "I highly recommend them."

"Shoo." She waved her hands at me as she left.

I hurried through my tasks and checked in with my team. As the morning progressed, work ran like clockwork.

It was funny. I'd taken this job because I'd been desperate. I'd returned from New York with no savings, drowning in grief, and struggling to help Ollie. Tessa had given me the job because it was all she'd had available.

Surprisingly, I enjoyed it way more than I'd ever enjoyed my advertising job.

I spotted one of the security team in the corridor, staring at a report. "Hi, Hugh."

"Allie."

"Is Caden around?"

The man shook his head. "He's locked in some security meeting with some of the international locations."

"Oh. I'll catch him later." I forgot just how much he was responsible for.

I'd already arranged with Marcy for me to clean the ESG's rooms again today. I pushed my cart onto level three and got to work. I made beds, dumped dirty towels, cleaned the bathroom, restocked the minibar. I avoided taking at peek at the bug, but I couldn't help having a little poke around.

Unfortunately, there were no traces of drugs left lying around. *Where were they keeping the stuff?*

I wondered if they had a car. I carried in some more shampoos and shower gels, then set them up in neat rows on the vanity.

My gaze fell on their suitcases. One was in the closet and the other on a stand in the corner. Clenching a dust-cloth in my hand, I crouched down and had a quick look in the case on the stand. I gently rifled through. All I found were clothes. Rising, I headed for the one in the closet.

I leaned over it.

"What are you doing?"

The voice made me jolt. I spun, clutching the cloth to my chest. My heart raced, trying to burst out of my chest.

Blake stood in the center of the room.

"I dropped my dust cloth." I held it up and prayed he couldn't sense the panic thundering inside me.

His gaze narrowed. His mouth was pressed into a hard line and suddenly, I didn't think he was that good-looking anymore.

"Sure you weren't having a poke around, Allie?"

I set my shoulders back. "I can assure you, house-keeping at the Langston Windward does not stoop in guest's property. I'm cleaning."

He scanned the room.

Play it cool, Allie. "I figured you'd be on the mountain."

"I came back to get some things."

Drugs? Maybe they were hidden in here somewhere.

He took a step closer. "You didn't come and have that drink the other night."

I cocked my head. "I was a little busy helping a woman who'd been drugged. You know anything about that, Blake?"

His eyes glittered. "Of course not."

My heart thumped, but I lifted my chin. "No other women better get drugged or hurt." I kept my gaze locked with his, then walked past him. "I'll get out of your way."

He gripped my arm. *Hard.*

I gasped.

His mouth twisted. "I don't take orders from nosy bitches. And I don't like people poking around in my business."

There was no sign of charming Blake now. "What?" I breathed.

"You're in my room. I've seen you in the hall, too. I saw you in the bar. I've seen you around a lot."

I swallowed. "I work here."

"I don't see the other housekeepers this often."

"Then you're not paying attention. We're usually invisible to guests."

His fingers squeezed and I fought back a wince.

"Well, I see you. And I know you're watching me."

Play the part. "You're easy to watch."

His cool eyes narrowed. "Then you should have let me buy you a drink and fuck you."

My mouth went dry. "My life is busy. I have a kid, remember?"

He released me. "I've no time for kids."

"Right." I couldn't believe I'd ever found him attractive. I hurried to the door.

"Allie..."

I glanced back. "If I catch you poking your nose where it doesn't belong, you won't like it."

"You have nothing I'm interested in." Heart racing and palms sweaty, I pushed my cart down the hall and into the elevator.

When I looked up, he was watching me as the doors closed.

The elevator started downward, and I sagged against the wall.

CHAPTER 16
CADEN

I hated meetings.

I'd been on video calls all day. There'd been various security fires to put out the other Langston Hotels around the world.

I hadn't seen Allie once yet today. Damn, I missed her.

I strode down the hall in the staff area. I could still taste her, hear the sounds she'd made. I shook my head. I wasn't supposed to be thinking about her. What I needed to do was check in with the security team, and Hugh, who was monitoring the bug.

These damn drug dealers were cunning bastards. I wasn't going to let them continue to peddle their poison, or hurt innocent women.

Hugh poked his head out of the conference room. His face looked like a thundercloud.

"What's wrong?" I clipped out.

"I was monitoring the bug. Allie was cleaning the room, and Moreland showed up."

My chest locked. "She okay?"

Hugh nodded. "But he threatened her. She asked him about the woman who'd been drugged in the Bluff Bar. He accused her of poking around."

Fuck. "Thanks, Hugh. I'll check on Allie. I want you and Gretchen to follow these guys. Be discreet. They have a stash of drugs somewhere and it isn't in their hotel room."

"You got it."

"Hugh, don't let them see you."

The tall man nodded and strode back into the conference room.

Ahead of me, Allie turned the corner. She was in her civilian clothes—fitted, well-worn jeans, and a gray sweater that made her eyes look silver. My cock twitched against the zipper of my pants.

"Hey." She smiled. "I heard you had meetings—"

I grabbed her hand, opened the nearest door—to a supply closet—and shoved her inside. I shut the door behind us.

Then I kissed her.

She made a hungry sound, her arms flinging around my neck. Denim-clad legs wrapped around me, and I cupped her ass.

We were both breathing heavily.

"This is one time I appreciate you being a man of few words," she panted. "I've discovered I prefer a man of action."

She was okay. Something inside me eased. She was unhurt, smiling, and in my arms. "Blake Moreland threatened you."

A look crossed her face. "How did you—?" Then she nodded. "The bug. I forgot. I was going to tell you."

"Are you all right?"

"I'm fine. Totally fine."

I kept watching her. She didn't seem upset or afraid.

"He was an asshole, but I already knew that." She pressed her hand to my cheek. "So, about being a man of action...you have any more for me?"

I couldn't stop my smile. My gaze dropped to her mouth.

"You have a sexy smile, Broody."

"Be quiet." I nuzzled her neck. "Apart from the ESG, how was your shift?"

"Better now."

I set her down, then stroked her cheekbone.

"It started well. I won't lie, I was still riding post-orgasmic goodness this morning."

Fuck. I liked knowing how much she liked what I did to her. I let my lips trace over the shell of her ear. "I fucked my hand in the shower last night afterward. I came hard."

She gripped my shirt and her lips parted. "I would've liked to have seen that." She tilted her head back. "You fixed my car." Her voice was low and husky.

"Yes." No way I was letting her run to work again.

"That's one of the nicest things anyone's ever done for me."

Damn. My gut was tight, my cock hard.

"And you left me more chocolate."

I was done. I couldn't fight this anymore. I wanted Allie. "Have dinner with me tonight?"

Her face fell. "I can't. It's cocktail night with the girls. Tessa organized it."

"Ah."

"That's right. They're going to interrogate me."

"Dinner tomorrow? Ollie as well."

Warmth crossed her face. "I'd like that. And so would he. He's staying with Tessa's aunt tonight. So I definitely want to hang with him tomorrow night."

"He's a good kid. We'll have fun." I ran my fingers down her neck. Her eyelashes fluttered.

"Now I'm all hot and bothered." She pushed the sleeves of her sweater up.

I glanced down at her arms. There were bruises on her forearm. Dark smudges that were definitely finger marks. Large ones.

White noise filled my head. I lifted her arm gently. "Did I hurt you?"

"What? No." She looked down. "Oh, that asshole."

"Moreland." My tone was measured, lethal.

Her face changed, her hands pressing to my chest. "Caden, stand down. I'm right here, I'm perfectly fine. You just kissed me like the world was ending."

I felt a muscle tick in my jaw. I was pissed and she was making me want to smile. I dragged in a deep breath. "You didn't tell me that he touched you."

"He grabbed my arm. He suspects something, and he warned me to keep my nose out of his business."

I growled. Moreland was a dead man.

"Hey." She pressed a hand to my jaw. "Look at me. You can't kill him."

"Yes, I can."

Her eyes narrowed. "I can't tell if you're joking, or not."

I met her gaze and let her see that I meant it.

"No killing. I want more orgasms, and I have plans to explore this." She waved a hand up my body. "So no killing."

"No one would ever find out."

She huffed. "Caden, I'm counting down to the day that he and his buddies are dragged off in handcuffs. That will be justice."

"Fine," I grumbled.

"Good. I have to go." She rose up on her toes and pressed a quick kiss to my mouth.

I hauled her back and kissed her properly.

"Well, ah..." She pressed her fingers to her lips. "Now, I feel a little dizzy."

"Dinner tomorrow night?"

She nodded.

"Allie, I'll be thinking about you tonight. Call me when you get home."

CHAPTER 17
ALLIE

The roar of the blender was almost deafening.

Sierra was manning it and mixing up a new cocktail. Jazz sat on a stool, sipping her drink. Piper sat beside her. Tessa was busy bustling around the kitchen, putting cheese and crackers on a wooden board.

"I made basil dip from this new recipe," Tessa said. "I hope it's good."

Looking around, I saw signs that she no longer lived alone. Ro's woolen sweater was draped over the back of a chair. There was a set of men's sunglasses on the kitchen island. And there was also a large vase of flowers—roses in a deep red—in the center of the table. My guess was Tessa's hot guy bought them for her.

I watched Tessa smile as she set out the platter. She was...glowing. Happy.

She deserved it. She was hard-working, an excellent hotel manager, close with her aunt and cousins, a good friend. She'd lost her parents so young.

Tessa gave me hope that Ollie would be fine.

A phone dinged.

"Oh, that's mine." Tessa grabbed a kitchen towel and wiped her hands.

"That better not be your man horning in on our girls cocktail night," I said.

"No, he and Caden were catching up on security stuff." Piper sipped. "And having dinner together."

At the mention of Caden's name, my friends all turned their heads to look at me.

Tessa grinned at her phone. "It's not Ro. Emily sent a picture of the kids." She held the phone out to me.

On the screen, a smiling Ollie was wedged between Caleb and Haley, who were pulling crazy faces. Tessa's young cousins were both wearing Pokémon pajamas. I'd had a crash course on learning Pokémon since I'd moved back to Windward. Although, most of the time Ollie preferred LEGO over the weird anime creatures.

"He's enjoying himself," I murmured.

Tessa gripped my arm. "You're doing a great job, Allie."

I blew out a breath. "Some days, I feel like I'm barely holding on."

She hugged me. "So, lean on us."

"You're already doing so much. I'm not very good at leaning."

"You don't say." Sierra handed me a cocktail.

I sipped it with a smile.

"I suspect wild orgasms will help loosen you up," she added.

I choked on my margarita.

"Well, they've kissed," Tessa said, "so it could definitely be heading into the wild-orgasm direction."

"I'm not sure I can listen to sex talk about Caden," Piper said. "He's like a brother to me."

"When I busted Allie and Caden kissing like the world was ending, and it was hot, hot, hot," Tessa said gleefully.

I took another sip of tequila-y goodness.

Piper shook her head. "I've never seen him show the slightest interest in a woman—despite several opportunities—let alone kiss one."

"Hmm," was all I could manage.

"Oh, they've progressed way past kissing." Sierra's face was smug.

Tessa gasped.

"You've been holding out." Jazz waved a finger at me.

"Tall, dark, and broody is quite talented, I hear," Sierra said. "Allie's had non-self-induced orgasms in the shadows of the Bluff Bar and on her front doorstep."

There were lots of gasps.

"The man has a good mouth." I fought off an uncharacteristic blush and sipped more of my cocktail.

"He must really like you," Piper said.

I pulled a face. "It's hard to tell."

She nodded. "He doesn't say much, but before he worked at Langston Hotels—"

"He was in the military."

Piper nodded. "From what I can tell, coming home wasn't easy."

I didn't tell her that he'd shared some of that with me. An ache bloomed in my chest.

"He's big and strong, but tread carefully with him," Piper added.

I nodded in acknowledgement. "We're having dinner tomorrow night."

Sierra let out a happy squeal.

I held up a hand. "Remember, he's not staying in Windward forever."

Tessa waved a hand. "Pfft, Ro said that, too."

"Guys, I have a kid. My life's a mess. I have no idea what this is..."

"Just enjoy yourself," Sierra said.

"I second that," Tessa said. "You deserve some fun."

I nodded. "I'll try."

"Okay, I have another recipe to test out," Sierra said. "We need a special cocktail to celebrate Allie hopefully getting laid soon."

Piper groaned. "I do not want hear sex details about Caden." She pinned Tessa with a look. "Or Ro."

Soon I was stuffed full of brie and dip. My second cocktail had left me with a pleasant buzz. I was laughing hard at a story that Tessa was telling about Coral.

"She caught Ro and me kissing." Tessa rolled her eyes. "God, the lecture was tart. She called me a hussy."

"Everyone's caught you two kissing," Jazz said dryly.

"I want to catch Allie and Caden next," Sierra said. Then she pouted. "I need a guy to kiss."

"No potential prospects?" Piper asked, twirling her glass around.

"No one who ignites any sparks." Sierra grinned. "I like muscles. Lots of muscles. There's nothing hotter than a big, fit guy."

"I have no idea what I like." Piper frowned. "Men are annoying. I'm thinking of freezing my eggs."

"Oh, the right guy is out there," Sierra said earnestly.

Jazz snorted. "He might even be right in front of your face."

"Spoken like a happily married woman," I noted.

"Nope." Piper shook her head. "I don't want a man."

"Has everyone got their costumes for the Halloween Spooktacular on Friday night?" Tessa asked. "I'm going as Wonder Woman."

"And Ro?" Jazz asked.

"Captain America."

I snort-laughed. I couldn't wait to see the suave billionaire playing dress up.

"It's for the kids and charity," Tessa said primly. "What's your costume?"

I winced. "No idea. Ollie hasn't made up his mind."

Tessa gasped. "You're almost out of time."

"I'll get it sorted out."

"Does Caden have a costume?" Sierra asked.

I burst out laughing. "You really think he'll wear a costume? Have you met the man?"

Tessa crossed her arms. "He *will* wear a costume. It's the rule."

Piper sipped her drink. "I bet he will if you ask him to, Allie."

"We'll see." Hmm, I wouldn't mind seeing him as Batman, or maybe a sexy Grim Reaper. I glanced at my watch and stirred. "I'd better get home. One thing about having kids, you can never drink too much, or stay out too late." I set my glass down. "Kids don't sleep in, and trust me, kids and hangovers don't mix. Ollie will be home first thing in the morning."

"I hate that you're walking home in the cold," Tessa said.

"It's not snowing, and it isn't far. I'll be fine."

I hugged all of them.

"And we demand regular updates on you and Broody," Tessa said.

"Not the gory details." Piper held up a hand. "I need to be able to look the man in the eye."

I smiled. "Night, guys."

I slipped my denim jacket on. The air was crisp and the sky filled with clouds, but thankfully no snow. As I headed down the street, I glanced across at Emily's house. No doubt the kids were in bed, but my money was on them giggling under the covers. It would be good for Ollie.

After a brisk walk, I turned onto my street. My condo building was all lit up. Pulling out my cellphone, I texted Tessa.

My apartment building is in sight. Thanks for a great night.

Then I was planning to text Caden, but my fingers hovered over the keyboard. I pressed the Call button instead.

"You okay?" His deep voice came across the line.

"Yes." I imagined him sitting in a chair, studying files. "I'm walking home."

"Alone? After you've been drinking?"

"I had two cocktails, and my building is dead ahead. No need to worry."

"I would've given you a ride."

"It was girls only, Castro. No men allowed. How was your evening?"

"I had dinner with Ro. Now, I'm reviewing some security files."

So, I was right about the files. "We still on for tomorrow night?"

"Yes."

"Good, I—"

Someone grabbed me from behind and I sucked in a sharp breath.

"Allie?" Caden's tone sharpened.

"Let me go!" Something dropped over my head, plunging me into darkness. My phone was knocked out of my hand, and I heard it hit the ground with a crack. "Caden!" I screamed.

Then I was dragged away. I struggled, but there were two of them and they were holding me tightly.

"Hurry up," one said in a quiet whisper.

"Over here."

I broke free for a second, but I barely took two steps before I was lifted off my feet. I kicked and struggled. I flailed my arms and legs, hoping desperately to strike one of them. My arm made contact with a body part, and I heard a grunt.

The next second, the side of my head slammed into something solid. Stars filled my vision as pain spiked through my skull, and I bit back a cry.

Then I was lifted bodily, and shoved down into some sort of enclosed space. Something slammed closed above me.

Oh, God. I was in the trunk of a car.

CHAPTER 18
CADEN

"Allie! Allie!"

The line went dead.

Let me go! Her words echoed in my ears. Someone had grabbed her.

My throat closed, my pulse thundering in my ears. I shot to my feet and grabbed my jacket and shoes, and I was out the door of my suite in an instant.

I jogged down the hall and ran down the stairs. I tried to call her back, but it went to voicemail. I tried again and again. By the time I reached the conference room, I hadn't calmed down.

"Hugh, Paul, with me."

The men rose.

"Problem, boss?" Paul asked, his brow creased.

"It's Allie."

"From housekeeping?"

I nodded. "I was talking with her on the phone. She was walking home, and someone grabbed her. The call dropped out."

Both men cursed.

"I'll bring the SUV around," Hugh said.

My jaw tight, I watched him race off. I had to get a grip on this. I had to find my control.

Paul stepped closer. "We'll find her."

I glanced at him.

"I've seen the way you look at her. I know she's yours."

She wasn't mine. But I couldn't let that matter too much. My fingers clenched into fists. All I knew was I had to find her.

And I wouldn't stop until I did.

"What's going on?" Ro appeared in the doorway, his face serious. His jacket was gone and his sleeves were rolled up, but he must have been doing some work in his office.

I dragged in a breath. I needed to go. I needed to find her.

Get your fucking head on straight. Allie needs you.

"Allie was taken."

Ro frowned. "Taken?"

"We were talking on the phone, and someone grabbed her as she was walking home from Tessa's."

"Shit," Ro said.

I shouldered out past him, Ro and Paul falling into step with me.

"Who'd take her?" Ro asked.

I had my suspicions. I knew that Moreland had threatened her.

But it wasn't enough. I needed proof.

"Paul, I need you to monitor the listening device for the men on level three. See if they mention Allie."

He nodded. "I'm on it." He turned back and headed for the conference room.

Ro and I swept through the lobby. When Enzo spotted us, he frowned.

"What happened?" the concierge demanded.

"Someone snatched Allie," I gritted out.

He cursed in Italian. "I'm coming with you."

I lifted my chin. Outside, Hugh was in the driver's seat of one of the hotel's Yukons. I slid into the passenger seat while Ro and Enzo hopped into the back.

A second later, we drove out.

"What the hell is going on?" Ro asked.

"Allie's been poking around the ESG's rooms."

"The suspected drug dealers?"

I nodded. "She wanted to help, so I had her help me plant a bug. I wanted to keep an eye on her." I raked a hand through my hair. "The ringleader suspected she was poking around, and threatened her. Not in any detail." A muscle ticked in my jaw. If that fucker was behind this, if he'd hurt her...

"Okay. Keep a lock on it, Caden. Let's gather the facts and find her. If this is the dealers, they're not going to do something stupid."

We didn't know that. I knew they'd want to protect their lucrative little business.

Ahead, her condo building came into view. Hugh pulled into a parking space out front.

I got out and scanned the street. There was no sign of Allie.

"Hugh, see if she's inside. Condo number 14."

"On it."

I knew she wasn't in there. My instincts were screaming at me. My chest felt like it had been filled with rocks. I walked down the sidewalk. "She said she could see her building. She was walking back from Tessa's."

Ro and Enzo spread out, both scanning the ground.

"Maybe she just dropped her phone?" Ro said hopefully. "And it's broken?"

"No, someone grabbed her."

"What's that?" Enzo asked, pointing.

A glint of metal on the ground.

I strode over. It was a set of keys. The keychain had a small plastic tag on it and inside was a photo of Allie and Ollie. I scooped them up, grinding my teeth together. "These are hers." I turned in a circle, and a second later, I spotted her phone. I snatched it up. The screen was cracked. "Fuck."

Ro gripped my shoulder. "We'll find her."

I pulled out my cellphone and called the security office. "Paul, do you have eyes on the men on level three?"

"Only two of them are in their rooms. They just ordered room service."

My chest expanded. "The other two?"

"I did a quick check. They left in their car. Blue Honda Civic."

I bit back a curse. "Thanks." I turned. "Two of those guys aren't at the hotel. They took her."

Ro's face hardened. "We don't know that for sure. We need to ask them some questions."

We climbed back into the SUV. "We can't tip our hand." My hand flexed. "We can't risk putting her in more danger." I had to think. Where would they take her?

We pulled back in at the Langston Windward. As I sliced out of the SUV, I saw Blake Moreland. He and his friend had just exited a car. They looked relaxed, were smiling.

He caught my gaze.

I glared at him, and the smug asshole just smiled back. He thought he was so smart.

I took a step forward, but Ro grabbed my arm and Hugh stepped closer.

"Take it easy," Ro murmured. "I don't need you locked up for assault."

Moreland gave me another long look, then sailed inside.

I hurried over to the valet. "Is that their vehicle?"

The young man nodded. "Yes, Mr. Castro."

Enzo waved at the young valet. "Will, I'll park it."

"Oh, okay, Enzo." He handed over the keys.

Taking them from Enzo, I slid into the driver's seat. Enzo sat in the passenger seat, looking through the glove box.

Ro leaned in the open door. "Any clues?"

I saw takeout wrappers, sports gear, old receipts.

"Pigs," Enzo muttered.

Leaning forward, I tapped on the navigation screen.

A map appeared. As I looked at it, my chest expanded. *Bingo.*

CHAPTER 19
ALLIE

I was cold.

And scared. But honestly, right now, mostly I was pissed off.

Yep, pissed off was winning against the scared.

I fought the ropes on my wrists. I was still blindfolded, so I had no idea where I was. The two jerks hadn't been gentle about manhandling me in here.

Wherever *here* was.

I was inside a building, but it was still cold and damp, especially since I was sitting on a freezing-cold, concrete floor. Every movement I made seemed to echo, so maybe somewhere industrial? Someplace empty, or abandoned? My face and hand were throbbing. I'd scraped my hand when I'd fallen, and then they'd banged my face against the car.

Assholes.

I suspected it was Blake and his friends, but they hadn't let me see them, and they'd spoken in low whispers.

Watch yourself, bitch.

Nosy bitches get what they deserve.

It had to be the ESG. Who else could it be?

They'd dumped me here, then disappeared. I hadn't heard a single sound in ages.

My rage ignited.

How dare they kidnap me? I had a kid who depended on me. They were criminal assholes who hurt people.

They were going down. I'd make sure of it.

Caden had been on the phone. He'd heard me get abducted. My stomach cramped. He'd be losing his mind.

Feverishly, I kept working the rope. It loosened.

"Come on," I urged.

But it wouldn't budge enough for me to get my hands free. *Dammit.*

I switched to trying to pull my blindfold off. I did some pretty impressive acrobatics, rubbing my face against my shoulder. They'd tied it tightly and it was digging into the side of my head. I had no idea where my kidnappers were, or if they were coming back. I wasn't planning to wait around.

The blindfold slipped down around my neck.

"*Yes.*" I blinked, glancing around. It was dark, but there was a faint light coming through some windows at the front of the building.

I was in a huge, empty warehouse.

Pressing my tied hands to my stomach, I took a quick stock of the situation. I was alive. I wasn't badly hurt. I was alone.

And I was damn well getting out of here.

I pushed to my feet, shivering. It was so cold.

I hurried to the front of the building, my footsteps echoing. The place looked like it had been abandoned for a while. The dust was thick on the scarred floor and there wasn't anything around. I peered out the dirty windows. There were several other warehouse buildings nearby, but no cars or people. It took me a moment, but I figured out where I was. It was a small industrial area just outside of Windward.

Okay, Allie. Get out. Flag down a car, and call for help.

Suddenly, I heard the sound of an engine and the crunch of tires on gravel. I ducked down, as lights flickered across the warehouse.

Oh, God. Had my abductors come back?

Gut churning, I tried to make a plan. *Get outside and hide.* That was the best I had.

I heard the low murmur of deep voices. *Shit.* It had to be my captors.

Hunching over, I darted across the front of the warehouse, then paused with my back pressed to the wall. The handle on the door rattled, the sound echoing through the warehouse.

My pulse went crazy.

Then I heard muffled voices out front. "I'll head around the back." It was a man's voice I didn't recognize.

Crap. I darted along the wall, away from the voices. I needed another way out.

I paused again. Were those footsteps? I bit my lip, my fingers numb from the cold. I reached another window and peered through it. All I saw was darkness and dancing shadows.

But as I stood there, the huge bulk of a man emerged from the darkness. I sucked in a breath and stumbled backward.

Oh, hell. He was looking around, then his attention centered on me through the glass.

Run, Allie.

He stepped closer and our gazes met.

Caden.

As I sucked in a breath, relief crashed through me. I watched numerous emotions cross his face.

Then he took several steps back, and suddenly ran toward me.

My mouth dropped open. As I watched, he lowered his shoulder and leaped through the window.

Glass shattered. I watched him roll across the concrete floor, then come up to his feet. My heart fluttered.

He'd come for me. Like some sort of superhero or a super-spy.

"Allie." He closed the distance between us.

I'd been doing okay up until now, riding my wave of fear and anger.

Now, I lost it.

I threw myself at him, and he caught me, yanking me into his arms.

CHAPTER 20
CADEN

T pulled Allie close, pressing her face to my chest.

She was alive. She was fine.

I held her tighter and breathed her in. So many terrible scenarios had run through my mind. I tipped her face up.

"I'm okay." Her eyes were watery, but that defiant tilt of her chin told me that she was holding it together. "I'm fine now."

I rubbed my thumbs across her cheeks. I saw the swelling around her eye and my jaw tightened. "They hit you." My voice cut through the space like a blade.

She pulled in a breath. "No, I banged my face when they were trying to get me into the trunk of their car."

They'd put her in the trunk of the car. Air hissed through my teeth. "I'll kill them."

"Hey." She pressed into me. "You're the good guy, remember?"

"No, I'm not."

"Caden." Her face softened. "I won't pretend I don't

find your scary protectiveness hot, but let's not kill anyone." She nuzzled into my shirt. "I'm all right."

I released a harsh breath, then gently touched her face. "This is going to bruise."

"It's not my first black eye. Sean accidentally elbowed me once and gave me a shiner." She pulled a face. "Oh, but I don't want Ollie to worry."

"We'll get some ice on it." I realized her wrists were bound and pulled out my pocket knife. I cut her free.

"Do you always carry a knife?"

"Yes."

"Even when you're wearing a suit?"

"Yes." I pulled her closer again, and felt her shudder. I pressed my cheek to her hair and breathed her in. I realized now how fucking terrified I'd been.

Afraid I'd be too late, that I'd miss something, and she'd pay the price.

"You're so warm," she murmured.

And she was cold. I slipped my jacket off and guided her arms through the sleeves.

The sound of voices made me straighten.

"You found her?" Ro appeared out of darkness. "Thank God."

Enzo followed Ro inside. I saw Hugh hovering behind them.

"I'm okay," Allie said.

A quiet, lethal rage built inside me. Moreland and his asshole friends were responsible for this.

Enzo claimed Allie for a quick hug. My gaze narrowed on the man, while the asshole shot me a grin.

Ro pointed a finger at me. "You can't kill them."

"People keep saying that."

"We need evidence. Then we'll let the police do their job." Ro touched Allie's shoulder. "I'm really glad you're all right, Allie."

"Thanks, Ro, me too."

"Did you see the people who took you?" I asked.

She shook her head, frustration on her face. "They grabbed me from behind, then blindfolded me."

"Did you hear them? Was it Moreland?"

She shook her head again. "I don't know. They whispered. I couldn't recognize their voices. I can't say for certain it was Blake."

Dammit. These fuckers were careful.

Her face fell. "God, they're going to get away with it, aren't they?"

I ran a hand over her hair. "No, they won't."

"Why would they do this?"

"To warn you off." I pulled her close again and met Enzo's gaze.

"She was getting too close," Enzo murmured.

I looked at Ro. "She needs to get checked out." She'd also need to give a statement to the police. We had no evidence that the ESG were responsible, but I wanted this on the record. I'd call Sanchez in the morning.

"No." She shivered. "I want to go home and just put some ice on my face." She grimaced and lifted one hand. "And take some painkillers."

Her palm was scraped. I fought back the urge to find Moreland and ram him headfirst into a wall. "You're going to the hospital."

"Caden, please." She lifted her face. "I'm not bleeding and nothing's broken. I want to go home."

I ground my teeth together.

"*Please.*"

I couldn't say no. "Dammit. Fine." Keeping an arm around her, I lead her out to the Yukon. Hugh and Ro got the front while Enzo and I got in the back with Allie.

As we drove, she leaned against me, her head resting on my shoulder. I fucking liked that. I still wanted to charge into the ESG's rooms and rip some heads off, though.

She shifted against me, and I wrapped my arm around her.

She needed me more. She was coping okay, but shock could hit her at any moment.

I'd be there. I'd protect her.

"This needs to be reported," Ro said quietly.

Allie quivered and I squeezed her arm. "I'll call Officer Sanchez in the morning."

We pulled up in front of her condo building. I got up and helped her out of the vehicle.

"Thanks, Caden. For finding me... It means a lot."

I closed the SUV door. "I'm not leaving. I'm staying at your place tonight."

Relief bloomed on her face.

After I waved the others on, we walked to the front door of the building. I pulled her keys out.

"Oh, you found my keys."

"Yes. Your phone was ruined, though."

"Damn."

I unlocked the door. "Don't worry about that now."

She nodded tiredly.

Screw this. I slid my arms around her, bent my knees, and lifted her into my arms.

She gave a startled gasp and slid her arm across my shoulders. "Caden, I'm too heavy."

"No, you're not."

I carried her up the stairs. At her front door, memories of pinning her there and tasting her between those lean thighs hit me. I remembered her sweet cries as she'd come for me.

Now wasn't the time for that. She'd just survived a scary abduction, and she was cold and hurt. I unlocked her front door and carried her inside.

"Sit." I lowered her to the couch, then headed for the kitchen. I found an ice pack in her freezer, then sat beside her and pressed it to her eye.

Her place looked...cozy. There were bright colors on the wall in one corner, and a basket filled with toys. A welcoming home for a kid.

She'd made a cozy spot for her nephew. She'd turned a small, bland condo into a home.

"I need this to not look so bad." She fidgeted with the ice pack. "I don't want Ollie to panic."

"You can't shield him from everything."

"I know. I know there are times I won't be able to, but I'm going to try." She shivered again.

"Go and take a hot shower. I'll refreeze the ice pack and make you a hot drink."

With a tight nod, she pushed to her feet. She set my jacket on the back of the couch. "Thanks for staying."

I watched those long legs as she headed down the hallway.

I looked toward the ceiling and muttered under my breath. I needed to keep my own needs on lockdown.

She needed comfort, care, and my protection tonight, and nothing else.

CHAPTER 21
ALLIE

The shower helped.

I was no longer cold. I'd carefully washed my hair and cleaned my grazed palm. I'd put some cream on it later. Stepping out, I dried off, then looked in the mirror.

Oh crap. I winced, which tugged on my eye. The side of it was swollen. I poked at it. It felt tight and hot.

Stupid assholes.

A quiver ran through me. What if it had been worse? What if I'd been hurt badly or killed?

What would happen to Ollie?

My chest tightened. He needed me. I couldn't leave him alone.

Shivers started and this time I couldn't stop them. I wrapped the towel tightly around myself. Staggering out of my bathroom, I curled up on my bed. I'd be fine in a minute. I would get a grip on this.

I would.

I wasn't sure how long I lay there, but then I heard

the creak of my door. Caden uttered a low curse, then the next thing I knew, his big, strong body curled around mine.

I lifted my head off the pillow.

"Shh." He wrapped his arm around me.

Finally, I felt warm.

I felt safe.

I snuggled into the pillows, into him, feeling secure under the heavy weight of his arm.

"You're safe," he murmured. "No one is going to hurt you." His lips pressed to my hairline.

Only my brother had ever protected me. He'd been the only person I'd trusted to be there for me, no questions asked.

Now, I leaned into Caden's strength.

Just for just a few minutes. Then I'd get up and get myself together.

Warm and cocooned, I drifted off to sleep.

I woke with a jerk, my pulse racing.

It took me a moment to orient myself and realize that I was in my bed.

Safe.

I was safe. I wasn't stuck in the trunk of a car, or tied up in a dirty warehouse.

Blowing out a breath, I tried to shake off the disquiet. I knew my brain needed time to process what had happened, but I needed to remind myself that I was all right.

Slowly, I started to feel better. I noted that I was alone, although the pillow beside me held the dent of Caden's head.

Now, every thought of my abduction was replaced with the memory of Caden's big body curled around me as I drifted off to sleep.

Where was he? I glanced at the clock on my bedside table and saw that it was still the middle of the night. My room was draped in shadows. I knew he wouldn't have left me.

Climbing out of the bed, I tightened the towel around my body and padded into the living room. I spotted his silhouette sitting on the couch, staring out the window.

Staring at what? Remembering what?

As soon as I took a step toward him, his head lifted.

"Allie? You okay?"

"Yes, I just woke up alone." I crossed over to him, then without stopping to think, I straddled him and settled on his lap. I felt the flex of his powerful muscles beneath me, and his hands gripped my hips over the towel.

"That's better." I melted against him, my face pressed to his neck. He was so warm. His shirt was soft against my chest and the denim of his jeans was rough on my bare legs.

His hands moved up my back, stroking.

"Did you have a nightmare?" I asked.

"No, I don't get nightmares."

I lifted my head. "You just don't sleep."

I felt him shrug. "I've never needed much sleep."

But the old memories still found him. I pressed a kiss

to the tendon in his neck. "You said you had no regrets about your work in the military."

"I don't." He sighed. "But the things I saw... There are some things no man should ever see."

I rested my hands on his shoulders. He'd taken care of me tonight. Now, I wanted to take care of him. "Talk to me."

One of his hands cupped my jaw firmly and tilted it up. In the dim light, I saw the glimmer of his dark gaze.

"I'll never talk about it. Never give those things to you. The things I saw, did... I did them so you'd never have to know anything about them."

My heart kicked. He was a damn hero. Doing the hard things to save others from suffering it.

"Okay." My mouth hovered over his. "So, let's chase those memories away. Make better ones."

His hands slid down and clenched on my ass. "Allie..." He released a long breath. "You've had a rough night. It was intense, scary."

"I'm not scared now. If anything, tonight put things into clear focus." I touched my lips to his. "You always do the right thing and follow the rules. You protect and take care of everyone else. Now, it's just the two of us. Taking care of each other."

He made a low, masculine sound, then he was kissing me.

His tongue slid into my mouth, his lips molding mine. Sensation exploded through me.

I'd been holding onto everything so tightly for months. Since Sean and Sylvie had died, I'd been working hard trying to hold things together, trying to do right by Ollie.

This, right now...

This was all for me.

I whimpered, rocking on his body. I felt his hard cock beneath me.

Caden growled, and jerked me down, grinding me against his cock. "It's taking everything I've got not to throw you down and get inside you as fast as possible."

My belly clenched and I felt those words between my thighs. "So do it."

"No." He kissed me, then bit my bottom lip. "I'm not rushing this. It feels like I've wanted you forever." His fingers dug into my ass. "Get that towel off."

I licked my lips and nodded. I pulled the towel free and dropped it to the floor.

His gaze moved to my breasts and he released a low groan.

"They're not very big," I said.

"They're perfect." He cupped them, his thumbs flicking my nipples. "High, firm, and gorgeous. They suit you."

On a moan, I arched into him.

"Look at these nipples." Leaning forward, he closed his mouth over one hard nipple and sucked.

I cried out. Soon, I was writhing on his lap. His fingers clenched on my buttock and desire pumped through me.

"So pretty, Allie. Sometimes I watch you at work, on the cameras. I can't take my eyes off you."

I slid my hands into his dark hair and clenched, my

belly squirming. I liked knowing that. I let one hand move down to his chest, kneading through the thin fabric of his shirt.

He groaned and his mouth moved to my other breast. "Once I'm inside you, I'm staying there. Deep. Nothing will drive me away."

I moaned, undulating on him. His big hand slapped my ass, and I let out another moan. I wanted his chest bare. I wanted skin. I tugged at his shirt, then slid my hands under it. He yanked it over his head. He had a smattering of dark chest hair, bronze skin, and all those glorious muscles. I dug my nails in and scratched a little.

He made a hungry sound.

His gaze was hooded, his lips parted. I saw it all etched on his face. Desire. Need. Want.

For me.

"Tell me what you want?" I panted.

"Everything, Allie. I want everything."

I jerked against him, his swollen cock sliding across sensitive tissues. "And I want to give it to you." A smile curled my lips. "This time, I will follow your orders."

Delicious tension swirled between us.

"Unzip my pants, Allie."

God. I was dripping and shaking with need. I fumbled between us and opened his jeans. He watched as I worked the zipper down.

"Fuck, Allie." His chest heaved.

I shoved his black boxer briefs down and his sizable cock sprang free. I circled his thick girth. He was hot and pulsing. *Oh, yes.* I stroked him, and his body jerked beneath me. I ran my thumb over the moisture that beaded on the tip.

"*More.*" His voice was guttural. "Harder."

I stroked him again, panting.

"You keep looking at my cock like that, I won't make it much longer."

Desire felt like a blowtorch inside me. Then his fingers were between my legs. When he stroked my pussy, I cried out his name.

"You're nice and wet for me."

I ground against his fingers and met his gaze. "I feel like I've been wet for days. Any time I look at you."

Something savage flared on his face. He slid a hand into the pocket of his jeans and pulled a condom. I watched, chest rising and falling, as he rolled it on. Nerves and need fluttered inside me and I rocked on his thighs.

"So impatient for my cock."

"I am."

He yanked me closer, and my hands dug into his shoulders. One of his hands was on my hip, the other reaching between us, guiding his cock between my legs.

I lowered my hips, letting him slide inside me. Our gazes locked, his hand rising to curl loosely around my throat.

Sinking lower, I moaned and arched my back. I felt so full. "God. *God.*"

"Fucking hell," he gritted out. "You were made for me."

"No," I whispered. "Your cock was made for me."

His hands came to my hips, pulling me down. I cried out, full of him. Full of Caden.

"Allie... *Fuck*. This feels different, better than anything I remember."

Then he thrust up.

"*Caden*."

"Move, Allie. Ride me."

I started to move. Up, down. "You feel *so* good."

"You feel tight and sleek. Perfect." His arms wrapped around me, locking us together.

I moved faster, each slide of his cock driving me out of my mind. I bounced on him, my ass hitting his hard thighs.

"You like my cock, Allie?"

"Yes."

Then his hand moved between my thighs, found my clit. He thumbed it, teased it.

My whimpers filled my ears. "God, Caden. I'm... It's..."

I rocked harder, taking him deep.

He pinched my clit and everything flew apart. Pleasure hit—hot, relentless. My movements turned jerky, my body shaking as the climax tore through me.

Caden bucked his hips up. "Goddammit, Allie...*baby*. You're clenching so hard, pulling it out of me."

I tugged on his hair, listening to the growly noises he made. "Don't stop."

Then he reared up.

My back hit the couch and Caden was on top of me. I held onto his sweat-slicked skin, watching the flex of his muscles as he slammed into me over and over.

"Come again," he said on a low growl.

I didn't think that was possible, but after two more thrusts of that thick cock, I let go.

There was no worry. No fear. No stress. Just Caden.

I cried out—part cry, part sob. Another smaller orgasm hit, pleasure rushing over me. Through it, my gaze stayed locked on his face.

He was so damn beautiful.

His thrusts turned wilder, then he stiffened. He groaned through his own release, pleasure suffusing his rugged features.

Then he dropped down, his face pressed to my neck.

We were both panting.

"Broody..." My voice was scratchy. "We nearly killed each other."

He gave a low chuckle. God, I loved that sound.

"It was worth it," he said.

I wrapped my arms around him. "It sure was."

CHAPTER 22
CADEN

I held Allie tight. I wasn't sure I ever wanted to let go.

She yawned and I could tell she was tired. She needed some sleep.

She nuzzled against my shoulder. "I know it's the middle of the night, but I'm *starving*. I need a snack."

I rose, then grabbed the blanket thrown over the back of the couch. I tucked it around her naked body, then hitched my jeans up.

"Let me make a quick trip to the bathroom, then I'll feed you."

"Mmm," she said sleepily. "I like having you around, Broody."

My chest filled with warmth. After dealing with the condom and washing my hands, I strode into the kitchen. "What have you got to eat?"

"Not much. But I know there's a bag of corn chips in there and there's my Dandelion chocolate." She smiled. "Courtesy of a scowly hot guy."

I had no idea how she stayed so slim eating like that. I opened the cupboards and found the snacks. When I came back to the couch, she was wearing my discarded shirt. *My shirt.*

Damn. I felt a punch of heat to the gut. I liked seeing her in something of mine.

When I settled beside her, she snatched the chips away. Soon she was munching away on them.

"It didn't end up being such a bad day, after all," she said.

"Because it ended with orgasms and corn chips?"

She laughed. "No, although those are good things. It ended up with you here. With me."

I cupped her jaw. "Yes, it did."

She reached out and grabbed the chocolate. She broke off a piece and popped it in her mouth. Her quiet moan had my gut clenching. "Want some?"

I shook my head. Then she snuggled into me. I slid my arm around her. I had to admit, there was something to be said for cuddling. I pressed my lips to her temple.

That's when I noticed the framed photo sitting on the shelf. It was of Allie and a man who had to be her brother. They looked so much like.

She followed my gaze. "That's Sean."

"You can tell you're siblings."

"Yeah. Ollie looks just like Sean did at the same age. God, I miss him."

"The missing never goes away."

She stroked a hand over my chest. "Tell me. Tell me who you lost. Not the gory details or the classified details, just... I'm here. I want to listen."

I was silent for a while. I wanted to open up, but it was so damn hard. "His name was Wells. Maxwell, but he never liked Max for short."

"Wells is a great name."

"He was a damn fine soldier. Brave, but so open and friendly." I shook my head. "Even before the military, I wasn't the loudest or friendliest person. Wells decided we'd be friends and wouldn't be deterred." I paused, remembering. "He made me laugh." The pain was a solid ball in my chest. "Our whole team was tight."

"I guess you have to be when you depend on each other for your lives," she said quietly.

I pressed my hand to her thigh and gripped. "We were on a mission." A chill raced over me, and the memory sank sharp teeth deep.

Swallowing, I forged on. I wanted to prove I could... open up to her.

She stroked my arm, not saying anything, just listening.

"It was dangerous. We were well in enemy territory. Our commander had gotten hit and was bleeding badly. I knew he needed medical attention, or he'd die."

She pressed into me even harder. That steadied me.

"With our CO down, I was in charge. We ran. We covered so many miles of dense, suffocating jungle, and we carried him. We ran and ran, and I thought we were almost in the clear. The bullets came from nowhere." In my head, I heard the grunts, the screams, and smelled the blood. "We fought back. Wells was yelling at me, covering my ass. He took a bullet to the head. He died instantly, right in front of me."

Allie let out a small gasp.

"There one second, gone the next. Drew took two rounds next. He was alive, but in agony. I caught some shrapnel. We had to keep moving. I carried Wells' body. I couldn't leave him behind."

"You made it out."

"Yeah." I scrubbed a hand over my face. "Pat, our commander, lost his arm, but survived. Drew is paralyzed and, in a wheelchair, and Wells is buried at Arlington. I still remember his pregnant widow standing at the funeral, sobbing."

"Caden." Allie kissed the underside of my jaw. "You brought them home."

"I missed the signs of the rebel soldiers creeping up on us."

"You aren't superhuman. Everyone on your team knew the risks. And you're all heroes for fighting, anyway. Honor Wells' memory. His bravery. From the sounds of it, he wouldn't want you to feel guilty. He'd be pissed you aren't living your best life."

I pressed my face to her hair. "Why did I survive, and he didn't?"

"That's above our pay grade." She rose up on her knees. "I'm glad you're here. I'm glad you made it."

Her words ripped through me, loosening things inside.

She looked at me, her face open and honest. Then she got to her feet, looking cute and thoroughly sexy in my shirt. She held her hand out. "I want you in my bed, Broody."

My gut clenched. I felt so much. All of it for her. All of it for Allie.

I glanced at the photo of her and her brother. We both knew that life could change in an instant. The things you loved most could be ripped away at any time.

I needed her. She'd almost been taken from me tonight, and I could have lost her.

With a low noise, I pushed to my feet and scooped her off hers.

She gasped, holding me tight. "I have to confess, I like when you carry me."

"Good." I strode into her bedroom. It smelled like her. Intoxicating. I'd been so focused on her when I was in here last time, I hadn't paid much attention to the room.

My gaze fell on her dresser and my eyebrows rose.

Allie cleared her throat. "Um, I have little thing about collecting fairy statues."

"You don't say." There were dozens of them sitting on the dresser. All long, elegant creatures with wings. All of them in a dazzling array of iridescent colors.

Color filled her cheeks. "Sean bought me my first one when I was ten and I got hooked. He told me that in the old myths about fairies, they weren't all cute and sweet, that they were dangerous and powerful." She shrugged a shoulder. "I liked the idea of a powerful creature that could also be beautiful."

"They suit you."

The color in her cheeks deepened. Damn, I wanted my mouth on her skin.

"Don't tell anyone."

"I promise. It's our secret." Laying her down on the bed, I pushed the shirt up. "I think you're beautiful and powerful." I kissed her breasts, her collarbone.

She arched up. "Caden."

I let my lips travel down her flat belly, over her hip bones, lower...

"*No*." She grabbed my head. "I want..."

"Anything." I nipped her belly. I'd give her anything she wanted. "Just tell me." I nibbled the skin of her lower belly, smelling her arousal.

She sucked in a breath. "This time, I want you in my mouth."

Goddamn. Every muscle in my body was rigid. "You want to suck me off, baby?"

Her lips parted and she moved restlessly on the bed. "Yes." She held her hands out to me.

Quickly, I unfastened my jeans and shoved them down. Her gaze was all over me—and it was clear she liked what she saw.

"I have to confess. Your thighs have driven me crazy from the day I met you."

"My thighs?" I straddled her body, and her face filled with hectic color. She pressed her hands to my thighs, her fingers digging into the muscle.

"They're so strong and muscular." Her voice was husky.

I moved forward on my knees. Intense hunger clawed at me. She owned me. This woman owned every part of me.

"But I might have a new favorite body part," she whispered, her gaze on my erect cock.

Her lips brushed the swollen head, and I hissed at the touch.

She licked me. That delicate, pink tongue lapped at the weeping head and the sound I made didn't sound human.

"I'm yours, Allie."

Her hand curled around the base of my cock, her eyes wide and hungry. She wasn't shy, my Allie. Then she sucked my cock into her warm mouth.

I cursed. With a moan, she found a rhythm, stroking me, her cheeks hollowing as she sucked.

I fell forward, slapping my hands to the mattress. Growling, I thrust my hips forward. Allie took me deeper until I felt resistance. I pulled back and thrust again.

Damn, I wasn't going to last.

Mindlessly, I pulled free of the temptation of her warm mouth.

Moving back down her body, I pushed her thighs wide. I fell on her, need throbbing through me. A second later, I thrust inside her.

"*Caden.*" Her scream echoed off the walls.

"This is where I need to be." My thrusts were savage, but she took me, gripping me hard. Her hands dug into my biceps, her knees pressed into my sides. "You need it, too. My cock between your thighs."

"Yes, Caden. Don't stop."

All I could do was feel. All I could do was drown in her. She felt so good. So tight and wet.

A thought popped into my head. *Fuck.* On the next thrust, I stayed lodged deep inside her.

She moaned. "Keep moving."

"Hell, Allie. I forgot a condom."

When I tried to pull out, her legs clamped onto me hard. "It's okay, Caden."

"No. I have to protect you." I gritted my teeth. "Baby, stay still or I'll come."

"I have an IUD. Please, don't leave me."

"Allie—"

"I'm clean. Before you, I haven't had sex in a really long time."

"I'm clean, too. And it's been a long time for me, as well."

She kissed me, then bit my bottom lip. "So move."

I started thrusting. This time harder, faster. "Allie. *Mine*. All fucking mine."

"*Caden*." Her nails scored my back.

We weren't Allie and Caden. We weren't separate. We were one.

With a cry, she started coming and I was a goner.

Her name was a harsh groan as I came. It felt ripped out of me. I felt her pussy gripping me, milking me. I shuddered through the pleasure until I was totally drained.

When I collapsed, I remembered to roll so I didn't crush her. But I didn't let her go. Her legs were tangled with mine, my softening cock still inside her.

She let out a happy, gusty breath. "I haven't felt this good in...maybe ever."

Something in me spasmed. I really liked knowing I made her feel good. I pulled her closer, my face buried in her hair. We were sweaty and sticky, but I didn't care.

"I like having you in my bed, Broody."

"I like your bed." My throat tightened. "I like you better."

She sent me a lazy smile, then she yawned. "Good. Think I need some sleep now."

I kissed her temple. "Sleep." I'd watch over her.

"Don't leave me." Her voice was already slurred by sleep.

"I won't."

And a few minutes after she'd fallen asleep in my arms, surprisingly, I felt myself drift off.

CHAPTER 23
ALLIE

I woke up to a light throb in my cheek and blazing heat along my front.

Opening my eyes, I saw a glorious sight.

Caden lying beside me, in my bed, asleep.

Slumber didn't make him look relaxed. He was still rugged and tough, but there was maybe something a little softer about him.

I nuzzled into him. God, I loved him right there. How would it feel to wake up with him every day?

Swallowing, I shut that thought down. He wouldn't be mine forever. He was a man who liked moving around, and now knowing the things he'd done and seen, the people he'd lost, I knew that maybe he needed it.

Suddenly, his eyes opened. Instantly, he was awake and alert.

"Hey." His voice was like gravel.

"Morning."

He glanced at the windows and blinked. "I slept."

He'd slept soundly wrapped around me. I smiled.

His dark gaze snagged on my eye and his face darkened.

I winced. "How bad is it?"

"It's bruised." His thumb touched the corner of my eye. "It could've been worse."

"It wasn't." I let my hands explore his chest and felt his muscles flex. "I'm okay." Then I glanced at the clock on my nightstand. I sat bolt upright. "Crap, I need to get Ollie. I promised I'd collect him from Emily's and we'd have breakfast together before school and work." I scrambled out of bed. "I need to shower, dress, then hide the worst of this bruising."

I'd barely gone two steps when strong arms closed around me from behind. Caden rested his chin on my shoulder. Then I was distracted by a hard, naked body pressed against mine.

"Relax. You aren't working today."

"What?"

"Strict orders. You're to rest and recover."

"I'm fine—"

"And Tessa sent instructions to rest up, and be ready for the Spooktacular tonight." He smoothed my hair back. "She wanted to come and see you this morning, but I assured her that I was taking care of you."

My heart melted. "Caden..."

"I'll take you to get Ollie, then make breakfast for all of us, then we can drop him to school."

I tilted my head up. "You cook?"

"Not often, but I can."

I licked my lips. "You're staying with me today?"

"Yeah."

"Playing bodyguard?"

"Yes, I'm not leaving you alone today." He paused. "You also need to talk with the police. Tell them what happened."

I swallowed. "It was the ESG who did this, wasn't it?"

"Pretty damn sure, but we have no proof. You need to be careful. What those men did to you...it was a warning."

I looked into his face. "You're going to stop them."

"I am." He brushed his lips over mine. "But today, you're my priority. And your nephew. Now, shower, and I'll make coffee."

I kind of floated through my shower. It was nice knowing someone else was here, someone helping out.

I quickly dried off and dressed in my favorite jeans and red sweater. Then I did the best I could with some makeup. I poked my tongue out at myself. My eye was still obviously bruised, but it didn't look quite as bad now. I really didn't want Ollie to worry.

When I walked out into the living room, Caden was leaning against the island, sipping a mug of coffee.

"What should I tell Ollie about this bruise?" Somehow, Caden made my compact kitchen look tiny.

"Tell him the truth."

"Caden, he's five."

He cupped my shoulder. "You can't shield him from everything. I'm not saying give him all the details, especially about these assholes, but tell him a bad guy hit you, but you're fine."

She sighed. "I want to shield him."

"I know, but it's better to teach him resilience."

"He's already had to learn that lesson."

Caden handed me a mug of coffee, which I took with a grateful smile.

He ran a hand over my hair. "Drink that, then we'll get Ollie." Then he pulled something out of his pocket. "For you."

I stared at the brand-new iPhone.

"Your data and photos from your old phone have been copied over."

A lump lodged in my throat. This man. I took the phone. "Caden...you're spoiling me."

"Just say thank you, Allie."

I went up on my toes and kissed his cheek. "Thank you."

Then he grabbed my hand and frowned at the grazes on my palm. "These could get infected. You have a first aid kit?"

"Under the sink. There's not much in it. I have a huge collection of Band-Aids. I learned pretty quickly that Band-Aids fix a lot of things when you're five."

He came back with the kit. I sat on the stool while he bent over my hand, cleaning my grazes with antiseptic wipes.

"You want a Band-Aid?" he asked.

My lips twitched, all kinds of flutters in my stomach. "No. A kiss will do."

Then badass Caden Castro leaned down and kissed my grazed palm.

Everything inside me quivered. *Oh, God.*

I was falling in love with Caden.

My chest tightened. All kinds of thoughts flew at me, the biggest one being that he's not going to hang around forever.

Just one day at a time, Allie.

He took my uninjured hand in his, his fingers entwining with mine. "Let's go get your nephew."

~

"Anything I want?" Ollie asked from the backseat.

"Anything," Caden assured him. He expertly drove the SUV back toward my condo.

"Can you make French toast?" Ollie asked.

"Pretty sure we can work it out, buddy."

I smiled. They were so cute together. Ollie had been thrilled to see Caden and learn that he was having breakfast with us.

We pulled up at my condo. I climbed out, then opened the back door. Ollie was already scrambling out of his booster seat.

"I'm glad you had fun with Caleb, Haley, and Emily."

He nodded, then paused and reached up. I bent down and he gently touched my bruised eye.

"It doesn't hurt, Ol-ster."

"I don't like the bad guy who did this." His gray gaze shifted to Caden. "You'll catch him?"

"Yeah, I will."

God, they were both killing me.

Ollie's fingers brushed mine, and my chest hitched. For a second, I thought he was going to take my hand. Instead, he patted it, then headed toward our building.

Before I knew it, we were all in my kitchen, which quickly turned into a sugar-dusted mess. But I was grinning. I was happy.

Ollie was giggling as he helped Caden. Caden was smiling. Not a full-blown smile, but it was definitely a smile.

God. Careful, Allie. Don't like this too much. Don't get used to it.

I knew he'd leave eventually. I was prepared.

But for now, I was going to enjoy it.

Soon, we were seated around the island, eating syrup-soaked French toast. Ollie was eating enthusiastically.

"So, the Halloween Spooktacular is tonight at the hotel," I said. "You have to decide on a costume, Ollie."

He finished chewing and licked his lips. "I decided. I want to be Peter Pan."

It was a story I often read to him. "Good choice."

"I picked it because you like fairies, Allie." He smiled. "You can be Tinkerbell."

Oh. Tinkerbell was tiny and blonde, I was tall and brunette. But staring at his little face, all I could do was nod. "Sure thing. That'll be fun."

Large gray eyes settled on Caden. "Are you going to the Spooktacular, Caden?"

"I am, but I'll be working."

"Will you wear a costume?"

I leaned back in my chair. "He will. It's the rule. All the hotel workers will be in costume."

Caden's gaze narrowed on me, and I gave him an amused smile.

Ollie bounced in his chair. "You could match with us. You could be Captain Hook!"

Biting back my laugh was hard. A small sound escaped me. "I think he'd make an excellent pirate captain, Ol-ster."

Caden's look promised retribution. "I'll talk with Tessa. She ordered a bunch of costumes."

With the happiness bubbling inside me, my abduction and the ESG were the furthest things from my mind.

Clearing this throat, Caden started stacking plates. "What time does school start?"

I glanced at the clock and let out a squeak. I leaped up. "Ollie, we need to move."

Ollie got a stubborn look on his face. "I don't want to go to school. I want to stay with you and Caden."

"You have to go to school, little man."

"No!"

"Ollie—"

"You're staying home." He crossed his little arms. "I want to stay as well."

It was very rare for him to throw a tantrum. Actually, a part of me was happy to see it. His therapist had said once he felt safe, he'd test boundaries like any well-adjusted child.

I crouched in front of him. "School's important, Ollie. You need to learn, play, spend time with your friends. And I'm in charge, so you need to listen when I ask you to do something."

His militant look wavered.

"You shouldn't speak like that to your aunt, buddy," Caden said quietly.

Ollie's bottom lip wobbled. He sighed. "Sorry, Allie."

I ruffled his hair. "It's okay. Let's get ready, okay?"

He nodded, then cast a glance sideways. "Are you dropping me at school, Caden?"

"You want that?"

The little boy nodded.

"Then let's get you to school."

CHAPTER 24

CADEN

"I want you monitoring the perimeter of the party. Keep an eye out for any lost kids, anyone who needs help, or any trouble."

My security team all nodded. Everyone was wearing earpieces and dressed in costumes.

With a sigh, I lifted my pirate hat and sat it on my head. My trousers were black leather, tucked into knee-high boots, and my burgundy jacket reached my knees and was studded with brass buttons. A bronze hook was clipped over my left hand. I'd drawn the line at the long, curly wig.

Gretchen's lips twitched.

"Don't start," I warned.

"Aye, aye, Captain."

I glared at her. She was dressed as Medusa. She was wearing black pants, fitted black shirt, a long green wig, and a headdress of gold snakes. The makeup on her face was in a snake-skin pattern. She also wore a red sash to indicate that she was hotel staff. Hugh was dressed as a Viking, complete with helmet topped with horns. The rest of the team ranged from superheroes to vampires.

"The Spooktacular has officially began." Paul's voice came clearly through my earpiece. He was up in the conference room, manning the monitors and communications. He was pretty gleeful about not having to wear a costume.

"Acknowledged," I replied.

"And boss, I'm told that Peter Pan and Tinkerbell are waiting for you outside."

This time, I heard Gretchen chuckle. I fought my own smile. Ollie and Allie had come with Tessa and Ro. Ro had promised to keep an eye on them.

"You all know what you're doing and where your posts are. Any trouble, just radio."

We strode out of the hotel. Outside, Tessa had turned the place into a Halloween wonderland.

A low fence ringed the Spooktacular area. Everywhere I looked, I saw hay bales topped with glowing, carved pumpkins and cobwebs. Strings of fairy lights and pumpkin lanterns crisscrossed overhead.

There were kids everywhere. I watched two ghosts and a tiny Mandalorian rush past us, a young father in hot pursuit.

Trick-or-treat stations had been set up, with staff giving away a mountain of candy. There were food vans clustered around, a cobweb-draped bouncy castle, a petting zoo, and even a spooky maze made of hay bales. I shook my head. Tessa was a damned miracle worker.

I turned and spotted Peter Pan waving at me. Ollie

wore a green tunic top over brown trousers and boots, and a green pointed hat on his head.

Next, I saw Tessa dressed as Wonder Woman. I hoped she didn't freeze with how much skin was on display. I was sure that Captain America, standing beside her, would help keep her warm.

I didn't hold my smile back. Ro looked like he was enjoying himself.

Just a few short months ago, there was no way billionaire hotelier Ambrose Langston would have dressed up as Captain America.

Then my gaze fell on Tinkerbell.

Fuck. She was a punch to the gut. I felt every cell in my body respond.

Allie wore a leaf-green dress that was tiny. And I mean tiny. Her long, long legs were on full display, and I noted the sheen of stockings and cute little green ballet slippers on her feet. She hadn't bothered with a wig, either. The dress hugged every inch of her, and to finish off the outfit, she wore a set of sparkly, iridescent wings on her back.

I strode over to them.

"Caden." Ollie hugged me. "I mean Captain Hook. *Arrgh.*"

I lifted my hooked hand and the kid grinned. I felt like I'd won a prize.

But when I looked at a smiling Allie, I felt like I'd won the world. There was heat in her gaze, along with happiness.

She'd hidden her bruise well under her makeup—I could barely see it.

"Ollie, stay with Tessa and Ro... I mean Wonder Woman and Captain America." Allie grabbed my hand. "I need a moment with Captain Hook."

She dragged me off back toward the hotel. We stepped through the door, and she marched me down an empty corridor.

"Allie—"

"Shh." She pushed me against the wall, then pressed her body flush against mine. "How can you make Captain Hook look so sexy?"

Then she went up on her toes and pressed her mouth to mine.

The taste of her flooded my senses. I wrapped my non-hook arm around her and cupped her ass.

"You'd better have panties on under this tiny dress," I growled.

She grinned at me. "I do. I couldn't risk flashing some poor kid."

I let my hand wander down and under the hem. My fingers brushed a silky pair of panties. I nipped her ear. "I'm going to enjoy taking these off you later."

I loved the sound of her needy gasp.

"I'll also enjoy fucking you...while you're only wearing those fairy wings."

She rewarded me with another gasp, her hands clenching on my burgundy jacket.

"Now my panties are wet," she complained.

I kissed her lips again. "Come on, Tinkerbell."

We rejoined the Halloween party. Ollie was bouncing on his feet. "Come on, Allie. I *need* candy."

She shook her head, but she was smiling.

We walked through the crowd. All around, people were having fun. The kids most of all.

"Ooh, look." Ollie pointed to a stand. Stuffed toys—all of the spooky variety—hung on the wall. I saw targets set up in front of small plastic rifles.

"Everyone who hits a bull's-eye gets a prize," the young attendant in a ghoulish mask called out.

"Give it a go, Ollie," Allie said as she paid the attendant.

The kid tried. He lined up, gripping the plastic gun hard. Every shot went wide, and disappointment was stamped all over his tiny face.

"Can I have a try?" I asked.

He handed the gun over. I checked it out, testing its weight, then aimed and pulled the trigger.

It was not surprising that this piece of plastic crap was not accurate. The shot went to the left and missed the target. I re-adjusted and fired again.

Bam.

The shot hit the target dead on and lights lit up.

Ollie let out a whoop.

"Which toy do you want, buddy?" I asked.

"That one!" He pointed to a small stuffed Frankenstein's monster. It was green with little bolts on its neck. When the attendant handed it over, Ollie clutched it like it was made of gold.

Allie was watching me. Her lips moved and she mouthed *thank you*.

"Oh, I see Sierra, Jazz, and Piper." Tessa slipped an arm through Allie's. "I'm stealing Allie for a girls' only moment."

Allie pulled a face. "I'm fine, Tessa. I told you that I'm perfectly all right."

"I have some experience getting—" she glanced at Ollie "—tangled up with bad guys. You need to debrief with your girlfriends."

"Go," I told her. "I'll hang with Ollie."

"Are you sure?"

I nodded. "Go."

Ro glanced around. "I'd better do a lap and schmooze."

"Sucks to be the boss sometimes."

"I don't mind a little bit of schmoozing. I'll catch you later."

"Right, what next, Ollie?"

He lifted a little pumpkin-shaped bucket. "Candy."

We hit a few of the trick-or-treat stations, and I bought him a hot chocolate overloaded with marshmallows. I checked in with my team a few times. Everything was running smoothly.

Let's hope it stayed that way.

"Well, that's a hell of a uniform," a deep voice said.

I spun.

A muscular man stood nearby. He was roughly ten years older than me, with broader shoulders, but a few inches shorter in height. He kept his hair shaved short, and I saw the touches of silver in it and his stubble. He had piercing blue eyes and a hard jaw.

I grinned. "Gunnar."

"Hi, Castro. Or should I say Captain?" He glanced at my costume.

I stepped forward and hugged him, and we slapped each other's backs. "It's good to see you."

"You too, Caden." Gunnar glanced around. "I didn't expect to find this, or you playing dress-up."

"It's Halloween." I pressed a hand to Ollie's shoulder. "And Peter Pan asked me to play Captain Hook, so I couldn't say no."

"Hi, Peter. I'm Caden's friend Gunnar." He held out a hand to the boy.

Ollie shook it. "Hi, Mr. Gunnar. My real name's Ollie." The kid smiled. "Caden likes my aunt Allie."

Gunnar lifted an eyebrow. "Does he?"

"Yep. Caden, can I go on the bouncy castle?"

I glanced over at the large inflatable. There was already a horde of kids jumping on it. "Sure, buddy." I handed him some dollar bills. "Come straight back to me afterward."

With a whoop, he raced off.

"Caden Castro babysitting and liking a woman. Times really do change."

I glanced at my friend. "Allie works at the hotel and Ollie is her nephew. His parents died and she took custody of him."

"Shit, that's rough."

"Luckily, his aunt loves him. She's amazing." I felt a small knot in my chest. "Hell, I took one look at her, and it just...happened. I couldn't stay away from her, even when I told myself I should."

"Good. You deserve a good woman."

I dragged in a deep breath. "Not sure I'm good enough for her."

Gunnar made a sound. "Bullshit. You're just afraid."

My brows drew together.

"You're a good man, Castro. We've all been through shit, us more than most. You've waded through some of the worst of it, and you lost people, lost Wells. Some things, you need to let go."

I knew it wasn't that easy.

Gunnar wasn't finished. "Other things, the good things, you've got to grab onto them and never let go. We never know how long we've got. Trust me, if I found the right woman, nothing would stop me claiming her."

Now I felt a knot my throat, my mind churning.

Ollie came back, face flushed and his hat askew.

I cleared my throat. "What's next, buddy?"

His face screwed up in concentration. "I'm not sure."

"Ollie!"

"Hey, Ollie."

Two kids—a boy and a girl—rushed over to Ollie. The girl was wearing a yellow outfit with ears and a tail that looked like a lightning bolt. The boy was in an orange outfit that I thought was maybe a dragon.

"Caleb. Haley." Ollie beamed at them. "You're Pikachu and Charizard. Cool!"

I had no clue who or what those were. I glanced at Gunnar, and he shrugged a shoulder.

Then I saw Tessa's aunt Emily. She was out of breath, and dressed as a witch in a black dress with a deep V neckline, hat, and bright red lips. "You two, no running away from me in this crowd." She smiled. "Hi, Ollie. Hi, Caden."

"Emily." I turned to introduce Gunnar, then paused.

He was staring at Emily like he'd just been hit by a bomb blast.

Emily looked up at him and the smile on her face froze. She stared at him, her lips parting, and he stared back.

What the hell?

"Emily, this is an old military buddy of mine, Gunnar O'Neill. Gunnar, this is Emily Hawkins. She's the aunt of Tessa Ashford, the Langston Windward's hotel manager."

"A pleasure." Emily held out one elegant hand.

"Hello." Gunnar's large hand engulfed hers.

They held on for a moment too long.

Blushing, Emily ran her hands down her long skirt. "Right, my two are starving, so I'd better get them fed. Leo's around here somewhere."

"Your husband?" Gunnar's voice was gritty.

"No, my teenager." She paused. "I'm a widow. I have one at college as well. It was nice to meet you, Gunnar. I'd better find some food for these kids before they hit hangry mode."

Gunnar was still staring at her. "Actually, I just arrived and I'm hungry."

She blinked. "Oh, you're welcome to join us."

He nodded. "That would be great."

I bit back a smile. "I'll catch you later. Take a good look around." I looked back down at my sidekick. "Just the two of us, buddy. What's next on our agenda?"

Ollie wrinkled his nose. "Maybe the petting zoo? Or the spooky maze?"

We walked through the crowd and out of habit I

scanned around. No one seemed to be getting too rowdy and everyone was having fun.

Then the crowd parted, and I saw a tall man wearing a black leather jacket. Light glinted off his blond hair.

Moreland.

He smiled at me.

The crowd swallowed him up and I couldn't see him anymore. I took a step forward.

"Caden?"

Ollie's voice made me stop.

"What's wrong?" he asked.

I shook my head. "Nothing. Let's—"

Screams broke out.

I spun.

"Caden." Paul's voice in my earpiece. "We have a problem near the hot dog stand. A teenage girl has collapsed."

"Heading there now." I pressed a hand to Ollie's shoulder. "Stay close to me."

He nodded. We pushed through the crowd toward where a group of panicked people were gathering.

"Move back, please," I ordered.

I spotted a teenaged girl on the ground, dressed as a zombie, with fake blood splattered on her dress. Hell, she couldn't be more than sixteen. She was frothing at the mouth and seizing.

"Ollie, stay back, okay?"

Wide-eyed, the boy nodded. "Okay, Caden. You help her."

I dropped to my knees beside the girl, and it only

took me a second to realize that she'd overdosed on something. *Fuck.*

I touched my ear. "Paul, looks like a drug overdose. I need the Narcan from the security kit. And get the paramedics over here. I also need more security for crowd control."

"On it, Caden."

I checked the girl's vital signs. She wasn't breathing and she had no pulse.

Hell. She was so young.

"No, you don't." I started chest compressions. "You're not dying tonight."

CHAPTER 25
ALLIE

"You're sure that you're all right?" Sienna, dressed as Wednesday Addams complete with thigh-high socks and a black, braided wig, squeezed my arm.

"I'm fine." I smiled at her. "Caden took care of me."

Tessa re-adjusted her Wonder Woman headband. "I knew you two would work it out."

"Well, we had hot, delicious sex, but we haven't really talked. Well, we talked a little bit. He shared a bit about his time in the military."

Jazz clasped her hands together. She was rocking the Cowboy Barbie look in a lipstick-pink pantsuit and white cowboy hat. "He opened up to you. And we've all seen the way he watches you."

Sierra nodded. "Like he wants to wrap you up in protective bubble wrap and keep you all to himself."

"With this sort of sexy, slightly obsessive glint in his eye," Tessa added.

"I like it." No, I loved it.

But how I felt about Caden was too new to share. It was something I needed to work out with Caden first.

Still smiling, I turned.

And saw Blake.

My heart hitched. He was across the crowded area, standing by a food truck.

He winked at me.

The asshole. My hands clenched. I lost sight of him.

"Allie?" Tessa said.

"I just saw Blake. The ESG ringleader."

Tessa stiffened. "Where?"

I scanned the crowd. "I can't see him now. The prick winked at me."

Sierra's gaze sparked.

"We need to tell Caden," Jazz said.

I nodded. I wanted Caden. "Let's go and—"

A commotion broke out on the other side of the Spectacular.

"What's going on?" Tessa said.

We pushed our way through the crowd. Then it parted, and I saw Caden on the ground. He was giving a girl chest compressions.

I gasped. *Oh God.*

Tessa swung into action. "I see the paramedics coming." She raised her voice. "Clear the way. Move out of the way, please."

Hugh shouldered into view. "Everyone move back." Unsurprisingly, people started leaping out of the way of the giant Viking.

Enzo was with him, wearing a hooded, black Grim Reaper robe. "Narcan." He tossed something at Caden.

Caden leaned over the young girl and administered the medication, spraying it into the girl's nose.

A second later, the girl's eyes opened and she gasped in air.

Caden sat back on his knees and blew out a breath.

Then the girl started sobbing. The paramedics arrived, dropping down beside her, and setting their bags on the ground.

It was so scary. Then I looked around for Ollie.

There was no sign of him.

I spun, looking everywhere. I saw other kids in costumes, some clinging to parents and grandparents.

No Peter Pan.

"Ollie! Ollie!"

I hurried over to Caden who was talking with Hugh and Enzo.

"Caden, where's Ollie?"

His face hardened. "He was just here. I told him to stay back." He turned and pointed. Then his mouth flattened.

There was no Ollie.

"Ollie!" Caden called.

Fear and panic twisted inside me. I hadn't felt like this since the day I'd gotten the phone call that my brother and sister-in-law had been murdered. "You lost him."

I was too panicked to see the way he stiffened.

"You lost him," I yelled, fear choking me. "We have to find him." My voice cracked.

I couldn't lose Ollie.

"We'll find him." Caden touched his ear. "Lock down

the perimeter. We have a young child missing. Male, five years old, Peter Pan costume. His name is Oliver Ford."

"What's going on?" A tall muscular man I'd never seen before stepped up beside Caden. He wasn't wearing a costume, had silvery-brown shaved hair, and massive, muscular shoulders. Emily was with him, worry on her face.

"Ollie is missing," I said, my voice shaking.

"Oh no," Emily said. "He can't have gone far."

"Gunnar, you're with me," Caden barked. "Hugh and Enzo, check near the food trucks."

Enzo gave a clipped nod. "Sure thing, Caden."

The men splitting into pairs, stalking into the crowd.

My throat closed. God, I shouldn't have left him. He was mine. It was my job to take care of him.

"Hey, calm down." Tessa pressed a hand to my back. "Slow your breathing."

I pulled in two ragged breaths.

"He'll be fine." Her voice was calm and reassuring. "Caden has security at all the exits. Ollie can't leave."

"Okay." I pulled in another breath. "Okay."

"Caden will find him."

I nodded. I knew Caden wouldn't stop until he did. "God, what if he's hurt, or some sicko took him—"

"Deep breaths," Tessa ordered.

Suddenly, I saw Caden striding toward me.

He was carrying Ollie on his hip.

"*Thank God.*" I raced forward and snatched Ollie into my arms. "Where did you go?" I hugged him tightly.

"Allie, you're squishing me."

"I was so worried." I set him down and cupped his cheeks. "I couldn't find you."

"Caden was helping the sick woman." Ollie looked at his feet. "It was scary. Then your friend came and said you wanted me to go with him."

I stilled. "My friend?"

"In the black jacket. He was nice. He took me to see the animals at the petting zoo."

The air shuddered out of me. "Blake."

Caden's face turned into a terrible mask.

Ollie read the tension and his face fell. "He's not your friend?"

"No, Ol-ster, he's not."

"I'm sorry." He started crying.

"It's okay, baby." I pulled him back against me.

"I'll find him." Caden shoved a keycard at Tessa. "Take them up to my suite."

Then he was gone.

I shivered, pulling Ollie close.

"Come on, you two," Tessa said. "Let's get you inside and find some hot chocolate."

I let her lead us inside, still feeling numb.

Blake had taken Ollie. He was messing with me. He'd touched my kid.

I couldn't think about him right now. For now, my focus needed to be on Ollie.

CHAPTER 26
CADEN

I let myself into my suite.

My shoulders were tense. I hadn't found Moreland.

The ESG were in their rooms, and I'd paid them a visit. Blake Moreland hadn't been there. They'd claimed they hadn't seen him. That he was in town, and nowhere near the Halloween Spooktacular.

The asshole was clearly enjoying his sick game. He'd focused on Allie and was having fun tormenting her.

Fuck, if he'd hurt Ollie...

This was my fault.

I was supposed to take care of Ollie and I'd failed him. I'd failed Allie.

I saw Tessa and Ro sitting on the couch. They rose.

"Hey," Tessa said.

"No sign of Blake Moreland." I glanced at the closed bedroom door. "How are they?"

"Fine. A hot shower and fresh clothes did the trick.

Thankfully, Allie had some clothes in her locker, and Ro found some things for Ollie. They're sleeping."

"Good." I slid my jacket off. I'd ditched the ridiculous hat ages ago. "Thanks for looking after them. You two should get some sleep. I'll watch over them now."

"She doesn't blame you," Tessa said suddenly.

I felt my muscles tensing up. I didn't respond.

"She was panicked, Caden, and not thinking straight. Her entire focus was on Ollie."

"I know."

"You saved a girl's life," Ro added.

"It was a ploy so I'd take my eyes off Ollie. It worked. It was just dumb luck that Moreland didn't hurt him."

It could've been worse. For a second, I thought of Wells and my team, and the day we'd run out of luck.

"Caden, Ollie is fine. Allie is fine." Ro's voice rang with authority. "Tomorrow, we'll find Blake Moreland and end this sick game he's playing."

I gave him a clipped nod.

Tessa eyed my face and sighed. "Get some rest. Everything will feel better in the morning."

There'd be no sleep for me. I already knew that.

After they left, I walked to the bedroom and cracked open the door. Allie was curled around Ollie in the middle of my bed. They were both asleep.

They were a unit. A team.

They didn't need me. I didn't know how to fit into their life.

At the first opportunity, I'd let them down.

It seemed I was good at failing the people who mattered most, who depended on me.

This is just a reminder.

I quietly closed the door.

Back in the living room, I poured myself a glass of bourbon and sat on the couch.

Then I stared out the windows at the darkness of the mountain.

CHAPTER 27
ALLIE

Something nudged my side. Then a small hand whacked me in the face.

I cracked open my eyes. I'd had Ollie in my bed enough times to recognize his octopus tendencies.

He was still fast asleep despite the sunlight leaking into the room. Warmth flooded my heart. He looked relaxed and he was safe.

Then I blinked. This wasn't my bedroom.

I recognized the Langston Windward suite.

Caden's suite.

Last night was a blur. All I remembered was the volatile, paralyzing mix of panic, worry, and fear. Then the sweet relief as soon as I'd had Ollie back.

God, Blake had lured Ollie away.

I ground my teeth together. He was a first-grade asshole to mix a kid up in his games.

Anger stirred and I welcomed the hot burn.

He had to be stopped. The entitled prick thought he could get away with anything.

I'd help Caden bring him down.

Caden.

I sat up. I'd yelled at him. He'd found Ollie, and I'd been so absorbed in my kid that I hadn't even spoken with him afterward. Hadn't thanked him.

Oh God.

I knew that deep down he felt like he'd failed Wells and the others on his team. He'd take the blame for this, and it wasn't his fault.

Carefully sliding out of the bed, I noted my leggings and wrinkled, long-sleeved shirt. I vaguely remembered having a shower and pulling on clothes Tessa had gotten from my locker. I smoothed out my tangled hair and found a new toothbrush in the bathroom.

When I came back out, Ollie was still asleep.

I headed into the living area, but there was no sign of Caden.

Damn. I needed to talk with him. I needed to explain where my head had been last night, and thank him for finding Ollie.

God, I hoped the girl who'd OD'd was okay.

The front door opened, and I spun.

Caden appeared, wearing workout gear. *Yum.* I was so used to seeing him in suits, but looking at him in a tight, black compression shirt and black shorts made my mouth water.

"Hi."

He quietly closed the door. "Good morning. How's Ollie?"

My mouth went dry. His tone was cool and his face was all closed down.

"He's still asleep, but he's fine." I dredged up a smile. "Thank God everything worked out okay. Is the girl who overdosed all right?"

Caden nodded. "I called the hospital this morning and she's going to be fine. She got lucky."

Silence fell.

"So you hit the gym this morning?" God, that was lame.

He lifted his chin. "With my buddy from the military, Gunnar."

"The man who was with you last night."

"That's him."

"With everything going on, I didn't get a chance to meet him." This all felt wrong. We were talking like two strangers having a polite conversation about the weather. He wasn't coming to me, touching me. I wanted to close the distance, but I got the sense he wouldn't welcome that. Instead, he was cold, and I felt like there was a wall between us.

"You'll get the chance to meet him," Caden said. "Gunnar is going to be the new head of security for the Langston Windward."

My heart stopped. "You...found someone for the job."

"Yes. Now I can get back to my work."

And leave.

I felt nausea crawl up my throat. "Caden, I wanted to thank you for finding Ollie last night."

"He was missing because of me. I lost him.

"No," I gasped out.

"I let Moreland take him. You knew last night that it was my fault. I didn't protect him."

"God, no, Caden." I took a step forward and reached my hand out.

He inched back.

It was the smallest move, but it cut me deep. I let my hand drop and felt the yawning gulf between us. "It wasn't your fault. You were busy saving that girl's life—"

"It was a distraction that Moreland planned." Caden straightened. "This just...put things into perspective. You and Ollie don't need anyone. You're a unit, a family. That isn't for me."

I felt small bits of my heart crumbling to pieces. I was losing him. He was standing right in front of me and I was losing him.

"We do need you. We want you. *I* want you."

He shook his head.

"Caden..." My voice was a broken whisper.

"This is for the best, Allie."

Anger poked through my pain. "Best for who? Me or you?"

His head jerked.

"You came home from the military, and it was tough and there were challenges, and then you left your mom and sisters."

A muscle ticked in his jaw. "It was better for them."

"No, I think it was better for you. Your job means that you don't have to get too close to anyone, you don't have to care. This way, you won't lose anyone, you avoid the pain."

His face hardened to pure stone.

"You move around, you don't plant roots, you don't let people in." I took a step forward. "Until me."

He stayed silent.

I shook my head. "You're running away, and that's not for my benefit." I stared at him, willing him to talk to me.

He stayed silent.

I looked away, trying not to lose it in front of him. I'd hold myself together. I was good at that. "As soon as Ollie wakes up, we'll get out of your way."

Spinning, I faced the windows and wrapped my arms around my middle, trying to hold all the broken pieces together.

I waited for him to say something, anything. I wanted him to say something.

A moment later, I heard the front door open and close, and knew I was alone.

My heart felt like it was going to fall out of my chest. A tear ran down my cheek, then another.

God. I hurt so much.

There was a knock on the door, then I heard it open.

"Hello?" Tessa's voice. "I saw Caden leaving, and he said to come in."

Swiping at my tears, I turned. "Hey."

"How are you and Ollie? I thought—" My friend stopped in her tracks, staring at me. "What happened?"

"What I should have known would happen. Caden pulled the plug on us."

"No." Tessa moved to me and threw her arms around my shoulders.

"He's shut down and pushed me out."

"He'll come to his senses, Allie. Things are just a little raw after what happened last night."

I felt cold, then hot. "I...need some air. Will you stay with Ollie?"

She nodded. "Sure."

I slipped into the only shoes I had, the green ballet slippers that matched my Tinkerbell dress. I remembered how excited I'd been for Caden to take that stupid dress off me, for me to make love to him with those silly wings on. The pain made my lips tremble.

If I was going outside, I needed better shoes than these. I had some running shoes in my locker.

"I won't be long." I pressed a hand to my aching chest. "I promised Caden we'd get out of his suite once Ollie was awake."

"That man..." She shook her head. "He's shaken up after last night. He's out of practice with feeling and dealing with his emotions. It's going to work out."

She hadn't seen him. Hadn't heard the resolution in his voice. I needed to get out of there. "I'll be back in a bit."

I used the stairs to avoid running into anyone. I didn't want to talk and I certainly didn't want to run into Caden.

I made it to the locker room and opened my locker. That's when I saw the block of Dandelion chocolate resting on the shelf. I picked it up, smoothing my fingers over the pretty wrapper. He must have left it for me yesterday.

Before he decided that we weren't worth the risk.

I closed my eyes.

After a shaky breath, I pulled my shoes and hoodie off the shelf. I pulled the hoodie on and slipped the chocolate bar into the pocket. I sat down and laced up my shoes.

Some fresh air would help me clear my head. I just needed to shake this off enough so I could deal with it. Just like I'd dealt with every other shitty situation. I was Allie Ford. I wouldn't break. Not when I had a little boy depending on me.

When I reached the lobby, I scanned around to make sure there was no sign of Caden. I was halfway across the space when I heard masculine laughter. My head whipped up

Blake and the ESG were walking into the great room.

I stood there, rage filling me. It welled up, oozing into every corner of me like acid. It was far better than the pain.

Blake had instigated all of this. He'd terrified me, he'd taken Ollie, all as part of his sick game. Indirectly, he'd driven Caden away.

I sucked in a breath. I was sick of being a pawn. Hands balling, I strode into the great room, aiming right for Blake and his cronies.

His friends saw me coming and elbowed each other. When Blake's gaze hit me, he rose from the chair, a superior look on his face.

Walking right up to him, I shoved him in the chest. "You touched my kid. You crossed a fucking line."

"I have no idea what you're talking about."

"Don't be even more of a cowardly asshole than you already are." He had to be stopped.

I was going to stop him.

I'd find his damn drug stash, get the evidence we needed, and watch him get locked behind bars.

A plan snapped into place in my head.

Lowering my voice, I leaned in. "Do you know why I was interested in you and your...side gig? Why I kept hanging around? Because I wanted a fix."

His eyes widened. "Bullshit."

"My brother and his wife were both shot in the head by a carjacker. I had to identify them. I inherited my five-year-old nephew. I gave up my dream job and life in New York City to come back to the bumfuck mountain town that I escaped. All I do is clean other people's crap and take care of my kid. That's it."

His gaze turned assessing. "You're cozy with that security guy."

I cut a hand through the air. "I like a good fuck when I can." Ugh, I hated spilling these lies, but I needed him to trust me. "I need some relief from the grind." I cocked my head. "I was hoping you had one for me. Of the chemical variety."

He watched me for a moment. "Maybe I had you wrong."

"Obviously. You didn't need to shove me in the trunk of a car or take my kid." I crossed my arms. "Now I think you owe me."

He cocked his head. "Okay, Allie. I can hook you up."

I made myself smile. "Now?"

"Now." He took my hand, and I had to fight the urge to yank away. "We'll be back later, guys."

He towed me out of the great room. Discreetly, I glanced up at one of the security cameras.

Come on, Caden.

Things between us might be messed up, but I knew he'd want to stop Blake.

As we crossed the lobby, I looked for the cameras again. Behind the reception desk, I saw Coral frowning at us. I gave her a long look.

Before I knew it, we were outside.

"Where are we going?" I asked.

"For a little walk."

The Halloween Spectacular area was mostly packed up, but there were a few trucks and workers taking things down and cleaning up. We walked past the biking area, but I didn't see Sierra thankfully.

Then Blake led me up one of the hiking trails and into the trees.

God, how would Caden find me here? There weren't any cameras.

We walked along the path, and I slipped my shaking hands into the pocket of my hoodie.

My chocolate bar.

I pulled it out.

Blake glanced back. "What's that?"

"Chocolate." I unwrapped it and popped a piece in my mouth. "Want some?"

He shook his head and looked back to the path ahead.

I tore a piece of chocolate off, including a piece of the gold and white wrapper. Then I dropped it on the ground.

Find me, Caden.

241

CHAPTER 28
CADEN

It was easy not feel anything when you kept busy.

In the conference room, I had camera schematics spread across the table. I needed the system upgrades completed for when Gunnar started.

I scribbled some notes on the plan.

But my mind kept trying to go to Allie.

To her stricken face, the way she'd stared at me, her eyes pleading.

You're running away, and that's not for my benefit.

My hand curled into a fist.

"You look ready to punch the table."

Ro stood in the doorway, hands in the pockets of his suit pants. I hadn't even heard him walk in.

"I'm fine. Busy. Gunnar wants the head of security role, so I want the upgrades completed for him. It'll make the transition easier."

"We both know that's not why you're as tense as hell and ready to hit someone."

Dammit. Allie would have spoken with Tessa, and Tessa with Ro.

"I did what I had to do."

"Last night, you saved a young girl's life. She still has her entire life ahead of her, thanks to you. Then, you found Ollie. Today, you should be comforting your woman, and instead you wrecked her."

I thumped my fist on the table. "Ro, stay out of it."

"No. You're my friend. You're a good man and you deserve her. *Fight* for her."

"I hurt her. I failed her. I'll do it again."

"You never failed anyone. You never give up, even in the toughest of circumstances. You didn't fail Wells. When are you going to accept that there was nothing you could have done to a save him? You brought him home, Caden. Now, it's time for you to come home."

I sucked in a breath.

Then Ro focused on one of the monitors and frowned. "Caden..."

His tone made me stiffen. I shifted to see the screen. "What?"

"It's Allie."

My gaze found her straight away. She was in the great room.

Talking with Blake Moreland.

Dammit.

They were having some sort of confrontation. Then, the bastard took her hand and pulled her out of the room. And it looked like she was going willingly.

I watched her glance up at the camera for a long beat.

What the fuck? What was she up to?

I touched the keyboard and flicked the view to the lobby cameras. I followed them through the lobby, and right before they went outside, she stared at the camera again.

Like she was sending me a message.

"What the hell is she doing?" Ro bit out.

There was a knock on the door and Gunnar entered. "Everything okay?"

"Ro, this is Gunnar O'Neill."

Ro held out a hand. "I hear you're joining the Langston team. We might need your help before you've officially signed your contract."

Gunnar arched a brow.

"Allie just left the hotel with Blake Moreland," I said.

He frowned. "The asshole drug dealer who took her kid last night?"

I nodded. "She's up to something."

"And she wanted you to make sure you saw her," Ro added.

"She wants me to follow." I cursed. "She's going with him to find the drugs. So we've got evidence to arrest him." My heart started pounding. I spun to the locked cabinet in the corner and quickly dialed in the code. I opened it and pulled out a handgun. "Gunnar, you armed?"

My friend shook his head.

I handed him a Glock.

"I'll call the Windward PD," Ro said. "Be careful out there."

I nodded as I attached the holster onto my belt and slid my own Glock into it.

"Bring her home," Ro added.

Oh, I was going to. My gaze went back to the cameras, and I saw her and Blake outside, walking near the outdoor activity area. A moment later, they slipped out of view of the cameras.

Hugh appeared. "What's going on?"

"You're with us," I said. "I'll explain on the way."

The big man just nodded and didn't ask any questions. The three of us got outside and I brought Hugh up to speed.

"Hell," Hugh muttered.

"By the way, this is your new boss, Gunnar O'Neill."

Gunnar gave the man a chin lift. "Nice to meet you, Hugh."

"Likewise." Hugh's brow creased. "What the hell was Allie thinking?"

That she wanted this nightmare over.

Once again, I'd let her down. And I only had myself to blame.

I couldn't lose her.

She was right, I'd been holding myself back. And even while doing that, it didn't stop the pain of knowing that she was in danger.

She needed me.

Fuck. I was pretty sure that I was in love with Allie Ford.

Ignoring the tightness in my chest, I strode toward the trees.

I was bringing her home.

We reached the edge of camera range and the spot

where I'd last seen Allie and Moreland. I scanned around and saw no sign of them.

Where the hell did they go? My jaw worked.

"They could be anywhere," Hugh said.

"He's likely got his stash in the trees on the mountain." I let my gaze drift over the colorful Fall foliage. "That way he can use bike rides as an excuse to stop there and top up his supply without anyone noticing."

"It's a big mountain," Gunnar murmured.

Too big. For a second, unfamiliar fear cut into me. *What if I couldn't find her?*

Wait. I spotted a glint of something on the ground.

I crouched and saw a wrapper and a square of chocolate.

I sucked in a breath. It was a familiar white and gold wrapper. I smiled. "Allie left us a clue." I rose. My little Gretel was leaving me a trail to follow. "This way."

My hand clenched on the chocolate as I strode into the trees. After a few more yards, I spotted another wrapper. I snatched it up.

"Let's move."

CHAPTER 29

ALLIE

I was a little bit out of breath as I followed Blake up the hill.

The trees closed in around us, the leaves all vibrant and beautiful. But I couldn't appreciate the beauty right now.

Had Caden noticed I was gone?

I was almost out of chocolate. I was spreading the distance out a bit more before I dropped a piece, but any more, and I'd risk him not finding me.

Hell, I hoped no animals were eating it.

"Are we almost there?" I huffed out.

"Yeah." Blake wasn't even breathing hard.

We turned the corner on the trail, and he suddenly stopped.

A clump of rocks sat just off the track. He stepped closer, and pushed aside some sticks and dried leaves.

I spotted a black sports duffel bag.

He pulled it out and rested it on top of one of the rocks, then unzipped it.

It was filled with baggies. My mouth went dry. I could see some had pills and others were filled with white powder.

"So what's your pleasure, pretty Allie?"

Shit, I didn't know anything about drugs. I'd smoked weed a few times in high school but that was it. "Ecstasy?"

He nodded. "You got cash?"

"Back in my locker at the hotel."

"Okay." He handed me a baggie filled with several pills.

I took the baggie and stuffed it in my pocket. I needed to remember this location so I could bring Caden here and get the entire stash.

"I need to take a leak," Blake said. "Don't run off."

He stomped into the trees. I quickly pulled out my phone and took a few pictures. I was sliding it away when he reappeared.

His gaze narrowed. "What are you doing?"

"Nothing."

"You were taking photos."

"No. God, you're a paranoid prick. Can we just go?"

"Show me the phone." His tone had turned cold.

My pulse kicked into overdrive. "No."

He held out a hand. "Now."

"Fuck off, Blake."

His face twisted. Then suddenly, he backhanded me. *Shit.* His palm cracked against my cheek and I fell to one knee. My face throbbed.

I shifted and realized I was kneeling right beside the duffel bag.

"Allie, Allie, Allie." Sticks crunched as he took a step closer. "I should have known you were playing me. You can't play a player."

I grabbed the duffel bag, leaped up, and ran.

As I bounded into the trees, I heard Blake shouting behind me. I picked up speed, sprinting as fast as I could, dodging around tree trunks.

I needed to get back to the hotel.

Running as fast as I could, I crashed through the undergrowth, branches slapping me in the face.

"I'm going to fuck you up, Allie." Blake's shout echoed in the trees. "No one messes with my business."

My chest hitched, but I kept running.

Air was sawing in and out of my lungs. Ahead, I saw a small clearing and some rocks. I detoured around a boulder.

Suddenly, a weight tackled me from behind. I hit the ground with an *oof*.

No.

The duffel bag slipped from my hands.

"The game ends here." Blake's voice was low and angry in my ear. His weight pinned me to the ground. "I make too much money from my business to risk it. I've no desire to go and sit in a fucking cubicle being a lawyer like my father wants."

Bucking my body, I tried to kick him off. But he was too damn heavy and too strong.

"Quit that." He smacked a hand into the side of my head.

Ow. Pain throbbed through my face.

Then I felt him reaching around my body and in the

pocket of my hoodie. He pulled out my phone, then tossed it into the trees.

He also pulled out the packet of pills.

He reared back enough to turn me over, then pinned me down again. He smiled. "You're going to get to sample my goods. When they find you, you'll be another sad statistic. An overwhelmed single mom who took the easy way out."

No. I thrust my body up.

He jostled and almost overbalanced. With a growl, he pressed his forearm against my chest, shoving me back down.

This couldn't happen. I couldn't leave Ollie alone.

I didn't want to leave Caden. We had something special, I knew it in my heart. If the stubborn man would just let me in. Let me love him.

I wasn't going to let Blake Moreland ruin my life.

I kept fighting, but he was too strong.

He gripped my chin with one hand, holding my jaw still. Then he opened the baggie of pills with his other hand.

"Time to take your medicine."

"Fuck you." I pressed my lips shut.

He shoved the pills against my mouth, mashing my lip against my teeth.

No.

His fingers squeezed cruelly into my skin. I tried to shake my head.

If you get those pills in your mouth, you die.

He squeezed my jaw harder, and slowly I felt my muscles giving way.

No. No. No.

I was going to die.

Then a gunshot echoed through the trees.

CHAPTER 30
CADEN

My shot hit Moreland in the shoulder.

I watched his body jerk and swing to the side.

It was taking everything I had not to place a well-aimed bullet between his eyes. The bastard was straddling Allie. She turned her head, saw me, and relief filled her face.

Fuck. That look.

There was a lot I'd do to see this woman look at me like that.

I raced across the clearing. As I neared them, I saw the redness and swelling on her face.

He'd hit her. He was trying to force pills into her mouth. They were now scattered all around on the dirt.

I kicked him and he fell off her with a grunt. Leaning down, I pressed the gun to the side of his head, and he froze.

"How's it feel when someone bigger and stronger has you pinned down?" I growled. "You like preying on people who are more vulnerable than you. It makes you feel strong." I shoved the gun barrel harder against his temple. "You're nothing but a pathetic, cowardly parasite."

Moreland whimpered. "Please...don't kill me."

I smelled the sharp stench of urine. He'd wet himself.

I glared down at him with disdain. Then Gunnar and Hugh flanked me.

"We've got him, Caden." Gunnar gently pushed my arm down.

Hugh pulled handcuffs off his belt. "You take care of Allie."

I slid my handgun back into the holster and turned. She was sitting there, huddled on the ground, and shaking.

I approached her. *God*. She was alive. She was okay. I felt a little light-headed.

"Caden, the duffel is filled with drugs." She pointed to a bag nearby. "I took pictures. My phone's here somewhere. He threw it."

"You came out here with him to find the drugs."

She nodded. "He had to be stopped. I was sick of being his chew toy. And last night, after Ollie, after making you blame yourself..."

I crouched. I wanted to touch her, but I'd pushed her away, I'd hurt her.

Now, I wasn't sure she wanted me to touch her.

"He hit you. Do you have any other injuries?"

She shook her head, gently touching her cheek. "I knew you'd come. I left a trail."

253

"Yes, I found it. This was dangerous, reckless, and... brave. So damn brave."

Her stormy gray eyes met mine. "I knew you'd come."

Simple words filled with conviction.

My chest heaved. "When I saw you leave with him..." I held her gaze. "I knew you'd hold on until I got here. I knew you'd stop him." My heart felt like it was being squeezed. "Allie, you were right. I've been running for a long time. I left my family, I haven't settled anywhere, I haven't let myself get close to anyone or feel anything... Until I met a woman with mile-long legs and gray eyes. A woman who loves her nephew fiercely, who's a hard worker, a good friend. I couldn't stop looking at her, couldn't stop wanting to touch her, couldn't stop feeling so much for her."

Her lips parted.

"I'm in love with you, Allie Ford. And—" I dragged in a large breath "—I don't want to fight it or hide from it anymore."

"Caden..."

Then we both moved. I hauled her into my arms, and she burrowed against me.

"I'm sorry I pushed you away."

"It's okay. I'm falling in love with you too, Broody." She cupped my cheek. "My big, protective, paranoid Broody. Who always follows the rules and keeps people safe."

Jesus. Emotion flooded me. This woman loved me. I felt like I'd won a damn jackpot.

I lowered my mouth to hers and kissed her.

I was still kissing her when I heard a throat clearing.

Reluctantly, I broke the kiss and looked up. Gunnar was smiling at me.

Behind him, Hugh had Moreland at the edge of the clearing, his hands cuffed behind his back.

"We're ready to take this asshole down the mountain," Gunnar said.

With a nod, I rose and pulled Allie up with me. "I'll carry Allie."

"No way. I can walk." She leaned into me. "But you can help."

I grabbed the duffel bag and slung it over my shoulder. Then with an arm wrapped securely around Allie, we set off.

At the base of the mountain, once we cleared the trees, I saw a crowd waiting for us.

"Allie!" Tessa and Sierra ran toward us. Then the women pulled Allie away from me, hugging her and talking a mile a minute.

Ro was standing with Officer Sanchez and a detective from the Windward Police Department.

I handed over the duffel bag. "This is Moreland's drug stash. He also tried to kill Ms. Ford. He tried to force pills down her throat."

Sanchez took the bag, her face serious. "We have his friends detained inside. I think Ms. Ford has broken the back of this little drug ring." Sanchez glanced over at the huddle of women. "I'll need to get her statement."

I growled. "Not now."

Sanchez shared a glance with the detective, who nodded. "Later will be fine."

That's when I saw Ollie peeking out from behind Ro, watching everything with wide eyes.

"Hey." I crouched down in front of him. "Allie's okay."

The boy looked at the handcuffed Moreland. "You caught the bad man. He can't hurt her again. Can't kill her."

My heart squeezed. He was worried about losing the people he loved. I understood that. "He'll never get near her again. You want to see her?"

He nodded.

With my hand clamped on his shoulder, I led him toward Allie.

When she spotted him, she raced to him. "Ollie." She threw her arms around him.

"*Allie.*"

The pair hugged, and I saw Allie was fighting back tears.

"Buddy, how about we get Allie inside?" I suggested.

"Okay, Caden."

Then, I scooped Allie into my arms.

"Caden..."

"We're going up to my suite." Where I was going to check her out for injuries and ice her face. "We'll get some breakfast. Your choice, Ollie."

He didn't hesitate. "Anything I want?"

"Yes."

"Ice-cream and Pop Tarts." His eyes were gleaming.

In my arms, Allie winced.

I smiled at both of them. I'd do anything to make

these two happy. "Ice-cream and Pop Tarts, it is. I'll call the kitchen. I'm sure they can hook us up."

Allie pressed her face to my neck. "You're making me fall even more in love with you, Caden Castro."

My arms tightened on her. "Good."

CHAPTER 31
ALLIE

I woke with a start.

The fading dream of Blake looming over me slowly dissipated. My pulse evened out.

I was safe.

I was in Caden's bed at the hotel.

It was late afternoon now. I'd spent the morning with Caden and Ollie, gorging on ice cream and Pop Tarts. Then I'd crashed, and Caden had gently bullied me into his bed for a nap.

Now I wanted to see him.

Caden was in love with me. Giddy warmth filled me.

I rose and ran my hands through my hair to tidy it. As a walked out of the bedroom, I heard Ollie's familiar giggle.

In the living area, two males—one big and one small—sat crouched by the coffee table.

God, could a heart burst open with happiness? They were making a LEGO build together. Ollie was chattering away as he placed blocks, and Caden was nodding.

"Hello, what are you two doing?" I asked.

"Allie!" Ollie bounced up, raced over for a hug around my waist, then raced back to the table. "Caden got me a LEGO set."

"I see that." A large set, by the looks of it.

"It's a police station. It's got a prison cell and everything. I'm going to lock the bad guys up in there. Then they can't hurt anyone."

My heart squeezed. I knew he must be working through what had happened. I'd need to talk to his therapist to make sure he was processing it. When he smiled up at Caden, I was happy to see that he seemed fine.

Caden rose, his dark gaze scanning my body from head to toe.

I held my arms out. "I'm fine." My face was throbbing a bit, but Caden had iced it earlier and given me several painkillers.

Gently, he ran his knuckles over my cheek. Then his mouth was on mine, and the kiss was slow and thorough.

"*Mmm*." I pressed my hands to his chest, enjoying the drugging warmth.

Then I spotted Ollie watching us, grinning.

"Is Caden your boyfriend now?"

"Um, well—"

Caden slung an arm across my shoulders. "Yes, I am. Is that okay with you?"

The little boy cocked his head. "So you're not leaving Windward?"

Caden looked down at me. "No, I'm not. If that's okay with you two. I'd like to stay with you."

I leaned into him. "Yes. It's more than okay."

"I might have work trips away sometimes, but I'll always come home."

Ollie nodded. "When moms and dads go on trips, they bring presents home for their kids." He paused. "Like LEGO sets and stuff."

I laughed. My kiddo.

"Right." Caden nodded. "I can do that."

Ollie beamed. "Good."

"Girlfriends like gifts too," I murmured.

He nibbled my lips. "I can handle that."

"But you coming back to us will be the best gift of all."

He touched my hair, running the strands through his fingertips. "I want that. I want to move in. I want to sleep beside you, cook together, help with Ollie."

Everything inside me melted. I felt those tingles again that had freaked me out at first, but now, I loved.

"I want that too. You're mine, Caden Castro. Every overprotective, paranoid inch of you."

~

A few weeks later

"Two KIDS just spilled two giant cups of soda in the restaurant. Wade, can you take point on that?"

"You betcha, Allie." The young man grabbed his gear and headed out.

Swiveling, I tapped on my tablet. It was a busy day at the Langston Windward.

Winter season had started and snow was falling. Once we got a good amount of powder, the hotel would be bursting at the seams with skiers and snowboarders. I wrinkled my nose. They'd be tracking slush and mud inside in no time. It was a lot of extra work for my team.

I grinned. But we could handle it.

I didn't miss New York at all. While I still missed my brother fiercely, I was glad I'd come home to Windward. My life before was now just a faded memory. My life after, a vibrant tapestry of love and happiness.

And now I had an amazing man in my life, my happiness levels were off the charts.

Ollie was blooming with a man in the house. The condo wasn't really big enough for the three of us, and Caden and I had talked about house hunting in the spring.

Caden was blooming too. He smiled a lot more and he slept more too. He still had nights when he couldn't sleep. My lips curled. Luckily, I had a few tricks for helping him clear his mind.

"She's daydreaming again."

Sierra's voice made me look up. She, Jazz, and Tessa were grinning at me from the doorway to Tessa's office.

"I don't daydream."

"These days, you daydream all the time," Tessa said. "We all know you were thinking about your Broody."

"I thought he'd seem less scary now that he's in love." Sierra shook her head. "But he's just as dark and scowly."

Not with me he wasn't. "That's how I like him."

I'd gotten him to call his mom and sisters. We'd done

a video call last weekend. It would take time, but his family were keen to rebuild their relationships. They loved him, they just hadn't known how to help him when he'd first come home. His mother hadn't hidden her joy to hear that he'd fallen in love.

We'd had one disastrous call with my mother. I'd introduced her to Caden, and she'd been surprised but polite. Then she'd started in on me about the clothes I was wearing and my terrible cooking. She'd accused me of not taking good enough care of Ollie.

Caden had snapped. In his coldest, calmest voice, he'd told her that I was an exceptional, loving mother, a hard worker, and the most beautiful woman he'd seen, whatever I was wearing. He also pointed out that I was here, with Ollie every day, while his grandmother and grandfather were conspicuously absent. That had shut my mother up fast. I'd been so giddy, that I'd kissed him, then and there.

I didn't think my mom would call again for a while, and I was okay with that.

"When's Caden back?" Jazz asked.

"This afternoon." He'd been gone for two days in Denver doing something at the Langston Denver. At least he hadn't gone far or for very long. I knew he'd have a trip to the Maldives soon to assess a new Langston acquisition.

Sierra gave a gusty sigh. "You three are in love with your hot guys, getting breakfast in bed and regular orgasms. Meanwhile, I need to order new vibrator. I've worn mine out."

I slipped an arm around her. "The right hot guy for you will turn up."

Sierra sighed. "It's lucky we have a busy winter season ahead. I think I'll be doing lots of skiing, and binging on sugar-packed baked goods."

My friend had a serious sweet tooth. I had no idea how she managed to stay so trim.

"This one is *perfectly* fine," a sharp female voice snapped, echoing off the walls. "These are the best uniforms on the market."

The three of us swiveled at Piper's tart voice.

We watched her and Everett come into view.

Everett was striding down the hall, wearing jeans and a blue flannel shirt. Piper—wearing a snug black skirt and Louboutins with sky-high heels—was trotting after him. She held a khaki work shirt in her hands.

"Murray, you'll wear this. You've turned down all the other options." She tossed the shirt.

It hit him in the center of the back. He spun fast and caught it. "I don't need a uniform, big city."

"My name is Piper."

He balled the shirt up. "I'll wear this on the day you wear a flannel shirt."

Piper gasped. "I'll *never* wear flannel shirt."

He grinned at her. "I know."

She set her hands on her hips. "I'm doing my job. Trying to upgrade and improve things around here."

"More like making rule after unnecessary rule."

"Making things better."

"You need to loosen up, big city."

She hissed in a breath. "Wear the damn shirt."

Everett crossed his arms. "I'll make a deal with you. I'll wear it on the day you wear a flannel shirt—" he leaned in so their noses almost brushed "—with nothing else under it and crawl to me."

Outrage filled Piper's face and she let out a strangled noise. "Murray, I'm going to—" They stalked off down the hall and disappeared, still sniping at each other.

The four of us were silent for a moment.

"How long until they bang each other's brains out?" I asked.

"That, or murder each other," Tessa mused. A speculative look filled her face. "Let's start a betting pool. I've got fifty bucks on them doing it next month."

"Three weeks," Jazz countered.

I tapped a finger on my chin. "Two weeks."

Sierra smiled. "Two days."

We all burst out laughing.

"We are due for a cocktail night," I said. "We can interrogate Piper then." That's when I saw a man enter the back office area.

Dark eyes locked on me and my heart leaped.

Caden was back.

"And we've lost her," Tessa said. "Bye, Allie."

Tessa, Jazz, and Sierra walked past my man, calling out hellos.

He didn't slow down as he walked toward me. Then he picked me up and his mouth was on mine.

Yum. I kissed him hard and coiled my legs around his waist. Spinning, he pinned me to the wall, his hard body against mine.

"Missed you," he murmured.

"Missed you too."

His hands slipped down my back and into the waist-band of my work pants. He cupped my bare ass and groaned. "It drives me crazy knowing you have no panties on under your uniform."

I wriggled against him. "You drive me crazy every time I look at you."

He kissed me again. Things were just getting inter-esting when I heard a *harrumphing* sound.

I looked over Caden's shoulder. Coral was staring at us with her arms crossed over her chest.

"Hussy," she muttered.

"Hi, Coral."

Caden didn't turn to look, and I could see him fighting a smile.

"This is a luxury hotel, not a brothel." With a sniff, she stomped past us.

I laughed and Caden grinned.

"Did you get Ollie a gift?"

"That dinosaur LEGO set he wanted."

I nipped Caden's bottom lip. "And me?"

"I got you something too."

I undulated against his hard cock. "I know. I can feel it."

He snorted and set me down. "You can have that later." He reached a hand under his jacket, then pulled out a small, wrapped gift.

Grinning, I tore it open. Then I gasped. It was a tiny fairy made of delicate metal. Her back was arched, her head thrown back, and she had a set of magnificent, deli-cate wings.

He'd bought me quite a few fairy statues over the last few weeks. My man liked to spoil me.

"She's beautiful," I breathed.

"She made me think of you."

"I love you, Broody."

He hauled me back. "I love you too, Allie." He nuzzled my neck. "When we get home, I'll show you how much."

Home. Our home. I loved hearing that.

"Have I ever told you that I love that you're a man of action?"

CHAPTER 32
CADEN

The new security room renovations were finished. The scent of fresh paint was still strong. We were bringing in the gear and installing the new monitors. It would be ready in a few more days.

"What do you think?"

Beside me, Gunnar nodded. "It's going to be perfect. Your design works really well."

He'd started the new job this week. He refused to wear a suit, and was wearing dark jeans and a blazer instead.

"Did you go over the camera and sensor installation plan while I was gone?"

"Yes. I made a couple of tweaks." He grinned. "But you do good work for an Army grunt."

"I'm really glad you're here, Gunnar."

"Me too."

I glanced at my watch. "I need to leave for Ollie's

school thing soon. I'm just waiting for Allie so we can drive over."

My friend's grin widened. "Caden Castro, family man."

"Hey, don't knock it until you try it."

A contemplative look crossed his rugged face. "Maybe I will."

Gunnar had moved into a suite in the hotel, and was acquainting himself with Windward. I knew that had included visiting Tessa's aunt's shop in town several times.

It appeared he was waging a full-on, romantic assault on the beautiful widow.

Enzo popped his head through the door. "Caden, I have a message from Allie. She's been held up. A plumbing leak's ruined a room on level five and the hotel's fully booked. Her team needs to get it cleaned before the next guests arrive. She said to tell you to go ahead, and she'll meet you at the school."

"Thanks, Enzo."

The concierge nodded.

"Go," Gunnar said.

With a wave, I exited the security room. Allie would discover the gift that I'd left for her in her locker. I'm sure she was going to give me an earful about it.

I drove to the school, I navigated the slushy road, and passed by the Windward Police Department building. My thoughts turned to Blake Moreland. The ESG had turned on each other, tripping over themselves to make deals. They'd all do some time, but Moreland would be spending a very long time as a guest of the State.

After I parked at the school, I headed to Ollie's classroom. As I neared, I heard the hubbub of young, excited voices. In the room, several parents were standing around the walls, along with a few grandparents. I nodded at the teacher, and scanned the kids on the mat. Unsurprisingly, they were all having trouble sitting still. Ollie spotted me, and bounced and waved.

"All right, let's get started," the young teacher said. "Lucy, you can start."

A tiny girl with dark hair walked over to a couple who were clearly her parents. She introduced them, then started talking about her sisters, her cat, and their house.

"Made it." An out-of-breath Allie appeared at my side. I hugged her and she waved to Ollie.

"Work drama sorted?"

"Yes, but I have a bone to pick with my sometimes-bossy hot guy."

I raised a brow.

"Imagine my surprise when I rushed to get my keys so I could drive here, and I couldn't find them." Her gaze narrowed. "Or my SUV."

"It was a piece of—" I looked at the nearby kids "—crap."

"It was fine. Then I got an even bigger surprise when I found keys to a shiny, new Jeep in my locker."

"Mmm."

"Caden, you can't buy me a new car without talking to me about it."

"I already did."

"We're a couple, a team, we talk about things like this."

"When it comes to you having a safe vehicle to drive in the winter, there's nothing to talk about. It's about your safety, it's about Ollie's safety."

I saw the fight go out of her. I knew she'd do anything for Ollie.

"Fine," she grumbled. "I'll let this slide." She took my hand and squeezed it. "Thanks for the new car."

"You're welcome."

"Oh, I also got a message from your mom. She's excited for our visit in January. She can't wait to meet Ollie."

Allie had encouraged me to reconnect with my mom, Clara, and Sara. It hadn't been easy, but Mom and my sisters had made it clear they missed me. We were heading to Texas for a visit in the new year.

"She wants grandbabies. My sisters aren't making any yet, so prepare for her to lavish the love on Ollie and spoil him."

"Next up is Ollie," the teacher announced.

Ollie bounced up and rushed over to us. He turned to face his class.

"My mommy and daddy died." His voice wobbled, and Allie touched his shoulder. He smiled up at her. "I miss them. In my life before, I lived with my parents in a house. Daddy was going to get me a dog."

A dog? Maybe that was something else we could do once we found a new house.

"Now, I live with my aunt Allie." Ollie beamed up at her. "And my Caden."

When he looked at me, I winked.

"Now, we all live together." Then Ollie reached out

and took Allie's hand. She froze, looking shocked, then she closed her fingers on his. He reached out with his other hand and took mine. "Now, we're a family."

Hell, the kid was killing me. I never thought I'd be the man I was before I joined the military again. I never thought I'd feel so much, care so much, or love so much. But now, while I'd never be that young idealistic man again, I was a new man. One who was in love with an amazing woman and her nephew.

I looked over Ollie's head at Allie. Her eyes were misty and her mouth moved. *Love you.*

I smiled at her. My life after was better than anything I'd ever imagined.

I'd happily spend my lifetime protecting them, loving them, and doing everything with this woman by my side.

I hope you enjoyed Allie and Caden's story!

Langston Hotels continues with **Never and Always**, starring city gal executive Piper Ellis and laid-back head of maintenance Everett Murray, coming in 2026.

For more action-packed contemporary romance, check out Ro's friends in New Orleans, the Fury Brothers. The first book is called *Fury*. **Read on for a preview of the first chapter.**

Don't miss out! For updates about new releases, free books, and other fun stuff, sign up for my VIP mailing list and get your *free box set* containing three action-packed romances.

Visit here to get started: www.annahackett.com

Would you like a FREE BOX SET of my books?

PREVIEW: FURY

MILA

Strong hands grabbed me from behind.

Adrenaline surged. *No.* I was no one's victim. I whirled and rammed my elbow back into my attacker. I heard a grunt, but I kept moving, my heart thumping hard.

I lifted my knee, ramming it hard into the guy's stomach, then I shoved him down. I wouldn't be anyone's prey. Not ever again. He hit the mats with a groan.

"Mila, excellent work."

As my instructor nodded and smiled, I straightened, bouncing a little on my feet. Around me, the rest of my self-defense class were grinning and nodding.

My "attacker" lifted his head. "Why did I volunteer for this again?"

Shay, the instructor, held out a hand and helped the young guy up. "Because you're my very good boyfriend, and didn't have a choice." Shay was a fit, thirty-something with a shredded body I envied. Her black, cropped sports top showed off her six-pack. Her blonde hair was in two long braids.

She looked my way again. "Mila, really great. You did everything exactly as I taught you."

I nodded, happy to hear her praise. "I have a great teacher."

Shay's smile widened. "And you're an excellent student."

Because I had no choice. I kept my smile pinned in place. I had to know how to defend myself. I wouldn't be caught out again.

"All right, everyone." Shay clapped her hands. "We're done. I'll see you at the next lesson."

I nabbed my water bottle and towel. Slinging the towel around my neck, I took a big swig of water.

The sounds of thuds, punches, and grunts echoed around the gym. Hard Burn was one of the most popular gyms in New Orleans. It was located in a large warehouse in the Warehouse District, and most of the space was filled with roped off boxing rings. A glass wall at the end separated the exercise equipment and weights.

I'd heard there was a wait list to get a membership here. Luckily, Hard Burn also ran some self-defense classes, and I'd managed to nab a spot when I moved here. It was perfect because I worked just a few doors down.

The gym was run by one of the notorious Fury brothers. People *loved* to talk about the five men. They weren't brothers by blood, but brothers by choice. I'd heard lots of stories about them, but the most common one was that they'd grown up together in foster care, then banded together to make a good life for themselves.

It probably helped that they were all rich and hot.

One of them also happened to be my boss. He owned the nightclub where I worked, and the bar next door, and two restaurants. In fact, he and his brothers owned the entire block.

Shaking my head, I watched two guys in gloves going at it with each other in one of the boxing rings. I'd gotten a job at the hottest nightclub in New Orleans because I'd heard the Fury brothers were tough. They protected their patch of the city, and stood up to the gangs, cartels, and criminals.

It made it the perfect place to hide under the radar.

"Bye, Shay." I waved. "I need to get to work." Glancing at my watch, I saw I had exactly fifteen minutes to shower, dress in my uniform, and hightail it to the club.

"Bye, Mila."

In the ladies change room, I tapped the code into the

locker and pulled out my backpack. The first thing I did was check my laptop was in there. It was a habit now. As I touched the cool metal, the pressure I always seemed to feel eased a little.

I also kept a stash of cash tucked into a pocket I'd sewed in the bottom of the backpack. My emergency fund. It was a little low right now, but I'd build it back up.

It took me two minutes to shower and dress. In the foggy mirror above the row of basins, I caught my reflection. It was still a jolt to see my dark hair. I'd dyed it black after I'd gone on the run, and it was half a step above horrible. I wrinkled my nose. Black didn't suit me. I missed my caramel-blonde hair. I'd loved it, spent hours styling it.

Now, my harsh, black hair was usually up in a careless bun or ponytail.

Now, all I could do was hide and survive.

I fiddled with the shiny gold halter top. All the bartenders and servers at the club wore black trousers and gold tops. Well, the men got black shirts with gold stitching, but I was just grateful my top wasn't low cut or strapless. The halter top was actually pretty comfortable.

After stuffing everything in my backpack, I headed out. It was a balmy summer evening in New Orleans. Growing up in Louisiana, I was used to warm temperatures and humidity.

I hurried down the street. I liked the Arts/Warehouse district. There were loads of art galleries and lots of places to eat, but it wasn't quite as crazy as the French Quarter and Bourbon Street. Most of the old warehouses had been converted into galleries or loft apartments, and I really wished I could afford to live in one.

I walked past Smokehouse. The bar was running a brisk trade. I saw several groups sitting out on the front patio, sharing drinks and laughing. One table had a bunch of helium balloons in the center. Celebrating someone's birthday. Another table held a couple clearly on a date, and yet another one held a family with teenagers hunched over their cellphones.

All people going about their lives. Enjoying themselves. Doing things that normal people did. I'd been like that once. Just four months ago, actually, although most days it felt like a lifetime ago.

My eyes burned. All things I couldn't have.

Dammit. I sniffed. Feeling sorry for myself was a waste of energy.

I reached Ember, the name glowing in gold neon above a set of beaten-gold double doors. Reggie stood out front. There was only one bouncer on this early, and another would join later as it got busier, in addition to the security inside.

The handsome black man smiled at me. He was built like a linebacker. "Hey, Mila. Ready for a busy night."

"Always."

He waved me through.

It always felt like stepping into sin. Everything was done in luxurious black and gold. The floor was polished black, and one wall held a row of gold urns almost as tall as I was. Lights strobed across the dance floor. The long bar glowed with golden light, and off to one side was the roped-off, VIP area.

My favorite thing, though, was the ceiling. I glanced up. It was covered in a sea of gold flowers. It looked as though if a breeze blew in here, they'd all flutter down on us. It was totally the kind of club I would have liked to spend time in.

As I passed the bar, I called out hellos to the bartenders already prepping for the night ahead. I punched the code into the door leading to the staff locker room and wasted no time stashing my bag in my locker.

Showtime. It was Saturday night in New Orleans, and soon, the club would be hopping.

When I got back to the bar, Venus, the head bartender, appeared. She was mid-forties, tall, with her curly, black hair cut very short. Her halter top showed off super-toned arms I'd kill for. She could make any cocktail a customer asked for, and managed the customers with an ease that I'd never, ever have.

"Mila, you're behind the bar tonight, but if the servers need help on the floor, then you're up."

"Got it."

"And you're okay to close tonight?"

"Yes. Happy to."

She blew out a breath. "Great, because Bryce has this dance concert tomorrow. First thing in the morning." She was a single mom to two boys. "If I can at least get a decent amount of sleep, I'll be mostly functional for it."

"I'm happy to close any time you need me, Venus."

"It's appreciated." The woman cocked her head. "Been working on any new cocktail recipes?"

I smiled. "Maybe."

Venus nodded. "Good. You have a knack."

I had a knack for mixing up new drinks because I'd also spent loads of nights at home, memorizing cocktail recipes. I'd lied my ass off to get the job here. I said I'd worked in clubs before, all the while praying my fake ID held up.

I wasn't Amelia Clifton, marketing guru anymore. I was Mila Clarke, bartender. Thankfully, I was a quick learner, and I'd picked up working the bar fast.

A large crowd of clubgoers surged inside.

"Time to water the thirsty masses," Venus said.

Soon, I was too busy to think of anything. I was grabbing glasses, scooping ice, pouring shots, and mixing cocktails.

"You can light me up any day, sweet thing."

Sweet thing? Really.

Leaning over the bar, I ran the lighter across the three tall glasses, turning the red cocktails from hurricanes into flaming hurricanes.

The customer licked his lips and smiled. He was already heading well toward drunk. I'd need to keep an eye on him and cut him off soon.

"I'll add that to your tab." I flashed him a practiced smile.

"Thanks." He reached for the glasses.

"And don't use that line again." I shook my head. "It's a bad one."

He wrinkled his nose and cocked his head. "I thought it was funny. The drinks are on fire. And you're hot." He gave a sheepish shrug of his shoulders. "I wanted to take a shot."

"Mila?" One of the other bartenders, Staci, leaned in beside me. "I need your help with an order."

"Sure thing." I gave Mr. Sweet Thing a nod, and turned.

"He's *never* gonna make it back to his friends without spilling those." Staci tossed her blonde curls back.

"Nope." I was pretty sure Mr. Sweet Thing would have cocktail all over his shirt soon. Such a shame. I noted that Staci didn't actually have another order. "Thanks for the save."

She rolled her eyes. "He was talking to your boobs."

I snorted. He totally had been.

"After years of working in clubs and bars, I can pick out that type as soon as they step in here," Staci said. "Easy life, enough cash to make him feel like a hotshot, and he thinks any woman slinging drinks would be grateful to let him get her naked." Staci sniffed. "No, thanks."

Staci was a veteran, so she'd know. Me, I'd only been bartending for four weeks.

Okay, three weeks, five days, and six hours, but who was counting?

Someone called Staci's name, and she whirled away.

There was an uncharacteristic break in the customers at the bar, so I quickly grabbed a cloth and wiped surfaces down. I glanced around. The crowd was starting to build. It wouldn't be long before the club was pumping.

This was light-years away from my busy career in PR and marketing. Emotions hit me like a kick to the gut.

Sucking in a breath, I wrestled them back down. I

thought time would help make things easier, but so far it hadn't.

My old life was gone. My challenging, corporate job was gone. My cute apartment was gone. My parents were...

The shot of pain almost made me double over.

I lifted my chin, fighting back the tears. That life was over. Now, I was a bartender. I rubbed the throb growing in the side of my head.

Just pour the drinks, Mila.

I threw the cloth back in the sink, scootching out of the way as one of the male bartenders, Eli, brushed past me. Time to get my focus back on work.

One of the servers, Jules, arrived at the bar. "Mila, need a Jack and Coke, one flaming Hurricane, and one blazing Vieux Carre."

"On it." I grabbed some glasses and set to work. I turned to the wall of alcohol and tuned out everything else. Flaming drinks were a specialty at Ember, and the customers loved them—especially the tourists.

I quickly made the drinks, lit them up, and slid them across the bar. Jules smiled and loaded her tray.

A large group of customers entered, all laughing and looking to party. Soon, it was too busy for me to think. My hands didn't stop. Glasses, ice, booze, slice of lemon, lighter to ignite the flames.

I spent the next hour slinging drinks. Some shifts I worked out on the floor—and let me tell you, carrying a tray loaded with drinks is nerve-wracking. I liked it much better behind the bar.

Suddenly, I felt a ripple go through the crowd, and

my belly tightened. Without looking up, I knew what caused it.

Or rather, who.

Finally, I couldn't stop myself from raising my head.

And there he was, sauntering through the crowd like he owned the place. Which he did.

Dante Fury. Owner of Ember.

My hand curled around a bottle of Jack Daniels.

He wore tailored, black pants, and a black shirt with the sleeves rolled up. The shirt showed off the corded muscles of his forearms and his olive-brown skin, and the fabric strained against his biceps. He had black ink on one arm. He moved in a powerful, supple way, his stride sure and measured. It made me think of a warrior...no, a king in his domain. His hair was black, thick, and tousled. Like he often ran a hand through it. A dark, sexy beard covered a strong jaw.

He cut through the crowd like some sort of midnight predator. My throat got tight every time I saw him. He had an aura about him that made it impossible to look away.

He had this lock of dark hair that always fell over his forehead, and my hand desperately wanted to push it away.

Dammit.

I made myself look away, and set the bottle back on the shelf.

It didn't matter how sexy and attractive Dante Fury was. I was in hiding. I couldn't get close to anyone, or I could end up dead. Plus he was my boss.

My pulse skittered, and I couldn't help but look back

at him. He was talking with one of the servers, Jessica. Checking in. He did that every few hours, chatting with the VIPs, talking with the staff, looking for problems.

Dante drew closer to the bar. I saw the way men eyed him, standing a little straighter and sucking in their guts. There was no gut on Dante. His was as flat as a board, and was the perfect complement to his broad shoulders.

Women watched him too—hungry and dazed.

"God, that man is prime fantasy material." Beside me, Staci let out a gusty sigh. "I've contemplated naming my vibrator after him, but I decided it was skeevy to call it Dante." She eyed him. "Still, the man is *so* fine in that dark, dangerous, just know he'd pin a woman down and fuck her hard kind of way."

"*Staci.*"

She rolled her eyes at me and grinned. "Come on, Mila. You're quiet, but I've seen you eye-fuck the man when no one is looking."

I choked, grateful that it was dim enough that she couldn't see the heat in my cheeks.

Staci slapped me on the back. "No judgment here. He's worth an eye fuck." She sighed. "It's a damn shame he never messes around where he works. Never flirts with the customers, never takes them back to his office, and that goes double for staff."

In my few weeks here, I'd never seen a single hint of him flirting, or anything.

Staci leaned in. "I heard he was seen with some fancy assistant district attorney a couple of times. Figures he'd go for smart and classy."

My stomach did a weird flip. And then I noticed Dante was heading our away.

I straightened. "How about we make some drinks?"

Staci leaned closer. "Are you blushing?"

"No."

She grinned. "You *so* are blushing."

"No, but I'm thinking about giving you a black eye."

Staci laughed. I looked up and locked eyes with Dante.

He moved toward the bar, and I couldn't look away. Every single part of me shivered, filled with energy.

He had dark eyes. They looked like chips of obsidian. Deep, dark, unfathomable pools.

"Mila. How's it going this evening?"

Gah. It was all kinds of unfair that on top of his looks, he had a deep, panty-melting drawl with a touch of grit.

"Great." I managed a nod. "All good."

He cocked his head. "You sure?"

I felt a cold tickle down my spine. I always got the sense he knew I was hiding something. Like he wanted to know all my secrets.

I straightened. No one got my secrets. They were too horrible and too dangerous.

I knew Dante and his brothers stood up to the darker underbelly of New Orleans—the gangs, the mobsters, the criminals. But that didn't mean I'd bare my soul. Not when it could end with me with a bullet in my brain.

"Very sure." I pasted on a smile.

He watched me for a long second with those endless, dark eyes. "Are you closing tonight?"

My heart did a little jump. "Yes. Venus needs to get home. One of her kids has a dance thing tomorrow."

"Good. I've got some whiskey samples from a local distillery. I know you like your whiskey, so maybe you can try them with me? I need to decide if I want to stock them or not."

I nodded, my belly twisting. *Oh, hell.* A late-night close with Dante. "Happy to help. Oh, and I have a new cocktail creation I think the customers would like."

His teeth flashed white against his skin. "You and your cocktails."

"Hey, the Fiery Phoenix has been super popular." I'd made up the cocktail a week ago and the clientele loved it.

"I know." He held up a hand. "You try my whiskey, I'll try your new cocktail."

I almost said 'it's a date' but managed to stifle the words. It wasn't a date. It would never be a date. "I'd better get these drinks made. Thirsty customers."

I whirled away, but I felt his gaze digging into my back.

When I glanced his way again, he was gone. I blew out a breath and my shoulders sagged. I needed to definitely *not* get too close to Dante Fury.

The rest of my shift was a blur—tipsy customers, lots of drinks, sore feet.

And somehow, from time to time, I still felt Dante's gaze on me.

Shaking my head, I reached for a cocktail glass. *You're imagining things, Mila.*

DANTE

Standing at the large window in my office, I watched the club through the one-way glass.

Mine.

As I took in the dark floor, the gold ceiling, and long bar along the wall—not to mention the clubgoers spending lots of money at my bar—I clasped my hands behind my back.

All mine, and I was fucking proud of it. I'd planned every detail, picked every staff member, managed every aspect. My staff was currently switching to clean-up mode, as closing time drew nearer. They were the embodiment of a well-oiled machine.

I wouldn't accept anything less.

Heading toward the low, wooden cabinet against the far wall, I reached for the decanter full of my favorite bourbon resting on top of it. I grabbed a crystal tumbler, and poured a splash.

I wouldn't have more than one, not while the club was open. I only indulged when I was at home, with my brothers. It was the only time I let my guard down.

Swirling the liquor, I turned back to the window. My desk was behind me, and I should be sitting at it, dealing with work. My laptop was open, and I'd been sorting through orders and paperwork.

I sipped and enjoyed the sweet, smoky burn.

Letting my gaze drift over the crowd, I took in the dancers on the dance floor, the people standing at high tables sipping their drinks, the small groups in the VIP area. Everyone was behaving, and I knew I could trust my security team to spot any trouble.

Movement at the bar caught my attention. My newest hire, Mila Clarke.

She moved well, and was good at her job. Organized and efficient. I frowned. I couldn't quite get a read on her. She didn't have the vibe of a seasoned bartender. The things that stood out the most were her bad dye job, and the fact that she was smart. Really smart. She hadn't had much experience at first, but she'd picked things up quickly. She was hard-working, I'd give her that.

She also had dark smudges under her eyes, and I wondered if she worked a day job, too.

The woman had high, thick walls. And she wasn't keen for anyone to penetrate them.

I understood that. Hell, I'd had my own version of that growing up.

My thoughts turned to her face. High cheekbones, perfectly shaped lips, and killer curves that her black trousers didn't hide. Plus, she had that glint in her gray eyes.

Sharp-edged secrets, but also a hint of challenge.

Like she was daring me to push her.

I muttered a curse and took another sip. She was my *employee*. One I suspected needed help.

There was a knock at my office door. I took another swig of the bourbon and set the glass down.

Speaking of employees who needed help...

"Come in."

The door opened. The man in the doorway was in his

early sixties, stocky and balding, and worked a ball cap nervously between his fingers.

"Hiya, Mr. Fury."

"Eddie, I've told you a hundred times to call me Dante."

The man nodded. "Yes, Mr. Fury."

With a shake of my head, I circled my desk and sat in my chair.

"Take a seat."

Eddie dropped into a leather armchair on the visitor side of my desk. "It's Tommy again." He pinched his nose, worry on his broad, weathered face.

Tommy was Eddie's teenage son. He had one more year of high school left, and a scholarship lined up for college.

Unfortunately, a few of his friends were mixed up with a local gang called the Big Gs.

"He's been hanging with his gang friends again?"

"Yes." Eddie's face creased with panic. "They've dragged him into a mess. There's a girl."

I nodded. "Ah."

"She was scared, tried to get out." Eddie smoothed a hand over his head. "She called Tommy and he went over there to get her. The gang, they'd broken into some shop. Someone took a video of Tommy. They said if he doesn't commit to the gang, they'll share the video with the police. His scholarship..." Eddie made a sound. "I want better for my boy."

Eddie was the kind of father that had been lacking in my life.

Anger ignited. I hated people who preyed on others,

especially the gangs. They promised a family, a sense of belonging, but it was all just to use people. They ruled with fear and violence. Growing up in foster care, I'd seen it too many fucking times.

"Who in the gang threatened Tommy?"

Eddie swallowed. "A banger called Evan Curtis, goes by Easy-C."

I nodded. "I'll deal with it."

Relief crossed the man's face. "Mr. Fury—"

I arched a brow.

"Dante..." Eddie's voice was a little shaky. "Thank you."

I rose and pressed a hand to Eddie's beefy shoulder. "You're a hard worker, a good employee, and a good man. Tommy is lucky to have you. He will go to college, I promise."

Eddie rose. "Thank you so much. I can never repay you."

"I don't expect payment. Now, get home to your wife. I'll deal with this tomorrow, and let you know when it's done."

Eddie nodded in relief and shuffled out.

I needed more of my drink now. Sipping, I stared at the paintings on the wall behind my desk—wild swirls of ink in black and gold. I needed to make some calls, and talk to my brother, Reath. He kept his finger on the pulse of the local gangs, and he would know this Easy-C.

Lifting my glass, I turned to the window. The last of the customers were leaving. Soon, I could get out of here and find my bed.

But first, I had a few whiskies to try, and an interesting woman to try them with.

Suddenly, the door to my office burst open. There were only four people in the world who would dare barge in without knocking.

Sure enough, it was two of my four brothers.

Colton had an arm around Reath, helping him inside. Reath's gray shirt sleeve was soaked with blood.

"What trouble did you find?" I asked.

"I was minding my own fucking business," Reath muttered.

I snorted. Reath never minded his own business. He was a former CIA...something. He'd been black ops, and that was shit he never talked about.

I was glad when he'd gotten out. We all were. Now, he ran his own small security company—Phoenix Security Services. He did security for all our businesses, and a few select customers. He was damn good at it. He also kept the local players from interfering with Fury businesses.

Reath dropped heavily into a chair.

"Don't get blood on my furniture," I said.

"It's leather," Colton said. "It'll clean."

With a sigh, I set my glass down, then went over and opened the cabinet. I pulled out a huge first aid kit.

"Shirt off," I ordered.

Reath slipped off his ruined gray shirt, exposing brown skin stretched over hard muscles. Black ink covered Reath's back—the intricate image of a rising phoenix. Colt and Reath couldn't look more different. Colt was six-foot-three and packed with lean muscle. He had a neat beard, a near-permanent scowl, and tattoos on his forearms.

He was a bounty hunter. A good one. Years spent in foster homes and on the street had made him good at sneaking around, and tracking things—namely people —down.

Reath was a few inches shorter than Colt—same height as me—but more muscular. He didn't know who his biological parents were, but he had some African American ancestry. He had brown skin, black hair he kept cut ruthlessly short, and a face that always caught women's attention. We'd teased him for being so pretty his entire life.

He also had this easy, liquid way of moving that made him seem relaxed. He wasn't. He could move faster and fight dirtier than anyone I knew.

Right now, he also had a knife gash on his muscled bicep.

"It doesn't look too deep." I pulled out an antiseptic wipe and started cleaning it.

Reath grunted.

"What happened?" I asked.

"I was checking out a few leads. I got jumped by a junkie with a knife who wanted my wallet."

The junkie had picked the wrong guy.

"Is he still breathing?" I pulled out the glue.

"Yes," Reath muttered unhappily.

"Through his broken jaw," Colt added as he poured himself a drink.

I glued up the cut. Reath's dark skin had a collection

of scars—knife wounds, a couple of puckered gunshot scars, old burns.

I blew out a breath. We'd all worked out our demons in our own way, and Reath had done it working for Uncle Sam. At least he wasn't flying around the world to God-knew-where, to take on the bad guys anymore.

"I need your help with something," I said. "A banger called Easy-C is trying to jack up Eddie's kid, Tommy."

Reath's dark eyes flashed. "He's part of the Big Gs. Yeah, I can deal with him. You coming with me?"

I smiled. "Fuck, yeah."

My brother nodded. "I'll find him and let you know."

No questions asked. The Fury brothers took care of their own, and I always knew my brothers had my back.

They were the only people I could count on.

A pair of clear gray eyes, swimming in secrets, filled my head.

Who could Mila count on?

"You're closing up now?" Colt asked.

"Soon."

"Want to come to mine for a drink?"

"I'm in," Reath said.

I packed up the first aid kit. "I have a few things to finish up here."

Colt glanced at Reath.

Reath raised his brows. "Those things include a cozy drink and chat with your newest bartender?"

I forced my face to stay expressionless. "I often check in with whoever is closing."

"Mmm." Colt flashed a rare smile. "Nothing to do with the curves and the pretty face."

The thought of my brother noticing Mil. face had me stiffening.

"I think it's those turbulent gray eyes." Re his ruined shirt back on. "You've had a few co...ks with her."

Damn security guards had big mouths. "We talk, that's it."

Reath snorted. "Not like you to lie to yourself, Dante."

"Fuck you two. You know I don't dabble with my employees."

My brothers shared another annoying look.

"You don't dabble with anyone," Colt said.

"Oh, and you do?" I stood. "Get out of here. Before I kick your asses."

They were both grinning as they left. *Assholes*.

If Mila needed help, I'd help her, but that was it.

I didn't get involved with women, especially not ones who worked for me. End of story.

Fury Brothers
Fury

Keep

Burn

Take

Claim

Also Available as Audiobooks!

PREVIEW: BILLIONAIRE HEISTS

Want more action-packed romance? Then check out the the **Billionaire Heists.**

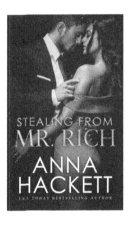

To save my brother, all I have to do is steal from a billionaire.

My brother is in trouble. *Again*. But this time he's in debt to some *really* bad people, and I'll do anything to save him. Even be blackmailed into cracking an unbreakable safe belonging to the most gorgeous man in New York. And one of the richest.

Steal from Zane Roth—King of Wall Street and one of the famous billionaire bachelors of New York—sure thing, piece of cake.

You see, some people can play the piano, but I can play safes. My father is a thief, safecracker extraordinaire, and a criminal. He also taught me everything he knows. I've spent my entire life trying *not* to be him. I own my own business, pay my taxes, and I don't break the law. Ever.

Now I have to smash every one of my rules, break into a billionaire's penthouse, and steal a million-dollar necklace.

What I never expected was to find myself face to face with Zane. Tall, dark, handsome, and oh-so-rich Zane. He's also smart, and he knows I'm up to something.

And he's vowed to find out.

Billionaire Heists
Stealing from Mr. Rich
Blackmailing Mr. Bossman
Hacking Mr. CEO
Also Available as Audiobooks!

Also by Anna Hackett

Langston Hotels

Night and Day

Hunter Squad

Jameson

North

Fury Brothers

Fury

Keep

Burn

Take

Claim

Also Available as Audiobooks!

Unbroken Heroes

The Hero She Needs

The Hero She Wants

The Hero She Craves

The Hero She Deserves

The Hero She Loves

Also Available as Audiobooks!

Sentinel Security

Wolf

Hades

Striker

Steel

Excalibur

Hex

Stone

Also Available as Audiobooks!

Norcross Security

The Investigator

The Troubleshooter

The Specialist

The Bodyguard

The Hacker

The Powerbroker

The Detective

The Medic

The Protector

Mr. & Mrs. Norcross

Also Available as Audiobooks!

Billionaire Heists

Stealing from Mr. Rich

Blackmailing Mr. Bossman

Hacking Mr. CEO

Also Available as Audiobooks!

Team 52

Mission: Her Protection

Mission: Her Rescue

Mission: Her Security

Mission: Her Defense

Mission: Her Safety

Mission: Her Freedom

Mission: Her Shield

Mission: Her Justice

Also Available as Audiobooks!

Treasure Hunter Security

Undiscovered

Uncharted

Unexplored

Unfathomed

Untraveled

Unmapped

Unidentified

Undetected

Also Available as Audiobooks!

Oronis Knights

Knightmaster

Knighthunter

Galactic Kings

Overlord

Emperor

Captain of the Guard

Conqueror

Also Available as Audiobooks!

Eon Warriors

Edge of Eon

Touch of Eon

Heart of Eon

Kiss of Eon

Mark of Eon

Claim of Eon

Storm of Eon

Soul of Eon

King of Eon

Also Available as Audiobooks!

Galactic Gladiators: House of Rone

Sentinel

Defender

Centurion

Paladin

Guard

Weapons Master

Also Available as Audiobooks!

Galactic Gladiators

Gladiator

Warrior

Hero

Protector

Champion

Barbarian

Beast

Rogue

Guardian

Cyborg

Imperator

Hunter

Also Available as Audiobooks!

Hell Squad

Marcus

Cruz

Gabe

Reed

Roth

Noah

Shaw

Holmes

Niko

Finn

Devlin

Theron

Hemi

Ash

Levi

Manu

Griff

Dom

Survivors

Tane

Also Available as Audiobooks!

The Anomaly Series

Time Thief

Mind Raider

Soul Stealer

Salvation

Anomaly Series Box Set

The Phoenix Adventures

Among Galactic Ruins

At Star's End

In the Devil's Nebula

On a Rogue Planet

Beneath a Trojan Moon

Beyond Galaxy's Edge

On a Cyborg Planet

Return to Dark Earth

On a Barbarian World

Lost in Barbarian Space

Through Uncharted Space

Crashed on an Ice World

Perma Series

Winter Fusion

A Galactic Holiday

Warriors of the Wind

Tempest

Storm & Seduction

Fury & Darkness

Standalone Titles

Savage Dragon

Hunter's Surrender

One Night with the Wolf

For more information visit www.annahackett.com

ABOUT THE AUTHOR

I'm a USA Today bestselling romance author who's passionate about *fast-paced, emotion-filled* contemporary romantic suspense and science fiction romance. I love writing about people overcoming unbeatable odds and achieving seemingly impossible goals. I like to believe it's possible for all of us to do the same.

I live in Australia with my own personal hero and two very busy, always-on-the-move sons.

For release dates, behind-the-scenes info, free books, and other fun stuff, sign up for the latest news here:

Website: www.annahackett.com

Made in the USA
Las Vegas, NV
18 August 2025

26503703R00184